McGRATH'S MURDER

A story of intrigue, murder, suicide, double dealing and intense love in the gentle, rolling countryside of the west coast of Ireland.

Laurence A. Booker

W & B Publishers
USA

Brandon Free Public Library
4 Franklin Street
Brandon, VT 05733

McGrath's Murder © All rights reserved by
Laurence A. Booker

No part of this book may be reproduced or transmitted in
any form or by any means, graphic, electronic, or me-
chanical, including photocopying, recording, taping, or by
any informational storage retrieval system without prior
permission in writing from the publisher.

W & B Publishers

For information:
W & B Publishers, Inc.
9001 Ridge Hill Road
Kernersville, North Carolina 27285
www.a-argusbooks.com

ISBN: 9780986280870
ISBN: 0986280879

Book Cover designed by Dubya
Printed in the United States of America

Brandon Free Public Library
4 Franklin Street
Brandon, VT 05733

To Lynn and
the Brandon Library
Staff!

January 11 2016

DEDICATION

For Marsha, Alexa, Thomas, Heather, and Bill, and
for the people of Ireland, one of the most beautiful of all
the places on God's green earth.

A bunch of fine people.

Hope you enjoy the
road!

ACKNOWLEDGEMENTS

This book, although entirely created from the depths of my imagination and two trips to Ireland, could not have been produced without the help of two special editors: Marsha, my beloved wife, who pointed out many glaring errors in the manuscript and to whom I am completely indebted for her critiques, and to Mrs. Carol Altruda, a professional editor and a dear an old friend from our NYU days, whose editorial assistance has been invaluable. She has corrected my manuscript, over the phone and through emails, in time lines, grammar and many other aspects. I sincerely thank them both for all their efforts, ideas and critiques. Any remaining errors in this book are strictly mine alone.

AUTHOR'S NOTE

Dear Reader,

After the online publication of my first book, *McGrath's Detail*, I thought I had finished with the proper Bostonian, Lieutenant William McGrath, USN. This was not to be.

There have been marvelous, and repeated, queries from relatives, and community members in our little Vermont town, as to when I was going to write another "McGrath book". Being a high school teacher, there was little time to do any writing during the school year. During the summer of 2006, my wife had corrective surgery in Boston – she's fine now and doing wonderfully – so no time was available then. The next two summers involved catching up on all the items that were left alone while we were in Boston.

Since that year, now in 2015, I have retired from teaching high school Business and Economics, and, when I am not called upon by neighboring high schools to be a substitute teacher, I have ample writing time on my hands. So, now is the time to again delve into the adventures of William McGrath. I thought I was done with him, but my readers will not let him rest.

So, thanks to all who encouraged me to continue the exploits of Mr. McGrath and have prodded me on to detail his new adventures. I appreciate your interest and hope you like the story.

--LAB

THE CHAPTERS

THE CAST OF CHARACTERS

William McGrath	Formerly a Commander in the U.S. Navy and a Meteorology Officer, Wealthy Bostonian, owns a shipping line
Lady Cynthia FitzHugh,	Daughter of Earl Trevor FitzHugh
Trevor FitzHugh,	Earl FitzHugh, a Nobleman
Sir Charles Tillingham,	Trevor FitzHugh's Brother-in-Law
Kathleen O'Shaunessy,	McGrath's Housekeeper
Patrick Riordan,	The FitzHughs' Butler
Mrs. Julia Lynch,	The FitzHughs' Cook
Jonah,	The FitzHughs' Gardener
Livy O'Toole,	Garda
Fergal Hanlon,	Assistant Garda
Father Joseph McDermott,	Parish Priest
Father Tim O'Neil,	Parish Priest in Kildunlee during the War Years
Col. Charles O'Meara,	Supervisor of the Garda for County Clare

Bridie Scanlon,	Lady Cynthia's Personal Maid
Edward, Timmy, and	FitzHugh's grounds men and tack keepers.
Edna and Lizzie,	Housemaids
Niamh Flaherty,	Publican
Edward Hillaire,	Husband of Siobhan Hillaire
Siobhan Rafferty Hillaire,	Edward's wife
Donal, Kathleen, and Deirdre Rafferty,	Siobhan's siblings
Margaret Hillaire,	Edward and Siobhan's daughter
Brendan Rafferty,	Siobhan's Father, a farmer
Ray and Marcie Hillaire,	Edward's wealthy parents from Montana
George and Beverly Huestis,	Friends of Ray and Marcie, also from Montana
Liam O'Banyon,	A Greengrocer
Willy O'Banyon,	Liam's Son
Sir Julian Brownlee,	Wealthy South African Gentleman
Lady Alice Stronton,	Sir Julian's South African

	Fiancée
Bobbee Fuller,	Friend of Lady Alice
Sean Pierce,	Garda in Training
Dr. Kieran McHugh,	Local Physician
Francis O'Farrell,	Regional Magistrate
Senan Neill,	Clerk of the Court
Joe Naughton,	Town Handyman
Tim Kearney,	Agricultural Worker
Jean-Luc Gaspard,	Vacationing Frenchman, a Dealer in Fine Art
Jose Luis Valenzuela,	A Vacationing Spaniard
Alejandro Arellano,	Another Vacationing Spaniard
Cormac O'Callaghan,	A *seanachie*. See the Glossary for an explanation

1.

PROLOGUE

"That's right, Commander, I seen him meself, didn't I? Dead as Brian Boru's corpse an' nary a drop o' red in his rigid body. Brains scattered all over the desk top blotter floatin' in blood an' soakin' in ter it like a jar o' the pure outter the blue on barren barley fields dyin' o the ragin' douth…"

2.

JUNE, 1944

Wind and rain lashed at the small boat, tossing it around like a toy in a bathtub, while Liam O'Banyon revved the engine to be sure the old girl wouldn't stall in the gale.

"Get out of the tunnel, out of the tunnel," Boats yelled at the Detail, herding them down to the slippery, cracked, twenty foot long by a yard wide, cement dock. "Here, into the boat. Fast. Step lively, now!" Boatswain's Mate First Class, Leon Koslowski, United States Navy, or "Boats" to the men of Lieutenant McGrath's Meteorological Detail, was as old a salt as ever sailed and he understood the sea as much as anyone, who had spent more than half his forty two years on it, could understand it. The others were mostly land sailors, taking weather observations, doing calculations, recording data. But the Boats knew the sea, and he knew deep in his heart that this night the witch of the sea was brewing a pig of a storm to lash out at them, to try to destroy them.

"Come on, do as the Boats says," Lieutenant McGrath told his weathermen. "We've got to make the rendezvous with the Corvette."

Wind, fierce and punishing, from the unforgiving, frigid and vindictive North Sea, whipped their faces, and tore at their clothes, driving the breath from their lungs, while a horizontal rain, like piercing needles, soaked their clothes and burned their cheeks and eyes.

"Captain, there's something going on up on the

cliff," Van Raalt called to the Lieutenant, and he pointed to the crest edge of a section of the Cliffs of Moher, Ireland's rugged and weathered ancient face, peering defiantly out to the fury of the North Atlantic. They stopped for only a second to look up and they saw several figures hovering near the edge of the cliff.

**

"We can't wait now, Van," McGrath shouted. "Everyone into the boat!" he called. Liam O'Banyon cast off the last line and revved the engine one more time, preparing to get to sea and to make contact with the Canadian Corvette, on patrol that night, and scheduled to pick up Lieutenant William McGrath and his Meteorological Detail.

A sudden *PRANG!* Ricocheted from the battered concrete dock.

"Good Lord, they're usin' guns! Someone's shootin' at us!" Willy O'Banyon, Liam's son, shouted over the roar of the wind.

"Get this boat to sea!" McGrath shouted to Liam, just as he was about to jump aboard. Another shot barked out in the night, but there was no *PRANG!*, only a dull thunk and a painful scream.

**

"Oh, me God, me God! They got Willy! They got me b'y!" Liam yelled. Boats took over the wheel as Liam hugged his son and tried to staunch the bleeding from his left shoulder. Boats drove the engines to full throttle and prepared to head away from the dock and out into the turbulent, black night, toward the lights of the heaving Corvette, a half mile away. Charlie Ziebel, one of the Detail, had had first aid training and he checked Willy's wound.

"It's not bad, Liam, but you'd better get him to Doc McHugh as soon as you get back." He jammed a large wad of gauze into Liam's hand. "This'll help stop the bleeding, but get him up the tunnel and back to town," he shouted at Liam over the screaming north wind, as they both lifted Willy over the side of the boat and onto the dock, Ziebel and Van Raalt guiding them to the tunnel's gaping mouth.

"Oh, me God, me Willy!" Liam kept crying.

"He'll be okay, Liam," Ziebel reassured him, "but get him to the Doc first thing." Ziebel and Van Raalt helped O'Banyon, father and son, to the tunnel, then, wishing them both good luck, made a break for the edge of the boat and got aboard. Boats pushed the throttle to full thrust and headed to the Corvette.

Suddenly, two dull thuds could be heard. One bullet tore into the side of the small cabin, shattering the glass window that protected Liam in rain storms, and the other slammed into McGrath's right thigh, tearing the flesh and shattering the bone.

"Charlie, they got the Lieutenant! They got the Lieutenant!" Van Raalt hollered.

Waves of scorching pain shot up McGrath's right thigh and burned into his hip. Nausea overcame him, and dizziness clouded his mind. The small boat tossed in the crazed North Sea and he was bounced from side to side, finally getting tossed onto an athwart ship bench. He felt Charlie tightening the tourniquet on his thigh, and the pinprick of pain killer, jabbed into his leg just above the tightening cloth, from the ampoule in Ziebel's fist, but less and less became clear.

"Lord, that Corvette better have a ship's surgeon on board!" Van Raalt yelled in his emotion at the sight of McGrath's wound, and trying to be heard above the sea's violence.

McGrath was rapidly losing consciousness from extreme tiredness, loss of blood, and the swirling, tossing of O'Banyon's boat. Turbulence of the present dissolved into a fading mist and was gone. Exhausted and in shock, McGrath's thoughts faded, and his last image was of her.

3.

NOVEMBER 1945

"You did a fine job, Lieutenant, in helping General Eisenhower and his staff with your weather reports. I know you can't control the weather, but you sure can tell us what it's doing."

"Thank you, Admiral."

"I'm sure you know we're still at war in the Pacific, and General MacArthur is preparing now to invade the Japanese mainland. If we have to do that, there will be many casualties, many of our soldiers and marines killed, despite all our efforts at bombing them into submission. I'm sure I don't have to tell you that. Consider our losses at the Normandy landing."

"Yes, Admiral, they were considerable."

"But we want the best for our troops, and we must have up-to-date weather reports for their landings and for the flyboys to pound the Japanese. We have to know about winds, any impending typhoons, storms and that kind of stuff. The General knows about the good job you did in Ireland and he's requested Admiral Halsey to let you take weather observations, and make forecasts in the Pacific, off Guam, to help with the possible invasion. You've been through a lot, especially with your wounded thigh bone, and you can refuse to go. We can always get someone else, but they wouldn't have your experience. And, it would mean a lot to us and the troops. The decision is entirely yours. You can keep your Detail from Ireland. Lieutenant, I'll need an answer by eight bells this afternoon."

Did McGrath really have a choice? Could he, in truth, refuse? Could he really say No and be responsible for "...*many casualties?*" Lieutenant Commander William McGrath, recently promoted for his work in Ireland prior to the D-Day invasion, found himself drifting off Guam, with all of the sailors of his previous Detail in Ireland, except Boats, the formidable Leon Koslowski, Boatswain's, or Bo'sun's, Mate first class, in Navy parlance, who had been reassigned to a troop carrier farther to the west of them.

McGrath and his detail were continuing to drift in a specially rigged weather ship, well protected by a large destroyer escort in the event an enemy plane or submarine approached, designed to take air temperatures, as well as that of sea water, plus tide directions and wind velocities, precise weather observations, barometric readings, sea current speeds, cloud covers and types and many other relevant data on a continual basis for the honchos in Honolulu to make their invasion decisions upon. They did these for twenty four hours a day, for four months, till MacArthur accepted the Japanese surrender aboard the Missouri. With the world's first two nuclear explosions, the dreaded invasion of Japan had been avoided, and, many said, tens of thousands of lives, on both sides may have been saved.

Then there was the voyage back to Pearl. The long mustering out in Honolulu; the flight to Alameda Naval Air Station; the goodbyes to the sailors in his Detail, and his promotion to full Commander, with personal thanks from General MacArthur and Admiral Halsey. He took a taxi from Alameda to San Francisco International Airport and caught a commercial flight to Logan International. To Boston. To home. The war was over.

4.

FAMILY MATTERS

November 1946. He had been home in Boston for almost a year, discounting the side trip to London to see Father Tim at Upper Kings Ridley. A year and a half ago, a lifetime of loss without her, he had wanted to continue to Ireland, to Galway, to where she lived, but the phone call at the Dorchester where he lodged had called him urgently and immediately back to Boston. His presence was needed. Decisions had to be made, and the Board of Directors felt it had to have his input. He was a former Naval Commander, a meteorologist, a scientist, rather well educated, but, above all, he was indeed a very astute businessman who could make immediate decisions that would benefit McGrath Lines, Inc., and his opinions were required. So, burying his yearning for her deep within his being, he allowed duty to draw him back to Boston just before Christmas 1945.

***

Back in the sumptuous and elegantly appointed ground floor living room in his family home, McGrath sat before a fireplace, luxuriously and tastefully designed of imported Cararra Italian marble, hand carved and then polished to a mirror-like sheen, which commanded the large room. Soft yellows and browns graced the walls, giving an atmosphere of total relaxation. It was here that the former Commander William McGrath, United States Navy, and highly respected meteorologist, would sit of a

November evening, submerged in thoughts of his World
War II experiences, and the adventures they had brought
him. From Hawaii, to Ireland where his Meteorological
Detail's weather reporting had helped influence General
Eisenhower's decisions for the D-Day landings on the
shores of Normandy. And, again back to the Pacific,
where the gentle sea, blue skies and blazing sun were in
direct opposition to the deep, dark, murderous turbulence
of the North Atlantic and its brother, the North Sea. Two
watery killers, who took sailors' lives at their pleasure; or
spared them if a rare moment of reprieve prevailed.

McGrath sat back in his favorite winged chair of
soft gold and brown hues, with a large splash of fine
Armagnac in his bell-shaped Waterford Crystal snifter. Its
fellows rested on the ancient carved oak colonial side
table, dating to the late 1770s and executed by some unknown Yankee master cabinet maker. McGrath breathed
deeply of the magnificent French brandy, slowly rolling
its spectacular bouquet over his palate and savoring the
flaming sensation that followed each swallow. He listened
intently to the crackling of the logs in the hearth, and
watched the mad, lace designs of the rain and sleet, driven
by the north wind, pepper the tall windows, glistening in
the glow from the gaslight on the street, just this side of
the cobblestone sidewalk on Beacon Hill.

"I've seen worse," he would tell the storm, as if to
taunt it with his own North Atlantic adventures. But the
nor'easter paid no attention, knowing full well that it had
caused blackouts in Portland, Cape Elizabeth, Saint
John's and Casco Bay; flooding the townships on the
coast of Newfoundland, and capsizing boats on Prince
Edward Island. *I don't care,* the storm answered
McGrath; *I'm here to flood everything I can and to ruin
everyone's day, and yours in particular, as much as I
possibly can.*

And ruin everyone's day it did. Businesses and

schools ground to a halt; civil services were left to another, sunnier time and offices were shuttered against the storm's wrath.

Still, McGrath and the storm understood each other. After all, his was a long time seafaring family, and he had ventured far, sailing on his families' cargo steamships, into the world's oceans in sunny, placid, calm, southern tropics as well as cloud-thickened, tempestuous, angry northern seas. His was a family that had interests in many of the major seaports of the earth: in Cherbourg, Southampton, London, Johannesburg, Oslo and others. Before the war, before and during his years at the Massachusetts Institute of Technology, where he earned a Bachelor of Science degree in a double major of chemistry and in meteorology, he had sailed to most of them, under the United States Flag with the McGrath Logo – a large green shamrock with the image of the state of Massachusetts, in blazing white, on each of the plant's three leaves – on the smoke stack.

Since he was the eldest of the three McGrath sons, his obligation was to oversee every aspect as the future Chairman and President of McGrath Shipping, Inc., and to know each of the twelve ships that sailed under the McGrath emblem. The only way to "…learn the trade is," his aging and ailing father said, quoting ancient great grandfather Josiah McGrath, the line's founder, "…you have to sail on McGrath ships. Go where they go, do what they do. Learn from the ships and the sea. There was no other way."

Old grandfather McGrath had departed the earth just before Archduke Ferdinand was shot at Sarajevo, and William McGrath's father, currently the Chairman and President, was getting on in years. He had survived the turmoil of several hurricanes in the Mid-Atlantic and four typhoons in the western Pacific. He was no stranger to the sea's power, and he respected it completely. His was a respect that the sea, with all its power, wind, gales and thunder understood in turn.

It was on evenings like this, while watching the nor'easter's wind and rain batter Boston to a standstill, that he raised his Armagnac in tribute to these outside forces, these formidable foes. And McGrath toasted the wind and rain. For the briefest of seconds, he knew deep in his heart, while his glass was in mid air, that the wind pounded the floor to ceiling windows especially hard, in its tribute to him. He understood and respected the sea and its power, although the sea had no respect for anyone, even William McGrath, and it did as it pleased.

Even so, now McGrath sat, content, thinking of his adventures, the shipping company he now controlled since his father had stepped down in light of his ill health; the second largest in the world, whose flags entered ports from Boston to Hong Kong, from London to Johannesburg, and now that the war was over, from Hamburg to Tokyo. His thoughts drifted to the turbulent North Atlantic; to the calm Pacific, and finally, to her

5.

THE RETURN

Rain slashed at the windshield, clouding his vision, making the typically narrow Irish road almost impossible to see. The comparatively smooth running of his tires told him he was still on the tarmac. But when they ground roughly, on that sharp Irish gravel, he knew he was riding on the edge of the road, dangerously close to landing in a ditch, getting soaked to the bone, freezing. And where would he ever be able to get a tow truck to haul him and his car out? Especially here in the wilds of eastern Ireland, a half hour west of Dublin? A nor'easter, he thought to himself, using his overcoat sleeve to clear the foggy steam from the windshield, and the intruding rain drops dribbling down the inside length of the driver's side window.

"A nor'easter," he said to himself. "That's what we'd call it at home in Boston, a nor'easter." Straight down from the wilds of the North Atlantic, bouncing off Newfoundland, Prince Edward Island and Maine, right in to Boston, dumping inches of sleet and freezing rain on the streets of Beacon Hill, where his family home sat.

But this wasn't Boston, with all its conveniences and comforts, and this car wasn't his Bostonian Cadillac, sporting its luxuries and elegant appointments. It was a pre-war, hard-used, four-door wreck, barely able to negotiate the slippery hill roads. He thought it may have been a reconditioned 1930s Rover Saloon, but he couldn't be sure. He had rented it through a long, hard phone call from London to Dublin, and had been assured that he would have a suitable vehicle for the trip to Ireland's beautiful West Country. To Galway. To her.

***

McGrath vividly recalled the few times they had been together back in 1944: the horse ride, the initial accidental encounter in the town store, his visit to her Manor House. Too brief, never a moment to tell her how he felt about her; never a time to say what he held in his heart. Always interruptions, as if they were planned. The war, items to be reconciled with his Detail, continually reporting weather data to Eisenhower's headquarters in London, her brother, wounded in the fighting in North Africa, her responsibilities managing the Manor and its farms, tenants and many herds, her ill father. Never a quiet moment.

She was Cynthia FitzHugh, Lady Cynthia FitzHugh, daughter of Lord Trevor FitzHugh, Eighth Earl of County Clare, in the west of Ireland and thoroughly Protestant. The first Lord FitzHugh had been granted the earldom of County Clare by the English Crown during the reign of Henry VIII. But, since Irish independence in the 1920s, the present Lord FitzHugh had no governing power, save over his hereditary manor and the farms and lands adjoining and supporting it. But Lord FitzHugh, a man in failing health, was very generous to his workers and tenants, taking only minimum payments and tributes. Whether this attitude was from a guilt feeling of the severe demands of previous Earls FitzHugh, no one knew, but the present earl was well liked and held in high esteem by the general populace of the Kildunlee area and beyond, as was his daughter, Lady Cynthia, who had been extremely generous to the FitzHughs' tenants and had been known, on many occasions, to forgive debts and right wrongs among people.

***

He had called her from Dublin just after he picked up his rental car, the blue Rover Saloon he was now trying to keep on the sodden Irish roads. It had taken fifteen minutes to get through from Dublin to Galway, then to the telephone exchange in Kildunlee, where her Manor was located, and finally to her.

6.

A VOICE FROM THE PAST

"Good evening. FitzHugh Manor. This is Riordan the butler speaking. How may I help you?"

"Ye... Yes. Please. Is... Lady FitzHugh available? It's a bit late, I know, but I'd really like to speak with her."

"I'll see if her Ladyship is available. Please hold the line." Riordan slowly works his way into the small ball-room, where a birthday party for Cynthia FitzHugh's wounded brother, Geoffrey, is in full progress.

"Excuse me, milady, there seems to be a telephone call for you. An American gentleman, I believe."

Lady FitzHugh's brow wrinkles at Riordan's message. "Telephone call? From an American gentleman? I don't know any Americans. Gentlemen or otherwise. Did he give his name?"

"No, milady."

Cynthia turns to her guests, "Excuse me. This must be some error." She swiftly glided to the small alcove, in the hall where the telephone had been placed. Curiosity builds within her, and yet, she feels a flash of trepidation; of fear of finding out.

The delay of several minutes, the waiting, and the conversations in the background, sharpened the edge that McGrath's nerves have already built. A number of people were talking at once. Voices in continual movement. A party. People making various conversations, which mean nothing to the listener. Nothing to him; only delay and intense waiting. Finally, after an eternity, he heard,

"Good evening, this is Cynthia FitzHugh. With whom am I speaking?"

The voice. Her voice. It excites him; takes his breath away. His heart ceased beating years ago. He almost loses control.

"Hello?" she said again.

"Hello…Cynthia. It's…William. William McGrath. How are you?"

There was silence on the other end. Not a word.

"Cynthia. It's me. William. I'm in Dublin."

"I'm terribly sorry. I don't know a William McGrath. You must have the wrong telephone number."

"No. I don't know your phone number. The operator connected me. I'm in Dublin. I've come back."

A brief moment of silence.

"I'm really very sorry. I have no idea who you are. I did know a William McGrath who was with the US Navy during the war. But he was killed at sea shortly before D-Day. I understand that he drowned in the North Atlantic during a crossing to America. I'm afraid you are quite mistaken."

"No. No, Cynthia. It's really me. I didn't drown. I made it back to Canada then to the States just after that. I've just docked in Dublin and I have a car. I'm going to make it to Galway and Kildunlee tonight. I think I can do it before midnight. It'll be late when I get there. I'd like to see you tomorrow when the storm has died down. Perhaps about one o'clock, just after lunch. I want to see you again."

"I've told you. I don't know a William McGrath. And the one I knew is dead. You have the wrong telephone connection. I must go. Goodnight." And the line went dead.

Lady Cynthia FitzHugh gently placed the telephone in its cradle, and stared at it for a moment. Her hand was shaking, and breaths came in small gasps.

"Cynthia, are you all right. You don't look well." She turned and smiled at the speaker, a large, powerfully built, ruddy-faced man, showing lines and signs of much outdoor activity and sport.

"Sir Charles, I'm fine. It was just a wrong telephone number. I think the man on the other end had too much Jameson's."

"Sir Charles? Bit formal, aren't we? What happened to Uncle Charlie?"

"I'm sorry, Uncle Charlie, but this call threw me for a loop. Strange kind of thing."

"It happens quite frequently. Telephones are new to some of us here, and people mix things up. Probably just someone with a bellyful. Won't happen again, I'm sure."

"Of course not. Come, let's join the guests." She takes her Godfather's arm and strolls back into the ball-room, a nagging irritation scratching at the back of her mind. An American gentleman, Riordan had said. No. Impossible.

7.

THE LONG ROAD TO KILDUNLEE

And so McGrath was on the road to Galway, then on to Kildunlee, his mind still reeling from the cold and confusing conversation. He had spoken with her, if that was the right phrase, just over two hours ago, and it was now almost nine o'clock. The night was black as the depths of hell, and the northern wind refused to let up at all, and, in fact, blasted the right side of his car with gusts calculated to drive him and his heap into the closest ditch, aiming, of course, for the ditch with the deepest pool of rainwater. His high beams penetrated into the Irish night, showing jagged rain drops and slicing pebbles of wet sleet, almost horizontal, racing ahead of the madcap wind, lighting up the asphalt road before him for a mere twenty feet. *At least,* he thought, *I can stay on the road and not miss a bend and end up in a cow field. Lord, what a night.*

McGrath was well accustomed to filthy weather, but he had been away from the miserable likes of this sodden lot for some time. Recent late winter weather in Boston had been almost benign, and the lack of storms from the northeastern Atlantic, passing by Quebec, had barely made any appearances except for the dynamic nor'easter that tore into Northern New England two days before he left for Dublin. But now the weather gods seemed bound and determined to make up for their oversight, and they continued to pound McGrath and his Saloon.

McGrath checked the time. Nine-twenty. He had

spoken to Cynthia around seven, so it was over two hours that he had been on the road, fighting the storm, trying to stay on the road. Yet he had made good progress. Two hours and he had already passed Tullamore and was, as he figured it, almost halfway between Tullamore and Ballinasloe. That would put him eighty miles west of Dublin, with another thirty to go till he made Galway. He didn't really have to enter Galway. He would swing south just east of the city and head down the west coast of Ireland to Kildunlee, ten miles south of Galway city itself. Then along the coast road, or what the locals called a road, south to Kildunlee; ten miles, about an hour in good weather. Coast road, he repeated to himself. The Detail – his Detail, the sailors who were sent to take the pre-Normandy invasion weather observations – called it the rut road, or just the rut. A dirt, barely a quarter paved, series of connecting stretches leading south from Galway to Kildunlee, Doolan and beyond, south to Hags Head. It got people where they wanted to go, but it was a murderous journey, jolting and bouncing around, especially when there had been a freeze and the ruts became rails.

McGrath turned south, away from Galway, heading toward Kildunlee. His watch read ten-thirty. He should make Kildunlee just before midnight. Maybe sooner, now that the north wind was behind him, giving him a boost. But, he had to keep this lurching heap of rusting pig iron steady and on the road. *I'm so close to Kildunlee, and her,* he thought, *that to push forward too fast might end me up in a deep water ditch and ruin everything. So onward, slowly and carefully.*

But it wasn't only the delay in tonight's travels that really irked him. Last November he had spoken with Father Tim, the priest who was in Kildunlee during the war. McGrath had fully intended then to go across the Irish Sea to Dublin and on to Galway, near to Kildunlee. Near to her. But, of course, he'd needed to overnight in Lon-

don. Can't drive in November storms if you're half
asleep, and after his interview with Father Tim he'd been
half asleep. So, to his hotel room in London it would be
for the night. He had no idea what was waiting for him. A
cable. From Boston, Massachusetts. Two words hit him
squarely in the eyes: "Respond immediately". Trouble in
the head office, and he was, after all, the Chief Executive
Officer and Chair of the Board of Directors. He really had
no choice. So he had the desk clerk put through a trans-
Atlantic call to McGrath Shipping Lines in Boston, and
went to his room to await the call. He ordered supper to
be sent up. Might as well have something to eat while I
wait, he thought. Twenty minutes later his telephone rang.

"Commander McGrath?"

"Yes. Speaking."

"Your call has gone through. The trans-Atlantic operator is on the line."

"Thank you."

"Commander McGrath," the operator said, "I have
you connected with McGrath Shipping. Please go ahead,
Boston."

"Thank you," came a voice from the other side of
the Atlantic. It was one of his vice-presidents, Francis
McCafferty.

"Evening, Commander, how's the weather in London, these days?"

"Bitter. A rain storm's hammering us. Tomorrow's
crossing to Dublin going to be a pig. But, what can I do
for you? Why'd you send me a cable?"

And Francis McCafferty, Vice-President for South
American Operations went on to detail to McGrath the
problems the shipping line was experiencing in acquiring
a Brazilian line. The intention was to acquire another local line in Brazil, and thus expand McGrath Shipping operations even further in the South American area.

"But some legal problems have come up, Commander, and it looks as if we'll need you here. Consultations and so forth. Your decisions and a ton of signatures are needed."

"Can't Fred handle it?" Fred Young, Corporate Counsel for McGrath Shipping Lines.

"Commander, he's got his hands full this very minute and he was the one who told me to contact you. It looks like you'll have to return to Boston for a while. A couple of weeks, anyway."

A couple of weeks, anyway, thought McGrath. *A couple of weeks delay from getting back to Ireland; to Kildunlee. To her.*

"I've taken the liberty of booking you on the Pan Am flight from London to Boston. There were a couple of last minute cancellations and I was lucky enough to pick one up for you. You flight leaves tomorrow morning at nine."

Thanks, thought McGrath. *Boston, not Kildunlee. Another delay in seeing her.*

What could he do? Business had to be taken care of, and he'd no choice but to catch the morning's flight back home.

A week or two turned in to four weeks, and negotiations were still in full force. Then came Christmas and he couldn't go anywhere. But, with the last week of January of the new year, all contracts had been signed, appropriate papers filed with the United States and Brazilian governmental agencies, and the acquisition was secure and complete. He could return to Ireland. But, with his current work schedule, the earliest flight was late the last day of February, so a bit more delay. He would be back in Ireland in early March. Still, he would soon be on his way to seeing her again. He could wait; it was only two weeks away.

***

Eleven-forty-five, just passing through the main four corner intersection of the West Country town of Kildunlee, near O'Brien's Tower, and slightly north of Liscannor. It was a small town, just a large village, really, and it was surrounded by farms populated with dairy cows, beef cattle, pigs, sheep and acres of vegetable gardens, especially potato, or, as the local populace called them, praties, gardens. Still, Kildunlee was a modestly prosperous Irish community sporting Niamh's pub, a grocery store, a dry goods store, an iron monger's to support the local farmers, a cattle feed store and its pride, a beautiful church that somehow escaped the ravages of Cromwell and the English.

Finally the storm has begun to subside; the wind dying down and the precipitation easing off. Another mile, and there it is. A warm glow spread across his chest. So familiar, now. The two standard thatched roofed Irish cottages, where he and his Detail spent almost a year, taking weather observations, forecasting and keeping meteorological records. But, the lights were on in both the north and the south cottage.

Why? He had told Mrs. O'Shaunessy just to get one cottage ready for him. He didn't need the second one. He told her that she could leave it unlocked against his arrival, since no one stole anything in this part of Ireland anyway.

He pulled his car into the circular driveway, put on the brake, grabbed his two suit cases and went inside.

"Well, yer honor, and 'tis a fine night for travelin', I'd say. And you in that soakin' outfit, lookin' like a fish just jumped out o' the lake. Take a minute to dry off and change yer clothes. I've got a nice beef stew bubblin' up fer yer, an' I left the lights burnin' in both cottages as a beacon ter welcome yer home agin'."

"Mrs. O'Shaunessy," McGrath exclaimed. "I didn't expect you to stay here till I arrived. It's late and you've got to go all the way back to town. I didn't think you'd be here."

"Sure, an' who is it that's going ter give you a nice warm feed on a ruddy pig of a night like this one?" Her smile spread across her rosy cheeks, her ancient blue eyes flashing. "Someone has ter take care of yer. Yer can't be expected ter start cookin' a meal by yerself this late, now, can yer?"

McGrath reached out and picked up the inimitable Mrs. O'Shaunessy and spun her around several times.

"Put me down, yer grand oaf!" she cried at him, both of them laughing like silly goats.

"Mrs. O'Shaunessy, you're the most beautiful lady I have ever seen, and your cooking is a gift of the gods."

"Argh! I may be beautiful, but 'tis not my old beauty that brings yer back here, now, is it?" He set her down gently; in spite of his formidable strength, both of them out of breath.

"No," he replied. "I've come back to see her ladyship, Cynthia FitzHugh."

"Did yer, now?" she asks slyly, knowing full well the reason he was here again. "Well, if it's any consolation, she hasn't got married, and there isn't anyone banging on her door with a diamond in his clutches, so there's a prayer for yer. And best o' Irish luck with her, but, as we say here in the West Country, yer never know what's ter happen."

"You're right. Definitely. But, I called her from Dublin and asked to see her tomorrow early afternoon. I'm not even sure what I'm going to say to her."

"Argh! Don't worry. The Good Lord will put the right words inter yer mouth, if it pleases Him. Now, I've got ter be goin'. Work ter be done tomorrow. Don't forget yer stew in the kitchen. Good and hot, the way yer always liked it, with plenty of praties and onions for taste."

She pulled on her long, heavy coat and clamped her

large, woolen hat on her head. "I'll be off, then, but I'll stop by after tomorrow and see what yer might be needin'. Till then, best o' Irish luck to yer."

"Wait. Why don't you let me run you home? It's a filthy night out and you'll get all wet."

"Nah. It's just a few steps up the rut, as yer and the b'ys called it, and I'll be home ter me old man, the fire and a drop o' the pure. Don't worry." And she stepped out into the clearing night. Stars had begun to appear, and the wind had died to a breeze. The storm was practically over.

McGrath turned to look at the inside of the cottage he and the Detail had called home for almost a year. The furniture was the same. The layout hadn't changed. Nothing had moved. It caused him to smile at the rustic comfort of the place. Nothing like his mansion on Beacon Hill, but it was fine for him. He went into the kitchen and ladled a large plate of Mrs. O'Shaunessy's stew out and sat down to one of her wonderful meals. *We never would have made it through the war years in Ireland without her,* he thought. He poured a generous portion of Jameson's whisky into a crystal tumbler. "Here's to you Mrs. O'Shaunessy," and he took a deep pull. *And to you, my Detail, the best sailors in the fleet.* A second mouthful. Then he started on his stew, with thoughts of Lady Cynthia FitzHugh drifting through his mind. *Tomorrow,* he thought.

8.

A TEMPESTUOUS REUNION

An intense fog enveloped his mind, wafting him further into the deepness of oblivious sleep. His night had been blissfully restful from the moment his head hit the soft goose down pillow. So complete was his tiredness that barely a dream provided entertainment or came to his conscious level. No dreams of her; no dreams of Ireland, his Detail or the upcoming day. Just marvelous, wonderful, restful sleep after a nerve tearing night of driving on washed out Irish roads, in a violent Irish storm in a rust bucket Irish car. The joy that only an excellent night's sleep can bring; the absolute paradise of escape from the concerns at hand. Release; relief. And yet something started to pierce his consciousness; something stroked his awakening mind, his vital senses. McGrath's eyes opened only a crack and he remembered that he was in the cottage in Ireland, with a challenging day ahead of him; one that he had planned for months; one that he had looked forward to, and anticipated with supreme desire, and, yet at the same time, one which he was terrified to face. To see her again. But what if she refused to speak with him? What if she rejected his request to see her? Well, he decided, in his dimming fog of sleep, the only way to find out was to go to her and plead his case. He'd sailed through typhoons and hurricanes, seen some action at sea during the war, and been shot in the right thigh during his Detail's escape from Ireland on another wildly stormy night. And, still, all of these incidents seemed to take less courage than a knock on her door at one this afternoon.

Yet what penetrated his morphed senses was the splendid, fragrant aroma of fresh, strong coffee being brewed. The pleasant scent of a rasher of newly cured Irish bacon and its accompanying musical sizzle in full swing. McGrath yawned loudly, basking in the sensuous pleasure of Mrs. O'Shaunessy's culinary achievements.

"Argh! 'Tis about time yer rolled outa bed, yer great thunderin' thing, and the Lord's day nearly half over," her ancient blue eyes twinkling and her ruddy cheeks aglow, a large grin, displaying perfect teeth, decorating the lower half of her intelligent face . "I've just been getting' a bit of breakfast ready fer yer. Yer'll have ter bathe later, 'tis almost ready."

"You're amazing, Mrs. O'Shaunessy. You appear out of nowhere and work miracles in the kitchen," replied a bleary eyed McGrath, arrayed in disheveled pajamas and wrapped in a large, blue wool robe.

"Begone wi' yer. I took care o' yer an' me Navy b'ys in '44 and I can do it again, especially since there's only one o' yer. Now, go and wash yer face. Eggs in five minutes. Fresh bread with marmalade I made meself last month, and new bacon, eggs and butter right from Brendan Rafferty's barn."

McGrath pulled the warm robe around him, against the cool Irish morning. "Six battleships couldn't drag me away," and he went into the well appointed bathroom to freshen up.

"And I hope yer've yer usual appetite t'day, yer honor," she said to him when he returned to the kitchen. "Yer always had a good one an' not an ounce on yer to spare.

"How d'yer keep so slim, seein' as yer've those broad shoulders an' strong hands?" She asked him, as she finished up at the stove top.

"I expect that it's from my days at sea," McGrath

answered her, as he pulled out a kitchen chair to sit in front of a massive breakfast. "Grandfather Josiah, and my father, Francis, after him, believed that the more a seaman worked, the tougher he became. And, if he was to run this company, he'd better be plenty tough. Life at sea is the hardest, and the most demanding and I think you know that." He sprinkled salt and pepper on his golden fried eggs, marveling at the half-inch-thick sliced bacon. "Mrs. O'Shaunessy, do you really think I can eat this banquet you've prepared?"

"Well, yer honor, yer've got ter keep yer strength up. As I ken it, yer've got a day an' a half in front o' yer this fine day." Her voice dropped an octave. "An' I'll be tellin' yer the truth, 'tis a job yer'll have, seein' as it's her Ladyship yer'll be wantin' to talk with, an' no doubt about it, mind yer." She bustled around the kitchen, keeping herself busy and out of his line of vision. McGrath's appetite didn't flag, and he relished his Irish breakfast, but her words did give him pause to reflect.

"How do you mean?" he finally asked her.

Mrs. O'Shaunessy kept her back to him, and hummed a little Irish tune for a minute or two. She washed two frying pans and the other utensils she had used to prepare McGrath's meal. He understood she was collecting her thoughts, and he waited for her response. At last, she finished the washing up.

"Well, yer know, yer honor, 'tis hard fer a woman when the man in her life ups and goes away."

"Yes, but…"

"None of yer lip! Yer'll be listening ter me, and no mistake, Commander William McGrath," she admonished him and a bolt of lightning shot through him jerking him upright and assuring her of his immediate attention and respect, if, in fact, she hadn't already gained it.

"Yes, Mrs. O'Shaunessy."

"I've been on this here earth twice as long an' more

as yer have, and when a woman has a man she fancies, then he's gone, 'tis no doubt she loses faith. In him and all he stood for." Mrs. O'Shaunessy took a long and deep breath, silencing McGrath with her raised right index finger. "Yer'll be listening ter me and no mistake. I know yer've talked ter the good Father in Upper Kings Ridley recently, in that heathen land ter the south. An' he told yer that I'd slit a man's gullet if he crossed me or the sod I was born on. 'Tis true I'd done the same an' worse. I were part of MI6 in the old days, in the first war, and that's gone an' forgotten, now, may God forgive me an' the work I done, an' that's all gone and past now like the carcass o' last year's Christmas goose. But I loved me Navy b'ys as was here in '44, and I loved yer as a son, me own lost in North Africker against Rommel, God bless his soul, me son, not Rommel, the Hun.

"But, yer left her an' was gone before we knew what was goin' on. T'wasn't yer fault. War is war. An' a bloody awful thing it is. But I'll be tellin' yer here an' now an' plain an' simple. She's there. Yer here. An' if yer carrying any manhood in that gut of yers, yer'd best be getting' ter the Manor ter see her. I ain't sayin' what'll happen. Maybe she'll toss yer out on the ruts, an' if so, be damned, an' go back ter yer Boston an' find a dainty fer yerself, one of yer blue bloods, or whatever yer call those wenches. But, if yer don't try, yer less of a man than I think yer are, Commander William McGrath. Now, let me get back to me dishes, finish yer breakfast, and go take a bath. Yer stink from travel."

***

Lost. Lost was the only word for McGrath. His head spun from Mrs. O'Shaunessy's tongue lashing. Was it really a tongue lashing? Or serious, heartfelt advice? He strongly opted for the latter, but with barely a touch of the former thrown in. *Why am I here?* He asked himself. *I thought I wanted to see...* He couldn't frame the words. *What is her name? Whose side is Mrs. O'Shaunessy on, anyway? Did I hear her right? Go get a blue blood? God in heaven, my head is spinning and I don't know what to do. Why am I here? Confusion. I have a multimillion dollar steamship company to run. Second largest in the world. A board of directors to supervise. Thousands of workers and seamen to oversee. I need management help, and I have to be there to oversee the company. Why am I wasting my time fiddling around in a speck of a town, which probably isn't even on the map, near Galway, chasing some nebulous woman who I haven't seen in months, over a year, and who probably doesn't even want to see my face again? Why am I here?*

A tension headache started deep in his skull. A headache he would rather not have had.

Stress. Tension. Impending fear. Experiences he hadn't had since the Zero torpedoes hit his ship in the Pacific in the Imperial Navy's last ditch effort to gain victory. But his ship held, and stayed afloat, with pounding help from the destroyer escort. But the anxiety... throbbing, weary, afraid. Fear of the unknown. He took a large swallow of Mrs. O'Shaunessy's hot, strong coffee, black, no cream, no sugar, U.S. Navy style, which for McGrath was frequently more effective in eliminating his headaches than aspirin.

"An' so, yer honor, I'll leave yer ter yer devices, now. If things are good, I'll be back this evening, about seven, with a nice leg of lamb. Thick brown gravy and roasted praties. It was yer favorite when yer were here in '44, do yer remember?"

"Mrs. ... Mrs. ..."

"O'Shaunessy, me b'y. Don't yer remember? Aye. I see I've put a thought or two in yer head and 'tis grand. Now, go do what yer came here for. I'll hear about it in the morning, no doubt. Sure, an' it'll be at Niamh's pub, aye, an' I'll be there for the news, an' won't we all? Best of Irish luck, an' remember, yer roots ain't far from here, just down Cork way," she said as her twinkling blue eyes winked at him, and she left for Kildunlee and her early morning's shopping, in a fine and bright West Country sun-filled day.

McGrath drained his coffee cup, confident that the strong, black liquor would banish his tension headache, which already seemed to be receding, jolt him back to the reality of the moment, and away from the fears of the unknown, and the aspect of seeing... *Cynthia!*

Her name came to him in a rainbow. He saw her exquisite straight, blond hair. Her flawless complexion and gray, flashing eyes. Her strong, athletic, voluptuous figure; flaring hips; bulging breasts. A marvelous woman. His heart yearned for her. His passion screamed for her. And, yet, was he man enough to go to the Manor and ask to speak with her? With Cynthia?

***

McGrath rinsed his coffee cup and put it in the sink Looking at the freshening day, bright with scalding sunshine and a flaming blue sky, a soft and gentle breeze from the warmth of the south, he took a long and deep breath and told himself, "Yes, Mrs. O'Shaunessy, I have the manhood to come here to see her Ladyship. I want to. I have to. She may throw me out onto the ruts, but here I am." McGrath tossed the dishtowel on the sink and went to the shower.

***

He started the engine in his rented rolling pile of rust and noise car, headed out the driveway and toward Kildunlee. McGrath remembered that the Manor was about three miles from the center of town, in an easterly direction, so, after he had entered Kildunlee from the south, the road paralleling the Cliffs of Moher, he swung his car off the quasi- paved road and on to the dirt road that ran east and led directly to the approach to the Manor.

The blazing sun, warm for mid March, entered his car through the rear and side windows, warming his right shoulder, encouraging and strengthening him for the tasks that lay ahead. His friend, the weather, had given him a beautiful day for his task, and urged him on, telling him you can do this; you can succeed. A crystal clear day, he acknowledged, not a cloud in the sky. He thought to himself, they must have all been blown out to sea by yesterday's storm. A clear and brisk day, the like you don't see in Ireland very often, and the like you don't see on the Cape as often as you may want to at this time of year. Although he did have some days like this one, sailing on Cape Cod Bay with Jack, his buddy, who lived down the road from the McGrath summer cottage. But that was before the war, and in a distant part of the world. Cape Cod seemed so far away just this minute, and here he was in Ireland's West Country, a world and a culture away from the surroundings he knew and understood. He didn't understand the Irish, not at all, especially the upper class Irish. Like Cynthia.

He was one hundred percent Irish heritage himself, all the way back to Grandfather Josiah McGrath, who married a Murphy, and beyond. But he was American, and that seemed to make all the difference. *Irish-American*, he thought to himself, *but I'm different. Will she see me?*

Verdant fields, filled with dairy cows and heavy beef cattle, spread to the horizon on both sides of the road. He saw pigs in the distance, and sheep grazing gently on the rich grass. So pleasant, so peaceful, he told himself. How could anyone want to leave such an idyllic place?

Finally, his car slowly nosed around a sharp bend in

the dirt road, continuing east, while a crushed rock drive tapered gently to the south, and a half mile away at the end of the well-tended crushed rock approach, and its surrounding grounds, stood the FitzHugh Manor House, its gray stone façade gleaming in the early afternoon sun.

**

"Well, Sir Julian, I'm really sorry you can't stay for lunch. It would be a pleasure to have you. I think the cook is preparing one of her usual delights."

"Thank you, Lady Cynthia, but I really must be off. Have to prepare for Alice's and my trip to South Africa, you know. I have already booked us a rental house in Johannesburg till we can find a proper home. Only a few more weeks till we leave and there's so much to be tidied up."

"I know, I know. Packing up and moving entails so much work, and we really will miss you and Alice. You've both brought so much joy to all of us."

"Ah, Cynthia, my dear, so good of you to say that. But I must be off, now. Alice will be expecting me soon." Sir Julian put on his topcoat and hat, against the bright, but chilly, day, and started for the front door, and Cynthia walked slowly beside him to see him out. She paused in the hall for a second. "Well, Sir Julian, we wish you and Alice all the best of luck in your new life. At least, it will be warm and sunny most of the time," she said smiling.

"Yes, it will be and we're looking forward to that. Ireland is lovely, but the rain and gray days sometimes get to be a bit much," he answered her.

"Excuse me, my lady. There is a gentleman here to see you. An American gentleman, I believe," Riordan, the butler, told her.

"American?" said Sir Julian. "I didn't know you were seeing Americans these days. They all left when the war was over last year, didn't they?"

Cynthia's heart doubled its beat, and her breath came hard. A bead of sweat sidled its way between her shoulder blades.

"Yes, they all left last year, when the war had ended. The group of American sailors that did the weather observations left before that, just before D-Day, I believe.

"No, I don't know any American gentleman. It must be some sort of mistake."

"Well, let me not keep you from your splendid lunch, Cynthia. So sorry to have to miss it and all that, but Alice is waiting. But, we'll be in touch before we sail for Johannesburg," and with that, Sir Julian warmly shook hands with Cynthia, and headed for the door and his car. As he stepped out to the gravel front yard, she saw a tall man just inside the entryway, his hair was almost black and his eyes the blue of frozen diamonds.

Cynthia couldn't move. She didn't believe the sight before her.

"Excuse me, my lady. This is the American gentleman I mentioned. Will you see him?" Riordan asked her, feeling the discomfort in the room, and with a questioning look on his face.

"Ah, Riordan..." she began, brushing a stray hair from her cheek. "I'm not sure... I mean, I don't think..."

"My lady, shall I call O'Leary and the men from the tack to put this gentleman out?"

"Cynthia. It's me. William. I've come back. It is really me. I'm not a ghost."

"No... Riordan. Wait. Let me think for a minute," Cynthia said, sounding quite confused. She brushed her hair away again.

"Cynthia, it's me. Can we go somewhere and talk? Please? I've come all the way from Boston to see you."

"My lady, shall I call O'Leary and the stable men?"

"No, thank you, Riordan. That won't be necessary."

Cynthia turned to the man who had spoken to her.

"Do I know you? Who are you?"

"William. William McGrath, formerly of the United States Navy, at your service. I was a meteorologist and I did weather forecasting near the Cliffs. My Detail—the sailors with me—took weather observations for my forecasts, and we were billeted in the two twin cottages south of Kildunlee. We all spent almost a year there. I received orders to leave with my entire crew the night before D-Day. I tried to get in touch with you before we left on that terribly stormy night. Liam O'Banyon was to run us out to a Canadian Corvette in his boat. The Corvette was bound for Halifax, and we had orders to rendez-vous with it. I called the Manor several times, but you weren't in. Now, I've come back and I'd like to tell you what happened so you understand."

"I knew a Lieutenant William McGrath almost two years ago, but he died at sea. He left before D-Day and his ship was sunk." She had to take a very deep breath to gain some form of composure. "I understand it was a torpedo or some such thing like that."

"No. It wasn't like that at all. Will you give me a few minutes to tell you what happened? Just a few minutes, Cynthia. Please?"

She could feel her heart hammering inside her chest. Breath was difficult to come by.

"All right then. Just a few minutes. Come into the morning room. Riordan, tell Mrs. Lynch to hold lunch, and give her my apologies. Thank you."

"Yes, my lady," and he started for the kitchen.

Cynthia couldn't even look at William, so she said over her shoulder, "Come this way," and he followed her into the morning room, where the bright sun glanced off the highly polished furniture with its blazing green upholstery. "Sit down. I'm listening. You have only a few minutes, as you asked."

"Yes. Thank you." McGrath took a very deep

breath and began his story. "I don't know how much you know, so I'd better tell the whole series of events." For a moment, he looked out the tall west window, displaying the lush, verdant lawns punctuated by numerous flower-beds like colorful sail boats on a green sea, to gather his thoughts. He had never seen a bluer sky in Ireland before. He turned back to face Cynthia, but her back was to him, as she gazed at the same vista through the tall south window.

"We were here in the cottages for almost a year, taking weather observations for Eisenhower's prepara-tions for D-Day. I was brought in from the naval weather station in Honolulu. It was quite a change." He smiled briefly. "We took our observations and sent them on to London and Washington. It helped Eisenhower plan for the crossing. At any rate, we got orders to leave the night before D-Day, using Liam O'Banyon's boat, and to meet up with the Canadian Corvette I just told you about a half mile or so out to sea. It all went well except that I took a rifle bullet in my right thigh. Then there was some trouble at the edge of the Cliffs, I think it was with Hilsblad, the Swedish Importer, and the IRA men. Maybe that's where you heard that I had been lost at sea. But I wasn't. I was only wounded, and it eventually healed although that wound still bothers me now and again. We then docked at Halifax and flew to Washington after that. The worst part was that we did such a great job in our observations and in helping Ike out that MacArthur learned of our work, and insisted that we do the same for him in the Pacific.

"We were recruited on a volunteer basis," he said smiling. "Of course, we could have refused, but can you really refuse? Germany was about to fall, since the Allies had crossed into France, but Japan was still in full swing. So we all got on a plane and flew to the West Coast, then on to Honolulu and out to a carrier in the Pacific. From there we went aboard a small destroyer escort to take more observations. Of course, we couldn't tell anyone what we were doing or where we were headed. It was all sort of top secret. But from early July 1944 until shortly before Hiroshima, we did the same thing we did in Kildunlee. Except that this time we sent the results of our observations to MacArthur. He wanted to know all about the winds, sea temperatures, currents and so on in the event of an invasion of the Japanese homeland." McGrath paused for a moment.

Cynthia continued to gaze out the south window at the verdant lawns outside. Edward and Timmy, the footmen and groundskeepers, were running their mowing machines up and down the lawn in a beautiful geometric pattern, keeping the grass low.

"Did Boats go with you this time?" Cynthia asked. Leon Koslowski, called Boats since he was a Boatswain's Mate, was a popular and colorful figure among the townspeople, and they all knew and liked the Boats.

"No. I wish he had, but we had no need of him in doing observations at sea. Unfortunately, he was killed by a Kamikaze pilot in the run up to the invasion of Iwo Jima. I was told that when the plane hit, Boats died instantly. He didn't suffer."

Cynthia shuddered at the thought of Boats being killed in such a manner.

"As they say, the rest is history. The surrender was signed on the Missouri, we were mustered out and we all went home. I had a very large business to see to, so I returned to Boston. As I mentioned, our work was secret, so none of us could let the folks at home know what was going on. I couldn't write you if I wanted to, and I did want to." Suddenly, his tone changed, from the matter of fact relating of the history of the last year and a half to a timbre of emotion entering his voice.

"Cynthia, I've wanted so much to write to you, to tell you where I was and what I was doing. But, I couldn't. And, then, when I was back from the Pacific, I had so much to attend to with my family and at my office that I had no time to even compose a letter to you. And a letter would be so cold and crass, coming out of nowhere that I resolved to come back to Ireland and speak with you face to face."

She continued to stare out of the window at the grounds men doing their mowing, apparently ignoring William and his story. Her golden hair gleamed in the sunlight and he longed to reach out and touch it. She faced away from him, tall, straight and exuding self-confidence he had seldom seen in a woman. At least, the women he knew. He recalled her deep gray eyes, like sapphires in a soft, creamy, beautiful face. He wished she would look at him, if only for a moment. But her eyes were fixed on the men working on the landscape. He had to tell her what was in his heart and on his mind, but the marvelous curves of her graceful, athletic figure distracted him.

"I tried to write to you, but I never could compose a letter with the thoughts and feelings I wanted to convey. After we were discharged, at the end of the war, in late September for me, I had to return to Boston to again take charge of McGrath Shipping. My management staff had done a wonderful job in my absence. But I had resolved to come back to Ireland to see you and I flew to London in November of last year, spending a day with your cousin, Father Tim O'Neill in Upper Kings Ridley. He brought me up-to-date on the events that had occurred after we left Kildunlee and encouraged me to come and see you. He is your cousin, isn't he?"

"Yes. He is. From the Catholic side of the family" she said, her voice strangely soft, but its tone was lost on McGrath.

"My last day in London, I got a trans-Atlantic call that I was to return to Boston immediately. There were

South American business affairs to attend to and my father had had a stroke and wasn't expected to live. I booked a flight right away and returned home. He died a week after my arrival." McGrath paused for a moment, breathed deeply a couple of times, then continued.

Cynthia still stared out the window.

"Then came Christmas and it was impossible for me to leave at that time. I spent Christmas with my family, and January and February being sure the company could run without me for a few more weeks. It made it through the war years, so why not a few more weeks while I came to see you? So, I tied up all the loose ends at work and at home, made reservations on another flight to London, and came to Ireland. Cynthia, I had to see you again." Her eyes lifted to some dark object far in the distance, a monument or dead tree. He couldn't tell.

"Cynthia, please listen to me. I've missed you all these days I was away. In the Pacific. Back in Boston. There has been little on my mind but you since we left just before D-Day. I thought of our horseback ride, our collision and the brief conversations we had. They always seemed to be interrupted, and we never got very far. But, I will never forget our ride on Sassy and Warrior. The few moments alone before your servant showed up to tell you about your father's heart attack. I've thought of nothing else. I haven't wanted to think of anything else. Just you. I realize now that I've loved you since I first saw you. That love hasn't gone away. It's still there and I had to tell you. I love you and I've come back. To you." He paused for a few seconds. "So. I'm done. I've said all I've had to say. I have nothing more to tell you."

McGrath looked at her.

Lady Cynthia FitzHugh stood looking intently out of the window at the grounds, watching the workers. Her shoulders began to shake, then rippled throughout her whole body, shaking as if in a grip of spasm.

"How... How can you stand there ignoring me after I've poured out my heart to you? Then you laugh at me. I told you I love you, that I was being honest; that everything I just said was true. And all you can do is laugh at me." McGrath wasn't angry. He was confused, upset, shocked.

Finally, she turned toward him, toward this room bursting with passion, away from the idyllic setting on the other side of the glass.

"You foolish American. You silly, silly sailor," she said to him. "Can't you see? Are you completely blind?" Her eyes flooded with tears. They cascaded from her gray eyes and down her cheeks, washing away her makeup, smearing that immaculate, and beautiful, face. "I'm not laughing at you, William. I'm crying from joy, relief that you're back. That you're mine. I've loved you from the moment you knocked the tin cans out of my hands in O'Banyon's so long ago. And I can't think of anyone but you. And here you go away to God only knows where and leave me with a broken heart longing for you. You silly, silly sailor. It's you and only you I love. It's been that way all along. There is no one else."

"I... Cynthia, I... had no idea."

"How could you? You were far away in the middle of the Pacific. But for all that, I thought you might have been killed at sea. I was told that and I really believed it. You can't imagine my upset at hearing that you were dead. In my room, I cried for weeks. No one knew my feelings, not even Bridie Scanlon, my maid. I told no one and kept my love for you, and my pain and sorrow, locked in my broken and tortured heart. Now, here you are. Safe. Sound. Mine again, and an old sea story is nothing but a story."

"That was it. Just a phony story. We were top secret, working directly for MacArthur. The Navy didn't want any reprisals on Kildunlee, so it was given out that we were killed at sea. Torpedoed. At the end of the war, when things had quieted down, we were released from our secret mission and silence. We could return and tell the truth. I got things fixed up in Boston and came here as soon as I could. Then..."

"William."

"Er, what?"

"Please stop talking and kiss me."

His arms went around her waist and he held her so close. Their lips met, sweet and passionate. The past year and a half forgotten in the happiness of their embrace.

"William, it's always been you, and now you're back. Thank God for miracles," she breathed on his neck.

"I'm not leaving for a while. You and I have some catching up to do. And, you know what?"

"What? Tell me."

"This is going to be the shortest engagement in the history of all Kildunlee."

She stood back and smiled at him, radiant and ecstatic at being with Commander William McGrath again, and for always. Mrs. William McGrath.

"Why should we wait?" She asked him. "We've lost a year and a half as it is."

"We'll go to the village and see Father McDermott this afternoon. We can start planning. I'm sure that he'll understand."

"The whole village will understand."

"I love you, Cynthia."

"And I love you, William," and she kissed him tenderly. "But, Mrs. Lynch is holding lunch, and we had better not keep her waiting much longer. She gets upset when her meals are ignored."

"Come, my lady, let me take you to lunch. I'm starved." They embraced again and then Cynthia rang for Riordan.

9.

.

A GLORIOUS MORNING

Sunrise came early and very bright that Tuesday morning. The sky still held its clarity but some high clouds were beginning to gather in the south, though they didn't seem to be particularly threatening. Sunshine struck Edward Hillaire's closed eyes and charmed him awake. His wife, Siobhan, was sound asleep beside him. He smiled in appreciation of her gently curving cheek; her long, black Celtic hair spilling all over the pillow. A thrill of warmth and love spread throughout his breast. He stroked her cheek till she murmured.

"Oh, Eddie me own. 'Tis you isn't it?"

"Of course. Who else but." He continued to stroke her cheek till she smiled in her sleepiness, her bright blue eyes finally opening to look at her young husband. He leaned over and gently kissed her lips and she responded, softly moaning in an early morning welcomed greeting.

"Oh, Eddie, I'm so glad yer came back to me. Aye, an' I'm lost without yer, especially having Margaret and all."

"Siobhan, I knew I'd be back. They shipped us out to the Pacific to work for MacArthur. I went over with Commander McGrath, but I always knew I'd come home to you.

"I had to go home to Montana to see my parents, then, when I had them calmed down, I came back to Kildunlee. And here I stay, learning how to be a pig farmer from your Da."

"Ah, an' a fine pigger yer'll be, an' it warms me heart ter hear yer call our little place home."

"We have a fine Irish home in this little cottage and I like the idea of being an Irish pigger, as you call me," and they both laughed at his comment.

"Siobhan, so much has happened. My parents are coming over from Montana tomorrow, in time for the Commander and Lady Cynthia's wedding. It couldn't have worked out better, especially after all the mix-ups from the war, my being sent to the Pacific and all that."

"Ah, Eddie, me own, 'tis done with and you're here with me and the babe. 'Tis grand," and she wrapped her arms around his neck, kissing him full on the mouth.

"Siobhan, I'm supposed to take you to Galway to get a new dress for the wedding. Lady Cynthia chose you to be a bridesmaid, you know. She's chosen the dresses for you and the other bridesmaids and we have to pick yours up."

"Oh, Eddie, 'twill wait. 'Tis you I want, not the dress."

"I know there has been a lot of emigration from Ireland to the rest of the world, but I think you're trying to repopulate the island singlehandedly," he said with a chuckle.

"With you, Eddie, me own, 'twill be a joy. *Is tú mo ghrá.*" Hillaire stopped talking and let the rising sun warm the room, his wife and him. "I love you, too, my graw." Siobhan's lips curved into a smile at his Gaelic. They fell into each others' arms.

***

Later, after bathing, as they dressed, Siobhan said to him, "And think, the Commander has been here just under a month, since mid-March, living in one of the cottages that you used to live in during the war, and with Mrs. O'Shaunessy takin' fine care of him, and now they have the weddin' all planned out. After being apart for a year an' more, they're not having any more time be wasted.

"I certainly wouldn't if I were them. The whole town approves of the two of them and is waiting for the big day," he said to Siobhan.

"Ah, sure'n 'twill be a grand affair. I know her Ladyship is taking Catholic instruction from Father McDermott. The way you did just before we got wed."

"Yes. I remember. He's a fine old priest, is Father McDermott, although I liked Father Tim, as he preferred to be called. He was young and understood things."

"Aye, but he's in England now in some place called Upper Kings Ridley. Mrs. O'Shaunessy told me that he does work there other than keepin' his parish."

"Rumor has it that he had been involved—with special permission from the bishop—with some cloak and dagger stuff, things he had done before he entered the seminary. I really don't know, but I'm glad we invited him to come to our wedding. I like the man."

"We all do," she said, as she finished brushing her long, raven tresses. "I expect the Commander will invite him ter his wedding as well."

"I'm sure he will, and I expect he's already done it," he said as he gave her a peck on the nose. "After all, he is Lady Cynthia's cousin." Eddie finished buttoning his blue work shirt.

"When I told the Commander that my parents and their friends were coming to see Margaret, their grand-child, he told me that they should come to his wedding and they should bring their friends, the Huestises. They're all nice people. And also, in their last letter, my parents mentioned that they'd like for you, the kids and me all to go back to Montana for a few weeks. You could see the place where I grew up."

"But, Eddie, it'll be such a long trip. The other side o' the ocean and then the other side of America. I don't know if the kids and I could do it."

"The kids", as she called them, were Siobhan's siblings, Donal, Kathleen, and Deidre Rafferty, whom Siobhan, as the oldest child of her widowed father, Brendan Rafferty, helped raise.

"And these people, the Huestises, do they also have a horse farm?"

"No. They opted for cattle and they make a good living at it. My father wanted to raise horses so he took over my grandfather's horse farm, or ranch, if you prefer, after grandfather Hillaire got too old and sick to ride. He also has a bad heart, like Earl FitzHugh, and he's quite up in age. But, my father does pretty well. When he's not there, my brothers, Roy and Peter, run the ranch. They're learning the profession."

"And what about you, Eddie? Are you going back ter 'learn the profession'?"

"No. You know that. I'm here to stay in Ireland. Your Da's teaching me all about pig farming, with a few cattle and a sheep or two mixed in, and, my dear, that's enough for me."

Eddie checked his watch and saw that time was passing. "Well, the invitation to Montana is there and it'll never go away," he smiled at her. "I know it's a long trip, but one day we'll have to do it. Maybe in a year or two when the kids are a bit older."

"Sure, we'll go. Maybe next year."

"OK. But come on, now, I can smell Deirdre's bacon frying. She's just come over from your Da's cottage to prepare our breakfast. And this Thursday morning, when the chores are done, we have to go to town for the wedding rehearsal. We can pick up your bridesmaid's dress in Galway tomorrow. I never dreamed that the Commander would ask me to be his best man. I really feel honored. That part actually belongs to one of his brothers, but, as you know, unfortunately, they were both lost in the war."

"I know, and 'tis a pity. But, Ah, 'tis a fine man he is and all the townsfolk like him, sure'n they do. I'd even say they love him for what he did for our town; put it on the map and made us proud ter be from here. We're lucky ter have him back."

"I know," Eddie said, then picking up his keys and stuffing them in his pants pocket. "He's been here since mid-March, when he first went to see her Ladyship one afternoon. Mrs. O'Shaunessy told me all about that."

"She sees and knows everything around here, doesn't she?"

"I don't know how she does it, but she learns everything. In Montana, engagements usually take a year or so, but the Commander and her ladyship decided to move things along. They waited only a few weeks to get the arrangements and paperwork in place, and now it's late April and we're getting ready for the wedding this coming Saturday. Seems like it's been one party in their honor after another, and always at Niamh's pub," he said smiling at her, admiring the beauty of his young Irish wife. "And, you know something else, it's like spring here. Not cold at all; probably around fifty, fifty-five, degrees. In Montana, at this time of year, we often hit thirty or forty below."

"Below what?" Siobhan asked, innocently, her blue eyes agog.

"Below zero, *a chara*, my dear." Eddie informed her, getting his clothes straightened out, ready to meet his father-in-law and his daughter's siblings.

"Get on with yer. Never is it that cold. Yer're telling me a story again."

"No, I'm not. Really, Siobhan. It gets so cold in Montana, what with the wind whipping down out of the Canadian prairies, that we have to stay inside some days. We can't go out. We have to clump around the fire to stay warm."

And at the thought, she put her long, sweet arms around her man. "Eddie, *mo ghrá*, 'tis a fine idea to me," and she kissed him softly.

"Siobhan, my dear," he smiled at her, while gently extricating himself from her loving embrace, "I have to have some breakfast, help your Da with the farm and get the chores done. Let me alone, dear lady, let me alone!" He pleaded, chuckling. "There's a big wedding coming up, and we're part of it. Work to be done!" He pulled her arms from around his neck and caught his breath. "The rehearsal's at one this Wednesday afternoon, and the Commander will be expecting us. We have to be on time, so the work with the pigs must be done."

"Ah, sure, the whole town'll turn out and what a party afterward t'will be. Since the war was done, Kildunlee has never been happier, an' 'tis a joy ter see. And did I tell yer, her Ladyship came ter see me and thanked me for being a bridesmaid. Said she had several cousins that had ter be used, but she also wanted someone outside of the FitzHugh family, and it was wonderful that I would be in the wedding party because the Commander had chosen you as his Best Man. She said she was happy ter have me accept as a bridesmaid. Can yer believe that? What a marvelous woman!"

"She really is lovely. The Commander chose well."

"Ah, Eddie, what a *ceili* 'twill be!"

"Not a doubt in my mind. Come. Let's just have breakfast. I'm so hungry I could eat one of your father's pigs right now, sight unseen."

And he gently grasped his young and beautiful wife by the elbow and whisked her out of the bedroom to the dining room where crisp bacon, skillet fried potatoes, fresh, scrambled eggs, warm bread with rich marmalade and newly churned butter provided simply a "… bit of a breakfast," to help keep "…everyone's strength up," at the Rafferty farm.

10.

A SECRET REVEALED

McGrath got out of the newly rented and up-to-date four-door Land Rover he had driven to town and grabbed several letters that were lying on the left front seat, which he had written to his staff in Boston, instructing them to stay in touch and to keep him informed of all the details that occurred with McGrath Shipping, Inc., and of any untoward business events that might arise. Today was Tuesday, and he was to be married on Saturday to Lady Cynthia FitzHugh. He really didn't want any problems to interfere with their wedding day. Neither did Cynthia, since they had spoken about the wedding and his responsibilities several thousand miles away in Boston. But they both understood the problem of trying to stay in touch with corporate headquarters staff, and, although the staff was truly reliable – and had, in fact, really run McGrath Shipping while McGrath was a Meteorological officer in the Navy, during the war. He knew that his primary responsibility was to keep McGrath Shipping "afloat", as Grandfather Josiah McGrath, the founder of the line, was accustomed to saying. So, McGrath picked up his letters and stepped into the Irish Royal Mail Office to send his instructions and orders to Boston.

"Well, if it isn't himself, and how are yer this marnin', Commander?"

"Fit as a fiddle." McGrath smiled at Sean Neill, who represented the Clerk of the Irish Royal Mail as well as being the Clerk of the Court whenever the Court was in session. Still, since there was seldom any serious crime committed in the town of Kildunlee, Sean made the bulk of his income from his job at the post office. Francis O'Farrell, the Regional Magistrate, who oversaw the prosecution of all criminal activities in the Kildunlee area—and they were few and far between—found himself dealing with the usual Saturday night raucous *bowseys*, the locals who had just a touch too much Jameson's or Guinness.

Sean Neill, of course, was understandably proud of his standing in the Kildunlee pecking order as, not only the Head Clerk of the Irish Royal Mails, but also as Clerk of the Court to Magistrate O'Farrell, regardless of the pettiness of the offense.

"An' are yer gettin' ready fer the weddin' now, Commander? Argh, 'twill be as grand a *ceili* the likes of which has never been seen this side o' the crowning of Brian Boru, an' will be talked about till icicles hang from the divil's doorpost, sure an' i'twill."

McGrath smiled at Sean's easygoing flow of Irish idioms. "Well, I hope so, Sean. Her Ladyship, I mean Cynthia, since she prefers everyone to call her that, and I are looking forward to our wedding day. It should be quite a fling."

"Argh, yer honor, quite a fling and then some, a clatter o' *craic,* aye, fun had by all. Oh, an' have yer heard? There's to be a story at Niamh's this very evening. An' won't Cormac O'Callaghan himself be there tellin' a tale or two. 'Tis always excitin' hearin' himself spin a yarn. Yer'd best be arriving' at Niamh's now ter see what the plan is fer this evenin'. Yer and her ladyship might want ter stop by ter hear the *seanachie*."

"The what?" Asked McGrath, forehead furrowed, but smiling at the sound of the word.

"Oh, aye, an' isn't Cormac O'Callaghan himself the finest *seanachie* in County Clare, Galway, Westmeath and all the way to the green slopes of Armagh? An' 'tis true, some say he has no equal in all the turf of the Holy Island. He's a *seanachie*, yer honor, a story teller and many tell of his ability to be a seer, someone who has the power ter see things that'll happen in the future and ter know how things are ter be in times to come. Aye, he's respected and welcomed all over this land."

Reaching in his pocket for the cash to pay for the airmail fee required to send his letters back to Boston, McGrath said to Sean, "In that event, I had better stop by at Niamh's and find out just when the story teller, the shanah-kee, will be around."

***

"Aye, an' welcome ter yerself, yer honor," Niamh said to McGrath. "'Tis true. Cormac will be here tonight, though we can never be sure of exactly when himself will be arriving. He keeps his own hours, yer ken."

"Yes. I understand that. Sean, at the post office, was telling me about him. He tells stories and is a seer as well?" McGrath asked the publican.

"Aye. That he is. An' what he sees always come true. He has the sight, an' no mistake. Everyone here tonight will be listenin' ter see what he's ter tell if he sees anything. An' though they'll all be half stocious from a drop o' the pure, they'll still understand what he says. And, argh, if there's a story ter be told, so yer and her ladyship ought ter be here fer a grand time. Now, will yer have a drop?"

McGrath smiled at Niamh's pleasant verbalizing, always intrigued and enraptured at the sound of the West Country voices and sounds of speech. "I'd better not. I can't show up at home half stocious, as you say. Cynthia will have my head. I would make John the Baptist's loss to Salome look like a child's party."

"Argh, 'tis fer sure, an' herself such a fine lady the

likes of which ain't been seen in these parts since Brigid herself set up shop in Kildare, don't yer know?"

"Actually, no, I didn't know, but I'm sure my future wife will be happy to hear it. We'll try to make it tonight, Niamh."

Niamh put her hand on McGrath's arm as he was getting up to return to the Manor.

"Commander, take a bit o' the drop o' the pure in a small jar, an' let me have a private word with yer." Niamh's voice was low and soft, almost a pleading whisper, kept in a quiet tone for only herself and the Commander to hear. McGrath saw the imploring look in her eyes, and, sensing her urgency, he re-took his seat on the bar stool at the corner of the bar.

Only Jean-Luc, the French Art Dealer, who had arrived three days previously to attend the Irish Impressionist exhibition at the new Galway Art Gallery, and two vacationing Spaniards, José Luis and Alejandro Basilio, were at the pub at this two o'clock hour. Jean-Luc flipped through the Gallery's Impressionist Art Catalog and sipped his Pernod distractedly. Jose Luis and Alejandro Basilio, who had driven in to Kildunlee after their recent overnight boat trip from Glasgow to Belfast, and were apparently oblivious to the conversation in English between McGrath and Niamh, continued an undertone of Spanish conversation, sipping their Fundadors. They had told Niamh in their very halting English that they were "...take vacation in north for fishin', an' fishin' good in Scotland, fishin' good here, yes?" They had a car load of poles, nets and reels with them to show their ardor for trout and salmon streams.

"What is it, Niamh?" McGrath asked softly. She poured him a very small bit of Jameson's, and a large one for herself, which she seldom did in the presence of a customer, and locked her gaze at McGrath. "Tell me about Boats, Commander."

If McGrath had been hit with a Louisville Slugger, he couldn't have been more knocked off balance.

"Boats," he stammered.

"Yes, Boats, Leon Koslowski, Bo'sun's Mate First Class, part o' yer crew here in forty-four."

McGrath took a sip of Jameson's, put his glass back on the oak bar, took a deep breath, then downed the rest of his whiskey. Niamh refilled his glass, which he gently pushed aside.

"Boats? Why Boats?" he asked her. Niamh took a sip of her own whiskey, closed her eyes and rolled her head back to her shoulders. When her face once again confronted McGrath, her eyes were flooded with tears.

"Because I had his baby last November. A beautiful little boy. I named him Brendan, after St. Brendan the Navigator, another sea-goin' man. He lives with my sister in Liscannor. A pub is no place for a child. But I see him each weekend. Sometimes, I take the bus down ter Liscannor just ter be with him. He looks so much like Boats." She took another sip of her Jameson's.

"I had him in Galway hospital, and everyone knows, yet no one knows, such as it is in Kildunlee. Boats had promised ter come back after the war, ter retire from the navy, marry me and tend the pub. Ter take care o' his babe. I've not seen him, nor heard a word, Commander."

She again lay an imploring hand on his wrist. "What happened to Boats? Where is he?" Tears streamed down her cheeks.

"I… I had no idea that you and Boats were… seeing each other. Intimate. He didn't tell any of us."

"No," she replied, "Boats kept things ter himself. But he did say one thing. He'd been around the world many times during his stint in the navy, and he said he'd had enough. He wanted to settle down, near the sea he loved so much, and Kildunlee was where he wanted ter be, after the war. He said he wanted ter be with me. And the babe. He wanted ter tend the pub, and that we'd have a good life together, he told me. A tough Chicago Polack, like me, he said, in Ireland. Commander, what happened ter Boats? I... don't know..."

McGrath dropped his gaze, ran his palms over his face, took a deep breath, and looked straight into Niamh's eyes.

"Niamh, I had hoped never to have to tell you this. But I must. Boats died, was killed, in the Pacific. He was aboard a troopship that loading Marines aboard an LST, getting ready to invade a Japanese held island. He was helping them get on board and load up the LST. But the troop ship was under attack from Kamikazes, the suicide pilots. Most of them were shot down, but one got through the anti-aircraft fire and hit the LST. It killed most of the marines on board and Boats," McGrath told her. Then, for some reason, he couldn't speak. Not a word could get out of his emotion-packed throat. He had to force his breathing down into his being. He had to collect himself so he could finish this story. He had to tell Niamh.

"Niamh..." he began, choking with emotion, "...you can tell Brendan..." McGrath said to her, "... you can tell Brendan..." he took a large sip of his Jameson's, "...that his father Leon Stanley Koslowski, Boatswain's Mate First Class, United States Navy, a tough Polack from Chicago..." McGrath breathed deeply, trying to hold Niamh's flooding eyes, "...died a hero's death, fighting for the U.S. Navy against the Japanese Air Force."

The tears flooded from Niamh's eyes, soaking her handkerchief and thick Irish sweater. "Did he really, Commander? Is it true? Did he really go as you said?"

"Yes," replied McGrath, barely able to speak, stifled in his own emotion at having to tell Niamh about Boats' death. "Yes, he did. Boats died a hero, defending his ship, this island, you and his son. He was a most wonderful and honorable man, Niamh, a wonderful man. You can be truly proud of your Boats. And your son, Brendan, when he's old enough to understand, you can tell him that his father, Leon Koslowski, died a hero, and Brendan will be proud of the father he never knew. After all," he managed a small smile, "it's in official U.S. Navy records."

Niamh rubbed her hands over her face to gather herself and clear her mind after all McGrath had just told her. She wiped away the tears, regaining self control and her breathing.

"I'll be thankin' yer, Commander. Thank yer," she said. "I can't tell yer how much of what yer just told me means ter me and 'twill mean ter me son, Boats' son."

They both took a moment to compose themselves. Jean-Luc, José Luis and Alejandro Basilio kept their attention to themselves. Niamh forced a smile, heaved a great sigh, and finally smiled with true relieved emotion.

"Thank yer, Commander."

McGrath returned her smile. "It's OK. You had a right to know. He was your man."

"Aye, I did. I did," Niamh finished her whiskey. "Will yer drink up, then?"

"Thank you, Niamh, but, no, I had better not. I have to drive back to the Manor, and I don't want Cynthia to think I've out boozing all day."

Niamh laughed at his remark, showing she had regained her composure. "Well, did you hear that Cormac O'Callaghan himself, the storyteller, the *seanachie*, will be here tonight?"

"Yes, I heard it from Sean at the post office," he told her.

"So, yer and her Ladyship ought ter be here tonight fer his story. 'Twill be a fine story, I'm sure, an' make no mistake."

McGrath stood up and headed for the front door. "I think we will be here tonight. This sounds like something

I wouldn't want to miss," and he waved his hand at her and strode out to his waiting car.

***

"So, you told Niamh about Boats?" Cynthia asked him.

"I did. She had a right to know. Now it's all in the open and clear, and she and her son can be proud of the boy's father."

Cynthia nodded, understanding what McGrath must have just gone through.

"Incidentally, they have nothing but high praise for you in the village. You're well liked, I hope you know," McGrath told Cynthia.

"It's the same with you, William. Ever since you inserted yourself into Kildunlee public life, and helped so many people, you've been a man revered and held in great esteem. I frequently heard town folks ask when you would return. Of course, at the time, I had no answer for them. Now, I do," and her flashing gray eyes bored into his of slate blue. Her long, slender arms encircled his neck and drew his lips down to hers into an embrace at once of tenderness, love and passion.

"My dear, we have to wait just a few more days. Then the wedding and after that we're together for a long, long time," McGrath told her, slowly easing himself from her embrace.

"Incidentally, Sean, at the post office, and then Niamh told me about Cormac O'Callaghan coming to the pub tonight to tell a story. Do you know about him?"

Cynthia jerked her head up. "Know about him? Why, I've listened to his stories since I was a little girl. My father took my brothers and me to the pub whenever he was in town, to hear his fabulous tales. He's there tonight?"

"That's what they're telling me."

"William, then I'll tell Mrs. Lynch to have dinner ready at six rather than seven. We'll eat early and go to the pub to hear Cormac tell a story. I'll give the staff time off, as well. I don't want them to miss it."

McGrath shook his head in bewilderment, entirely amazed at the apparent influence of this man, Cormac O'Callaghan, to mesmerize people with his power of *seanachie.* "Well, I guess we'll see," he told himself. "I guess we'll see."

11.

THE SEANACHIE'S VISION

With the word out that the *seanachie,* Cormac himself, was to appear at Niamh's pub this evening, the bar itself and the side rooms were packed with folks from town. McGrath and Cynthia made an early appearance, at about quarter to seven, so as to get a seat near the bar and to be able to hear the tale to be spun for the evening. They were greeted with pleasant, and warmly welcoming, comments: "An' how is himself this fine evenin'?" "Is he takin' good care of yourself, yer Ladyship?" "Well, yer honor, an' 'twill be a fine tale ter tell this evenin', an' no mistake."

McGrath felt as welcome as he had in all the homes of his Boston family and friends, in the city itself and out on the Cape, especially with his friend, Jack, who had also been in the Navy, only on a PT boat in the Pacific.

"Very well, thank you," McGrath and Cynthia replied to everyone, "Very well, indeed, thank you," and they took their seats around a small round table where Eddie and Siobhan had already been waiting for them. The talk, laughter and general noise all around them had grown in a steady crescendo to a mild roar. People were talking about what the teller of tales would relate tonight. Would it be about how the Moynihans undid the O'Brians in the famous sword duel two hundred years ago? Maybe the way the Milners stole the fatted sheep from the Connerys, blamed the Scanlons and laughed when the Connerys and the Scanlons slew each other on the field of battle, leaving the Milners to take over both their farms and lands.

"No," said a voice passionate in her conviction, "it will be the story, told only once in my lifetime, about how the Kellys and the McNeills fought for fifty years over fishing rights around the Aran Islands."

And the speculation and betting went on like this till the black hands of the large clock behind Niamh's bar reached ten minutes before the eighth hour of this fine evening. Then, the front door of the beloved Kildunlee pub opened slowly, revealing a diminutive rugged-faced man.

Barely five feet seven, and, if he weighed eleven stone, it was because his clothes were drenched from the rain. His shoes were worn, his pants baggy and dull grey. A heavy, well-traveled, wool, three-button jacket showing wear marks and patches covered a dark green woolen oxford shirt, and he sported an ancient necktie of various shades of brown. His duncher, a cloth cap, settled gently to the left side of his crown, shading blazing blue eyes and emitting stalks of light grey hair, while his face, dark from the sun and his travels, sported an impish smile, a large red nose and weathered cheeks. Cormac O'Callaghan had arrived.

The uproar that had filled the pub, just seconds before, was drowned in the appearance of O'Callaghan. Barely a speck of noise was heard. The apparent reverence was akin to that if the Bishop had entered the pub, which he had been known to do, and at which appearance the silence of reverence had descended like the silence for those under the falling knife of a guillotine. But, this time it was the reverence of the locals for someone who told magnificent stories and "...had the sight." All were watching the entrance of Cormac.

"Argh, Cormac O'Callaghan, 'tis good ter see yer again. Come over here by the fire and have a drop o' the pure. An' sure as there's coal in the pits of hell, don't we have a fine supper fer yer tonight."

"Ah, Niamh, yer were always grand at the meals, so yer were. An' after me travels 'tis meself dying o' the parch an' willin' ter give me last farthing ter the Divil fer a drop o' the pure, so I am."

"Here, Cormac, sit here an' Sheila's just now bringin' a wee dram o' Jameson's fer ter take away yer feverish parch."

Sheila appeared from nowhere and set a glass beside the *seanachie* with four ounces of Mr. Jameson's best whiskey in it, two of which immediately went down O'Callaghan's throat to eliminate the threatening parch.

"Now, what'll it be, Cormac? I've got nice beef from Casey's farm and grand pig from Rafferty's farm. Pratties and cabbage cooked to shame the best chefs in Dublin, and a trifle to top it off. So, will it be Casey's or Rafferty's?"

"Argh, Niamh, 'tis a fine puzzle yer lay before me, an' me just a simple soul, so I sez ter meself, I sez, why not a bit o' Casey's an' a bit o' Rafferty's so no hard feelin's around."

"Argh, Cormac, yer always had a way with words an' so a bit of each 'twill be," and Niamh rushed into the kitchen to get O'Callaghan's meal. Sheila stood diligent duty over the Jameson's in the definite event O'Callaghan's parch came upon him again. And she did her duty well, tipping the neck to meet the rim when the level went down. Steady conversation picked up again and people began to opine about the tale for the evening. The Jameson's and Bushmill's flowed and Niamh's Guinness had never seen a better night. And O'Callaghan enjoyed his supper of beef, ham, boiled cabbage and pratties, a drop at the right time, and a rich trifle to top things off. But, soon, as with Christmas and a birthday, all good things come to an end, and O'Callaghan signaled that supper was finished.

He gloriously downed the last few drops in his glass, licked the few remaining drops decorating his upper lip, stretched and then sat back in his chair, comfortable, satisfied and anticipatory. A gigantic hush fell over the crowd, awaiting the tale told by the greatest *seanachie* in the land. Sheila hastened to fill his glass, a full six ounces of Jameson's best. And the silence drowned the pub.

***

"And this is what it was," began O'Callaghan. *"Two hundred years after the time of the death of our beloved Christ; and two hundred years before the time of the arrival of the Great and Holy Saint Patrick himself; during the time of the conquering Romans who never really reached our beloved isle, thanks be to God Himself; and two hundred years before the time of the Saxons, who never invaded our shores, and eight hundred years before the time of the Normans, there arose a great ardrí, a high king, and wasn't his name Rory O'Connor himself. Aye. A great high king in the finest meanin' o' the words, and he was beloved by all the folks in this enchanted isle, wasn't he? And he was the first ard-rí ter be called Rory O'Connor, for in 1170, there arose another high king named Rory O'Connor. But we're talkin' about the first Rory O'Connor who reigned as ard-rí around the year two hundred after the death of our beloved Lord. And Rory himself, he had been elected ard-rí, high king, by all the other kings in Ireland so as ter have someone ter lead them together in battle if any o' the heathen tribes in Britain or Rome came snoopin' around our green lands. And there came one fine day in June that Rory himself decided to consolidate his power and ter unite the clans of Ireland into one strong and unbeatable army, with total allegiance ter himself, in the event o' some o' them heathens decided ter land on our golden*

shores o' this Hallowed Isle. And Rory O'Connor decided ter have a grand ceili, a grand party, and an ever grander fleadh, a festival o' sports and feasting, didn't he now? And it was ter be the grandest fleadh ever seen on this Blessed Isle. Rory O'Connor let it be known throughout all the land that there would be three days feastin', followed by two weeks o' sports ter decide the sport champion of all the greatest athletes in Ireland, then another week's feasting ter honor the great sportsman of all Ireland, and all those who had participated in the events. Finally, he let it be known that, whoever the greatest sportsman, the finest athlete o' all Ireland, came to be, that man would have Rory O'Connor's daughter, Bridget o' the raven hair and diamond eyes as his bride. And so it was."

Cormac began to cough and to wheeze here and Sheila, always so prompt with a drop of the pure, rushed to fill the *seanachie's* glass with Mr. Jameson's finest *uisce beatha*, whiskey. And with a large drop o' the pure in him, the *seanachie*, Cormac O'Callaghan began his tale again, with all eyes glued to his carven face and all ears straining to capture every word.

"And this is what it was. Rory sent his heralds out ter every city, town and village from Skibbereen ter Ballyhillin and from the Aran Islands ter holy Dublin itself, didn't he now? And the heralds had the charge ter tell everyone about the great fleadh and all the competitions ter be held and that all athletes from the Green Isle were invited ter attend and compete. And so it happened that there were two great clans that came from a certain place, and it was toward the competition that they sent their best athletes ter try ter win the raven haired Bridget, with the diamond eyes, and the ard-ri's gold, and it came to pass that the sports' competition and all the events that

were involved caused a great feud that threatened ter take the lives o' many a young warrior, bred from the farms, taught ter arms, called ter battle. But, so many young, and old, souls might have been lost that the population o' this blessed isle would be thrice what it now holds. And the cause o' this feud and loss of life lies here in County Clare."

Gasps of astonishment were heard. Here, in our own county? Murmurs of disbelief were heard, amid urgings from the crowd in the packed pub for the *seanachie* to continue his story.

Cormac, the teller of tales, and the seer, for many people had said that he had the "gift" for seeing events in the future, and when he did, and when he could see them clearly, he foretold these happenings to all those who would listen and believe, and didn't they always come to pass? Cormac cleared his throat, to assuage the onset "o' the terrible parch", and himself's throat no better than the sands o' the Sahara.

"Aye, and this was how it all began. The heralds came ter each plot o' the Green Isle, tellin' everyone o' the great feastin' and sportin' events ter be held near the high king's palace in County Meath, and didn't they come from every inch of Ireland ter compete and ter watch the competition. The young, blessed with the strength o' bulls and the speed o' deer. The old, bent with the toils of years of labor and eager ter see the gossoons do their best. And they all assembled at the high king's palace in County Meath, and they came from every inch o' Ireland for the feastin' and the competition. And ter start things off right, Rory O'Connor declared a three day ceili, a party, and all the cattle, sheep and pigs that had just been slaughtered, were put ter the roast, and fine scents filled the valleys and peaks till it was all a man could do ter stop him-

self from attackin' a roastin' side o' beef. But the ameni-
ties had ter be attended ter, and the guests welcomed, and
this took the whole first marnin'. But by noon time, as the
sun crossed the zenith of the day, and began its journey
toward the far stretches o' the sea, Rory O'Connor de-
clared the feast begun, and barrels o' mead, jugs o' the
pure, and hundredweights o' beef, sheep and pig were
devoured by all the people at the ceili, so that it might be
thought that they hadn't had a blessed morsel since they
first saw the light o' day. And the feastin', with all the
pipers, harpists and fiddlers playin' and dancin' till the
stroke o' the twelfth hour, when by common knowledge,
the ceili settled down and they all went ter sleep and ter
dream o' glory and passion. And this went on for three
days, didn't it now? Till finally, Rory O'Connor called all
the   athletes   together,   with   a   tremendous   crowd
surroundin' them and watchin' the events, and the
sportin' began in earnest, like a mad bull crashing after a
cow in heat."

Cormac stopped his tale here and availed himself of
a drop o' the pure. Sheila rushed to be sure his glass was
filled and ready to eliminate his dry, irritated throat, for,
after all, didn't story telling take its toll of the throat of
the teller. Everyone in the pub leaned forward, anticipating Cormac's next part of the story, for he was just about
to begin the section where all the ancient Irish athletes
were to take part in the grand festivities, to prove their
daring and valor. But Cormac hesitated. He didn't continue right off, but stared into the middle distance, as if seeing something; something no one else could see.

The pub goers began whispering to themselves.
"He's seein' somethin'."
"He's lookin' into the future."
"Cormac's seein' something. Something's goin' to
happen."

"Cormac, what do you see."

For they all knew that he had the sight; that he could see what others could not see, and that he knew when a strange event would occur.

"What do yer see, Cormac?"

"Argh. 'Tis nothin'. I kinna see no more." And he took a mouthful o' the pure, and continued his tale.

"And this is what it was. The grand contests began and the great Irish athletes competed with each other in runnin', throwin' the rock and throwin' the spear, hurlin' great weights and, finally, the grandest sport of all, wrestlin'. The contests went on for twelve days, with all the young men from every corner, hill, valley, town and city from the length and breadth of beautiful Ireland competin' for the gold and, o' course, the hand o' the lovely Bridget. And it happened that, on the twelfth day, there were only two competitors left, and there were only two days left till the end of the contests, and wouldn't yer know that one o' these athletes would gain the prize as Grandest Athlete o' all Ireland, be entitled ter the gold Rory O'Connor offered and lay claim ter Rory's beautiful daughter, Bridget. And, the two who were left came from no other than County Clare, right here where Kildunlee is this very day."

When Cormac, the *seanachie*, said these words, there was a mighty gasp that came from the crowded pub.

"No! Not here in Kildunlee!"

"Our little village?"

"Can't be. There's no history of it!"

"We've heard nary a word!"

And Cormac took a drop o' the pure, to slake his interminable thirst, which was replenished by the handsome Sheila, lest the *seanachie* lose strength.

"And this is what it was. In those days, there were no written records, so no one here would know of the feats and exploits of kings, lords and athletes, only in the major battles, defending our lovely isle, which are, of course, in the written records. But the final contests went on fer the last two days o' the competition, and, as luck and the gods o' the time would have it, the final two competitors were at a tie. And one was Brendan O'Neill from Clan O'Neill ter the north o' Clare, up near Galway town, and himself known as undaunted and fearless in battle, and the other was none other than himself, Killian O'Donnell, well renowned as a terrible and fierce warrior o' the Clan O'Donnell. And so it went. The competition came ter the very end, with only the wrestlin' left ter be the final sport, and weren't the two powerful young men tied in their efforts. Now, the two Clans, O'Neill and O'Donnell, swore before Rory O'Connor, the ard-rí, and all the lesser kings, lords, ladies and common folk, that, whatever the outcome o' the grand wrestling event, they would abide by the result and no hard feelin's either way. So, the fourteenth day dawned, and the two mighty youth, Brendan and Killian, took their places in the wrestling arena, surrounded by the high king and all the lesser kings, lords, ladies and common folk, and didn't it happen that way? And 'twas himself, the high king, Rory O'Connor gave the signal for the match to begin. And, then... and then..."

Here, Cormac stopped, and reached for his glass and took a deep draft. His eyes went to the middle distance again, and, though focused, for Cormac O'Callaghan could withstand the assaults of the best mountain dew, and was never worse the wear for a large drop of poitin, still seemed to be seeing a remote event not visible to the others.

"He sees something!"

"This is the second time tonight!"

"What do yer see, Cormac? Tell us!"

"Aye, 'tis somethin' on the horizon, somethin' comin' to Kildunlee, but I kinna tell what yet. Good or bad, I dinna ken." Cormac shook his head, sipped a drop and continued his story.

"And this is what it was. Rory himself gave the sign fer the grand wrestlin' event ter begin and the two slammed into each other, testin' the strength o' his opponent: Brendan slamming Killian in his massive chest and Killian returnin' the gift. They circled each other, takin' the measure and judgin' the power o' the opponent, tryin' ter find a weak spot, lookin' fer an advantage. Two hours this went on and both these muscular young men, sturdy as oak trees and powerful as northern bears were swathed in sweat and glistenin' with oil. Their war paint, for 'twas still used in those days, back in the dim mists o' time, don't yer ken? And the sweat and oil made the paint run till their faces and bodies were like a slick rainbow. And it was close ter the eleventh hour o' the marnin', and all the watchers were itchin' fer some real action, when what happens but himself, Brendan, sees, he sees, Killian drop his guard fer only a second. And Brendan, himself wild with passion fer Bridget an' the gold drives his fist inter Killian's face and flattens Killian's nose. Then he thrashes him again, an' again till Killian is unsteady on his feet, fer we must remember that punchin' an' kickin' were allowed in those days. And didn't it happen that Killian went down on his two knees? But, Brendan an honorable man, gave Killian a moment's respite, though he was bleedin' from his nose and mouth an' the blood from his eyebrows blinded him. Brendan went in fer the final attack, slammed Killian three, four, five times and then caught him in a fierce headlock that would have splintered Killian's neck inter a thousand toothpicks,

wasn't it so? And Killian had ter yield and he did. And he was proclaimed an honorable man and a fine wrestler and fighter, but the award o' gold and Bridget went ter Brendan, and King Rory himself, an honorable man and always true ter his word, declared Brendan O'Neill the Grand Champion o' Ireland, didn't he, now? And he told his servants ter bring the purple woolen cloak o' glory ter place around Brendan shoulders, and so they did. Then he told them ter bring the gold and place it at his feet and this was done. Then came the moment Brendan had waited and hoped fer, the reason, known ter himself alone deep in his heart o' hearts, the presentation o' Bridget O'Connor, daughter o' the High King, Rory himself, and she was presented ter Brendan in all her beauty and comeliness.

Her raven hair smooth and bright as the midnight skies, her blue eyes blazing in the midday sun and her heart racin' like a jackdaw's wings, fer it was known only ter herself that she loved Brendan as much as he loved her and herself was pleased as a child seeing a decorated tree on Christmas marn. Then it was at this moment that King Rory proclaimed a last day o' feastin' and the uisce beatha, the whiskey, ale, mead and all the roasted sides o' beef an' pig were borne out fer the grand ceili. An' the feastin' went on till the moon hit its zenith, isn't that so, and those that could took their way home, and those who had a mighty skinful an' were too stocious ter move just slept till the sun woke them fer their trek home the next day."

A hundred deep breaths were released at that moment, and as many smiles lit the inside of Niamh's pub. Glasses clinked and tipped and many a drop of the pure went down deep and well. It was a marvelous story and all the patrons exclaiming over it.

"A wonderful story, Cormac, a wonderful story."

"When will you be back these ways to tell another?"

"Are there many more ter tell, an' when will yer give us another, Cormac."

But Cormac, the great *seanachie,* simply wet his whistle, most thoroughly enjoying the delights of Mr. Jameson's labors, and sat back in his chair. His eyes were dark, and, again, focusing in the middle distance.

"Shhh. The *seanachie* is seein' somethin'. What do yer see, Cormac?"

"Is it bad, Cormac? Is somethin' goin' ter happen soon?"

"Can yer tell us, Cormac, can yer tell us?"

And Cormac O'Callaghan opened his ancient, lined and stubbled jaws, "'Tis hard ter say, but I see there's a happenin' upon the horizon. Just what, I can't say this minute, but 'twill be not good and 'twill be in a week's time or less. I see dark things formin' an' 'twill not be good, but as ter what they may be I kinna tell now."

"But, yer'll tell us when things take form, won't yer? An' sure, after such a fine story as that one yer just told, we can wait ter hear yer sight."

"An' who said it was the end of the story?" Cormac asked them. "'Tis only half and then some." Expressions of surprise were heard and gasps of anticipation.

"More story? Go on, Cormac, tell us!"

"Come, now, tell us the rest o' the tale. We're just after hearin' the first part an' now yer tellin' us there's more. Tell us, Cormac, tell us!"

And Cormac O'Callaghan, renowned as the finest *seanachie* in all the green of God's special isle began with the second part of the tale.

"And this is what it was. Everyone had gone back ter their farms, estates, villages and cities, an' life started itself back up again, didn't it now? But, as the days wore

on, and everybody had almost forgotten the great ceili and the wrestlin', what with the toils of takin' care o' the livestock, tilling' the fields, gatherin' the yield and keepin' out o' trouble themselves, the spirit o' the evil one entered the heart of Killian O'Donnell, fer he was mighty jealous of Brendan an' his winnin's, although he showed not a speck o' trouble when Brendan was proclaimed Champion Athlete o' all Ireland. But the evil entered his heart and he planned vengeance as mighty as rose from the pits o' hell itself, stinkin' an' screamin' an' lustin' for revenge, didn't he now, against his opponent, Brendan O'Neill, himself. An' he took his time, conjurin' an' connivin', plannin' each day how best ter get back at Brendan, fer, truth ter tell, Killian himself had his heart set on the beautiful Bridget, an' he wanted her all fer himself, didn't he, now?"

Cormac took a long pull at the pure and Sheila made sure his glass was filled to the brim.

"Now, 'tis well known in these parts that, over a thousand years ago, two hundred years before blessed St. Patrick stepped upon these holy shores, that the O'Neill clan had nothin' but pigs fer their herds and the O'Donnells had nothin' but sheep. That was the way it was in those days. Both had a few beef cattle, but not a great amount to speak of, fer beef cattle were the pride and joy o' the McCarthy clan over towards Dublin way, and the O'Neills and O'Donnells lived and farmed in what became County Clare, not far from where we see Galway, a fine town, this day. An' he took it inter his mind that he could cause trouble between the two clans, stir up fightin' and trouble, set the two clans against each other, be sure that Brendan was killed during the troubles and make off with the beautiful Bridget as his prize for bein' champion o' the battle field. 'Twas in his heart ter

do this mighty evil deed fer wasn't he the second only ter Brendan, an' who would stand up ter him, an' win, when the battles were over? And Killian schemed and planned that he would start the troubles a while after the grand tournament, an' he took it inter his mind ter make it look like the O'Neills were the dirty ones, the ones causin' the trouble, an' he would cause a great battle ter start, kill Brendan secretly, fer no man could stand up ter Killian, who was second only ter Brendan himself."

Cormac O'Callaghan took a large swallow from his jar containing many drops of the pure, and, for a moment, his stare remained on the middle distance, eyes riveted at the entrance door to Niamh's pub.

"Gawd, he's seein' somethin'! What's it to be?"

"Shhh. Leave him be. He'll tell us when the time is ripe."

Cormac continued his tale, focusing his glare from the front door.

"An' this was the way it was. Didn't Killian, spurned on by an evil spirit, take a half dozen sheep from one o' the O'Donnell folds, in the middle o' the night when the sky was blacker than Bridget's raven locks or the color o' Killian's evil heart, and spirit them away from the O'Donnell lands ter a distant corner o' the O'Neill lands, hiding them so they wouldn't be noticed right away. None o' the O'Neills made much trouble over this, fer they thought that the sheep wandered away from a farmer's pasture, not thinkin' they belonged ter the O'Donnells, an' that the farmer would come by soon ter take them back. But nothin' happened. And so, things went along smoothly as day turns inter night and every-one was about their business."

"So, a week or so later, doesn't Killian take another crew o' sheep from the O'Donnell family's lands – fer

*they had more than four thousand sheep an' 'twas told
there was a sheep for each star in the inky sky, black as
the pits o' the ocean, wasn't it said – and put them
amongst the pigs in the O'Neill's lands. The O'Neills
couldn't figure out where they came from and so they
waited fer some farmer ter come and claim them. Finally,
Killian, a true chancer if any lived upon these hallowed
shores, began ter lose his bap and ter become impatient
with the slowness o' things, an' so he took it inter his
mind ter get things grandly stirred up, like a storm from
the sea, he did. An' so he took it inter his mind ter steal a
hundred sheep from the O'Donnell fold, and park them in
the middle o' the O'Neill pigs, an' he did so when everyone o' the both clans were as deep in sleep as the sand is
at the bottom o' the sea, an' nary a soul heard a word or
bleat.*

*"An', the next marnin', he mounted his horse, Ter-
ror, a grand beast, tall an' mighty, a power o' strength,
and pretended ter count the sheep on the O'Donnell
lands. Knowin' there were over a hundred he rustled ter
the O'Neill lands, didn't Killian ride ter the O'Neill lands
and claim that the O'Donnell sheep had been stolen by
the O'Neill clan? The O'Neills knew nothin' o' this and
they swore they had nothin' ter do with the sheep, and
how did they get here in the first place? Killian demanded
the sheep back, demanded restitution an' threatened a
mighty battle if the O'Neills didn't do what he said. Then
he rode back ter the O'Donnell farms and told his father,
Dermot, the clan leader, what he claimed the O'Neills
had done, and his father grew terrible mad at the
O'Neills, and he sent out the word ter gather the clan fer
battle if the demands of Killian weren't met, an' a mighty
hue and cry went ter the far reaches o' O'Donnell lands
and many a farmer, trained in battle and the use o' the
sword assembled at the clan leader's door. The clan
leader told them o' Killian's story and they all affirmed*

that battle with the O'Neills was the best way ter right the situation. But, the men hadn't counted on the women, an' the women wanted no part o' a battle. What woman would want her man folk dead or armless? No, the women, hearin' this sent several o' their kin ter the O'Neill lands ter speak with the women there, an' a fine agreement came ter pass that the women would stop the battle before it began, and would appeal ter none other than Finn MacCool and Cuchullain themselves fer a judgement."

And Cormac stopped for a moment, his eyes avoiding the front door, and thereby not showing any emotion at what he might see coming in the next week or two. He took a large swallow of the pure and settled in for the rest of the story.

"An' this was what it was. To the end o' the story. The women from each clan refused ter cook, clean, do their daily work or complete their wifely duties ter their men until the situation was decided by the heroes, Finn MacCool and Cuchullain. For three days and three nights, they blew on their pipes and beat on their drums, till a mighty stirrin' came from the land o' the Ulstermen, may God spare their souls, and the land o' County Kildare, a lovely place. An' at dawn o' the fourth day didn't Cuchullain himself appear from the north and Finn MacCool arrive from the south?

An' at the sight of them both, taller than any tall man in either clan, each carryin' a sword o' five stone, an' no mortal man could lift with three arms, with shoulders wider than two male bulls together and muscles twistin' every which way an' the like o' which no human had seen. An' the women sent to them, one from each clan and they told their story ter Finn MacCool and Cuchullain, an' the story bein' short, only about the sto-

len sheep and Killian's threat o' battle, they were done within an hour an' returned ter their clans. An' this is what happened. They went back ter their own clans an' said that the feud – fer that what was brewin' – would be settled by Finn MacCool and Cuchullain himself. An' fer three days and nights the heroes sat on a mountain top and spoke about the events. Now, it must be remembered that Cuchullain was descended from a goddess and a god, and so he had powers the like o' which no seanachie ever possessed, he did. An' on the fourth day, both Finn an' Cuchullain called the two women an' Killian ter the mountain top an' they had a three hour palaver. An' it was determined that Killian did a wrong thing ter stir up trouble between the clans just ter get Bridget and kill Brendan, fer Finn MacCool and Cuchullain could well and true divine the truth. An' Finn MacCool and Cuchullain, both restrainin' themselves from killin' Killian, sent him to Rory O'Connor ter do three years hard labor fer the High King, and ter pay ten stones o' gold ter Brendan as a punishment. An' when Finn MacCool and Cuchullain made their judgement, they both sent Killian ter Rory O'Connor, watchin' him leave in shame, after he paid the ten stones o' gold to Brendan. An' the women went back ter their clans an' spread the news that there was no battle ter be seen, an' there was peace ter be held in the land between both clans. An' it finally happened that there were many marriages between the two clans, much tradin' o' sheep for pigs an' pigs for sheep. An' many a romance between members o' each clan grew into large families. An' it came ter pass that, whenever there was a dispute comin' up, weren't the women o' each clan consulted as ter what should be done, an' this happened fer several hundred years after the Brendan/Killian trouble, but, with all things, it finally come ter a stop. An' now-a-days, I sometimes wonder if the women o' families and the town – the clans don't do much together because o' all the intermarryin' an' so on – are consulted any more.

But, there has been peace in this part o' the hallowed isle fer so long that it surely doesn't matter."

And with that last statement, Cormac O'Callaghan took a long, and final, pull on his whiskey.

"Cormac, that was a wonderful story! It was grand!"

"Will yer be tellin' another in the next few days or so?"

"What's the next story goin' ter be about?"

"Oh, I wish 'twere still so that we women had the rule o' the land," said a female voice in the background, and this last brought laughter and jeers.

"Cormac, will yer be comin' ter the weddin' o' the Commander and her Ladyship?" Cormac's eyes darkened. He put down his glass.

"Argh. I don't know. I might. Then, again I might not. I see somethin' black on the horizon comin'. Somethin' I can't be sure of. I may be back fer the weddin' an' then again I may not. 'Tis not good comin'. And what I see tells me ter stay away, for 'twill be terrible an' black. Aye, I don't think I'll be back in Kildunlee till it's over an' done with." And with that, he picked up his duncher and pulled it onto his old, but majestic, gray head, and, placing the unopened bottle of Jameson's – a gift from Niamh for his tale-telling – in his side jacket pocket, walked, in a very straight line—for the pure didn't seem to bother him—out of Niamh's pub and into the night. The on-looking town folks watched him go, marveling at his self possession, and they began to talk amongst themselves about the grand story he had just told, but, behind each praising comment, there was a feeling of foreboding of what Cormac O'Callaghan, the great *seanachie,* had seen, and his pronouncement that he wouldn't be back till whatever it was he saw was all over.

***

The rays from the silver moon lit the countryside: the farms, the roadside fences; the barns and houses in the distance. Cynthia and McGrath watched the dirt road, now glazed in silver, unwind in front of them.

"William, just what did you think of the *seanachie's* story tonight?" she asked him.

McGrath smiled at his bride-to-be. "My great grandfather, Josiah McGrath, used to tell us kids stories about Ireland, as he remembered it. That's one of the reasons why I accepted command of the Detail in 1944. I wanted to come and see for myself. Grandfather used to tell us about the story tellers, and that the best tellers in the world were from Ireland. After tonight, I believe it."

"It's not just the wonderful story he told us, William, but it's the idea that he's supposed to be a seer, someone who can foretell, or divine, the future. With our wedding coming up in about a week, I'm hoping nothing will postpone it."

"Don't worry, my dear, nothing will postpone it or keep me from marrying you now, not even a hundred screaming banshees with pitchforks."

She smiled at his words. "It's not that. It's just that I wish he hadn't felt the need to say something dark was on the horizon."

"Grandfather also told us kids about the *seanachies* and that whatever they foretold was not of great consequence or was soon remedied. I don't think we have to worry. As I just said, there is nothing on this fair isle that will keep us from our marriage vows on Saturday. And if something comes up, we'll deal with it quickly and get on with our wedding."

"Glad to hear you say that, William, I'm so glad," and Cynthia cuddled closer to her future husband as he headed along the road that led to the Manor.

12.

ANTICIPATION

Wednesday dawned misty and with just a touch of
drizzle in the air, but no dampening of everyone's spirits
was to be found in all of Kildunlee, even though the
temperature was a few degrees below normal, somewhere
around forty-five. All the town was awaiting the
"...grandest o' events this village has ever seen, or will
see, till Gabriel himself bounces his notes off the Galtee
mountains, an' isn't it so'?"

"Now, Commander, if you will just step over here
with your best man, we'll begin the rehearsal right away.
You and Eddie here will be standing on the first step of
the altar, waiting for the bride-to-be. Eddie, after you and
the other members of the bridal party process down the
aisle, then you will please take your place to the right of
the Commander. Just here," and the priest pointed to a
step in front of the altar. "Are you ready, your Ladyship?"
asked Father McDermott, the parish priest. Beside him,
wrapped in a beaming smile, stood Father Tim, who was
the Kildunlee parish priest during the war years and who
had kept an eye on a former town resident, the Swedish
importer/exporter, Rolf Hilsblad.

In those days, Father Tim, by special permission of
the Bishop of Dublin, had resumed his old job with MI-6,
the British Secret Intelligence Service, the equivalent of
the United States' Office of Strategic Services, or OSS,
"Wild Bill" Donovan's group, precursor to the future
Central Intelligence Agency, or CIA. In the mid 1930s,

and after Trinity College and Theological and the foreign language studies at Cambridge, Father Tim worked for MI-6 as a translator, but left after three years to enter a seminary to become a diocesan priest. But immediately after his seminary years, and to help with the war effort, he applied for, and received permission, to resume his MI-6 work till the war's end. Suspecting that Rolf Hilsblad was working for the Nazis, an idea gleaned from several documents, which had been intercepted and translated by the Service's staff, MI-6 asked Father Tim to serve in Ireland and he had been posted at St. Paul's in Kildunlee, where he kept an eye on Hilsblad and his goings on, frequently reporting back to MI-6 in London and Dublin.

Now, he was back in the pulpit, in Upper Kings Ridley in Kent County, the garden county in the southeast of England, which supplied virtually all of the fruits and vegetables to English dinner tables and so named for the many farms found there, in a small hamlet just a few miles to the west of Maidstone, happy and content to be rid of his former cloak and dagger activities.

But, being a first cousin to Lady Cynthia FitzHugh, on the Catholic side of the family, which had remained loyal to the Roman Catholic Church and had nothing to do with Henry VIII's Anglican Church, the Catholic side had managed to retain its lands and titles in Ireland, and although Father Tim never went by his title of the Earl of Clare, he continued to pour his inherited wealth into every worthy charity he could find. As a special favor to Lady Cynthia and to McGrath, he had been asked, and had agreed, to attend their wedding and to co-celebrate it with Kildunlee's resident pastor, Father McDermott. Father Tim was happy and pleased to be here.

"You will want me at the back of the Church, I think, with Sir Charles."

"Yes, please, if you would go there now, we can get

started," Father McDermott replied.

"Years ago, when you were a little girl, you used to call me Uncle Charlie," said Sir Charles Tillingham, to his niece, Cynthia. Sir Charles himself was the very picture of a British ex-military man – a former Colonel of the royal Army, duty in India during the war, and knighted for bravery and courage, complete with a stiffened knee and clipped moustache.

She smiled fondly at her old uncle, "Oh, OK, Uncle Charlie. And thanks for agreeing to give me away. Since my father's not well and he loathed the thought of rolling down the aisle in a wheelchair to give me away, we're very glad you offered to take on the task. Anyway, thanks for helping out."

"I know and I don't mind. Trevor has had a bad heart for years now, and I will help out wherever I'm needed. He wants this marriage, you know. He and I spoke often, when the Detail was here before D-Day, and he thinks very highly of the Commander, doncha know? All right, we're here now, so I guess we just have to wait for the high sign, what?" They turned at the front door of the Church and faced the altar. "Bloody good man, this Commander of yours, eh? I approve. Damn fine fellow! Navy, but still a good man, what? Stout heart. Got what it takes. Heard he was in on the Iwo landings and all that."

"He didn't land, Uncle Charlie," she said with a chuckle, " he took weather observations for MacArthur to help for the invasion of the Japanese mainland," Cynthia explained.

"Worked with MacArthur? Good man, what?"

"Are you people ready down there?" Father McDermott's mellow voice echoed throughout St. Paul's emptiness.

"We are," Cynthia called back as she and Sir Charles took their places in line behind the groomsmen, the bridesmaids and Siobhan, the Matron of Honor.

"Are you ready, Uncle Charlie?"

"Never been more ready, my dear," he said, with an aloof military sniff. "Damn the Punjab! Blast the Raj! Royal army to the fore!" And he clutched his niece's arm well to his side and, Uncle Charlie, the former Colonel, the Honorable, Sir Charles Richard Tillingham, following the wedding party, strode forth in a military gait that would have made a Royal Army Sergeant Major beam with pride. Cynthia had to stretch her long legs to keep up, but his stride was slow and stately, and they approached the altar in grace and fashion.

"Excellent, Sir Charles, excellent," said Father McDermott. "Really good work. Now, here you pass the bride-to-be to the groom. Shake hands. That's fine. Now, Sir Charles, you can take your pew and Commander and your Ladyship, if you please, come up to the altar and kneel on these kneelers directly in front of the altar. Very good." The four groomsmen took their places on the kneelers to the right of McGrath and the bridesmaids, and the Matron of Honor, Siobhan, kneeling directly to the left of Cynthia. They formed a perfect semi-circle. Father McDermott was busy fussing around with the placement and last minute instructions for the groomsmen and brides maids. Four groomsmen and four bridesmaids.

The ushers, or groomsmen, were Edward Hillaire, as McGrath's Best Man, Dr. Kieran McHugh, the local physician, Francis O'Farrell, the Resident Magistrate, and Fergal Hanlon, the assistant Garda. Livy O'Toole was scheduled to have "the duty" on the day of the wedding, so Fergal had to stand in as a groomsman. Naturally, Livy would be on duty around town, to satisfy formalities, and then at the reception to "…keep an eye on things," while enjoying a pint or two himself. The bridesmaids were Kathryn, Elisabeth and Anastasia Tillingham, Cynthia's cousins, from Uncle Charlie's London side of the family, and, of course, Siobhan Hillaire the beautiful black-haired daughter of Brendan Rafferty, a local pig farmer, who would march down the aisle with her "… beloved Eddie, me own."

"That's it. I'll tell you when to stand, sit or kneel during the Mass. It'll go well, I'm sure, and that's really all we have to rehearse," Father McDermott told them. "During the wedding ceremony, as I just said, I'll give you instructions as to when you should stand, kneel and so on, so don't be concerned about what's going to happen and when. I'll be giving the directions," he said as they took their positions. And, turning to Edward Hillaire, the best man, he asked, "You do have the rings in a safe place, don't you?"

"Yes, Father, they're at home and I'll have them here with me on Saturday morning."

"Good. Good," Father McDermott replied, "We have to bless them before they get placed on the fingers of the bride and groom." Turning back toward Cynthia, he commented, "And you're coming along quite well with your studies to become a Catholic, your Ladyship. Congratulations."

"Thank you, Father McDermott. For him," and she looked up at McGrath, "I'd become anything, even an atheist," she said with a mischievous smile. "And that's the truth."

Ahhhs, smiles and red faces answered her comment.

"Ah, well, we don't want to go that far. And may I say this will be a grand event and finally it's come to pass," Father Tim announced to all of the members of the assembled wedding party. "This wedding has been a long time in coming and, believe me, no two people were more destined to be joined together than the Commander and her Ladyship. If I had a glass in my hand, I'd raise a toast."

A rousing cheer followed his words.

"As it so happens, Father Tim," McGrath said, "I've arranged to have a bit of a party at Niamh's pub this afternoon, and everyone's invited. It's a bit of a town-wide rehearsal supper. So, if the rehearsal's done, everyone to Niamh's on me!"

This announcement, of course, brought grand cheers from all the bridal party as well as the curious onlookers watching the rehearsal. Needless to say, the word had been spread widely and the rest of the townsmen, and all of the ladies from Kildunlee, were already at Niamh's, enjoying the liquid refreshments as well as the splendid roast lamb, beef, boiled potatoes and greens and the standard lasciviously rich Irish dessert, the trifle she provided. And they all trooped from St. Paul's to the pub, the two priests among the revelers.

***

McGrath and Cynthia pulled into the car parking lot behind Niamh's and went inside. He had just picked up some groceries to last him for tomorrow and Friday. In three days' time, he would be a married man, and Mrs. Lynch, the FitzHugh cook, could fix his meals. He would miss Mrs. O'Shaunessy's cooking, especially her roast leg of lamb smothered in her rich, thick gravy, but from the meals he had had with Cynthia, he was sure that Mrs. Lynch would do as well as Mrs. O'Shaunessy. He told himself that he would have to do more walking, since the thought of all this heavy Irish eating was definitely going to thicken his midsection, and that was something he did not want. He had kept himself lean, in spite of his injured right thigh, but to start putting on weight now was out of the question. *In the future, I can walk to town instead of driving,* he told himself.

***

"Ah, Commander, 'tis good ter see yer again,"

Niamh Flaherty called to him from behind the bar. "What'll yer have? A whiskey, will it be?"

Calls of "…plenty o' whiskey for the Commander!" rose from all the corners of the pub. Jolly cheers and shouts of good wishes filled the rafters, and well-wishers came forth to McGrath and Cynthia for half an hour and more.

"Congratulations, yer honor…"

"Best o' luck yer Ladyship…"

"'Tis good ter have yer back again, Commander…:

"Aye, yer've got a fine man ter watch over yer, yer Ladyship…"

And on, and on, and on till the sea of faces of well wishers mixed together and washed away in an ocean of music and joviality with Raymond Quinn and his three companions providing the appropriate sounds on two fiddles, a pennywhistle and a drum. *And this is only the rehearsal party! What of Saturday, three days hence*, McGrath asked himself.

"Ah, Commander, there you are. May we wish you and your fine lady our best wishes and the finest of luck."

"Thank you, Sir Julian, Lady Alice. We appreciate your good wishes."

Sir Julian raised his glass. "To the happy couple. Best of British!" And he downed his Jameson's in a twink.

McGrath and Cynthia answered with "Slaintha", and sipped Burgundy sparingly from their glasses; other-wise they would be out for the count with all the toasts being offered in their favor.

"Oh, Commander, I have a very special request to ask you," Lady Alice Stronton said to McGrath.

"What's that, Lady Alice?" McGrath inquired.

"My friend, Bobbee Fuller, whom I went to college with, is coming to town. She and I studied art together at the Sorborn, after I had left South Africa when my father,

Lord Stronton, passed away. He had wanted me to take over the family mining business but I wanted to study art and so off to Paris I went. So, I left the business to my brothers. Bobbee and I roomed together and we became close friends. She wired me last week that she's coming to Ireland. Unfortunately, it's on your wedding day and I'm afraid I'll be a bit late for the celebration. But, I'll be there and I'd like to bring Bobbee along. That is, if it's all right with you and her Ladyship. We won't be very late, but her train comes in to Galway station before the Mass begins, and so we'll be about an hour delayed."

"Lady Alice," Cynthia replied, "Don't worry about being late. As long as you can make it, that's all that counts. And, by all means, bring your friend Bobbee."

"Yes, of course," McGrath added.

"Thank you. I knew you'd both understand," Lady Alice smiled at them.

"Well then, when are you folks leaving for South Africa?" McGrath asked them.

"I think in a couple of weeks. We have a house rented for a while until we see what housing is available on the market. Then, of course, we'll buy. But, we'll train to Dublin, then cross the Irish Sea to London. There's a steamer sailing for Cherbourg, Lisbon and Casablanca, then straight on to Cape Town. I'll have a car waiting for us there and we'll drive to Johannesburg. Need a car in that country, don't you know? Lots of open space and long distances to travel, not like here. No bus service from town to town, but maybe one day."

"Well, Sir Julian, in the short time that I've known you, I've come to like you. So, let me wish you and your future bride our best wishes. You must be excited about getting married on the plains of South Africa," McGrath said.

"Yes. Quite. All of Alice's family is there and they really pressed us hard to get married in Johannesburg, or

Joburg, as they call it. So, we gave in to their wishes and off we go! I'd have liked to get married here, but her brothers, their wives and the rest of the family were all quiet adamant. So, there it is."

"I'm sure you'll love it in Joburg," Cynthia told them. "I've been there only once, and briefly, but it was very pleasant. The flower gardens are magnificent. Quite colorful."

"Yes, you're right, Cynthia," Alice replied to her. "Really bursting with color."

"Cynthia," McGrath, all smiles, said to his bride to be, "I think we're being paged. Niamh is beckoning to us from the bar. Do excuse us, Sir Julian, Lady Alice."

"Oh, no bother, no bother," Sir Julian told McGrath and Cynthia. "This is your day and Saturday will be even better."

***

And so, McGrath and Cynthia drifted from one conversation to another; one round of congratulations to another; one set of best wishes to another, all afternoon long, as the watery mid-spring Irish sun began to dip below the distant Cliffs of Moher and west into the Atlantic toward Canada. And although so many well-wishers kept the conversations going, and kept McGrath and Cynthia occupied, he was hard pressed to take his eyes off his beautiful future wife. And she could barely keep hers off him.

13.

THE MISSING GUEST

Saturday morning dawned warm, with a touch of humidity in the air. The sun rose bright with a smattering of high clouds covering the southern skies, toward Kerry and a slight western breeze in the air to keep the daily temperature comfortable. McGrath looked out the window and, even though he had no forecasting information in front of him, he ventured a guess that today would stay fairly warm and dry, for a spring day in late April. Perfect for having a wedding. And he could hardly wait to see his bride in her new gown. He looked around the cottage for a brief minute, thinking of all the times he had spent here with his Detail in '44, chatting, laughing, and enjoying each other's company. More like a family than a US Naval Meteorological Detail. Then these past two months here again, relishing Mrs. O'Shaunessy's company and masterful cooking. It's a wonder that his middle hadn't expanded with the way she took care of him. She always said she had "...to take good care o' me Navy b'ys." And that she did, for they all loved her for her care. But this was his last day here; even his last hour or two. Next Monday, he and Cynthia would leave for Shannon to catch a flight to Newfoundland with the new American airways company, Trans World Airways, which, after the war, had recently initiated regular twenty hour flights across the North Atlantic. From there, they would fly to Boston; a honeymoon in New England, showing off his new wife to all the family, introducing her to everyone at home and at work, to his friends, especially his long time buddy, Jack, also recently discharged from the navy, and who had done PT boat service in the South Pacific, and was aiming for law school and a career in politics, and wherever other introductions would be required to satisfy proper Bostonian protocol. Cynthia would like Boston, he was sure.

Still, that was several days away, and he had to get ready for the wedding. His tux was in the closet, and he knew that Mrs. O, as her "navy b'ys" liked to call her, would be here in a few minutes with freshly-ground coffee and hot baked bread. He just washed his hands and face, and decided to shower after he had had Mrs. O's wonderful breakfast. And here she was, just hopping off her bicycle, with a large bag of breakfast items, and several just-laid eggs from her henhouse.

"Ah, Commander, so this is the big day, is it? And 'tis a fine lass yer'll be weddin' this afternoon. But, yer'd best be havin' a hearty breakfast ter get yer through the mornin'. I wouldn't want ter send yer to the Church starvin'."

"Mrs. O'Shaunessy, I have never before starved, as you put it, as a result of your marvelous cooking," he said to her, a large smile splitting his face.

"Argh, get on with yer," she smiled back at him, "An' won't her Ladyship be wantin' yer ter be strong, well fed an' in fine form for the evenin's events, if yer get me meanin'," she chuckled as she began to bustle around the well-appointed kitchen.

McGrath stared at her in astonished wonderment. "Mrs. O'Shaunessy. I'm shocked!" He said in his best mock-offensive tone.

Mrs. O'Shaunessy laughed, and put a full plate of fried eggs, hot toast and four half-inch-thick strips of bacon before him. "Get on, with yer," she smiled, "'tis what's on yer mind, I'm certain. This'll keep yer strength up."

And with relish, Commander McGrath, formerly of the United States Navy, Meteorological Branch, tucked into his last breakfast as a bachelor.

***

Two and a half hours later, about eleven thirty, when he had finished his breakfast, showered, shaved till his face gleamed, and dressed himself in his tux, to the point of sartorial perfection, he stood before Mrs. O'Shaunessy for inspection.

"Oh, 'tis grand." She looked the Commander, as all the townspeople called him, up and down and gave her deepest approval. Tall, lean, strong and athletic despite his injured leg; blue-eyed with straight, black hair on a noble head set atop broad shoulders. "Yer look so fine, a credit ter yer Irish heritage and we'll be..." she stopped for a moment and turned toward the sink. "We'll be glad ter have yer in ..." Mrs. O'Shaunessy busied herself with the washing up from breakfast.

"Mrs. O., thank you for all you've done for me and my sailors, especially in these last few weeks. I really can't say how much I appreciate it. Thank you."

"Yer'd best be getting' ter the Church. The whole town's turned out fer yer and her Ladyship." She kept at her work, unable to face him in her emotion. Number one among her "navy b'ys."

"Thank you, Mrs. O. I'll see you at Church and at Niamh's. I have to go now. Eddie will be waiting for me for any last minute arrangements. Father Tim wanted us there a few minutes early. He is jointly celebrating the wedding Mass with Father McDermott." He picked up his topcoat and hat and opened the front door. "And don't forget to clean off that mantelpiece over the hearth. It really needs a lot of tidying," he called back to her over his shoulder, and closed the front door of the cottage for the last time. From now, his residence would be the FitzHugh Manor House, or Beacon Hill in Boston. But he wanted Mrs. O'Shaunessy to "tidy up" the mantelpiece, where he had left her an appreciative check. And she was worth every penny.

He got in to his Rover Saloon and drove to St. Paul's Church, careful to avoid any view of the Manor house and his bride-to-be before the wedding ceremony.

***

McGrath parked in the car park behind St. Paul's. *I'm glad I bought this new car last month*, he thought to himself. Leased cars, like the one he had driven from Dublin to Galway were expensive, and frequently out of repair, but something brand new, kept in top form was what he needed.

He opened the side door to St. Paul's and stepped into the Church. Every pew was occupied with townsfolk from Kildunlee, including all the Catholics who attended Sunday Mass regularly, those who got religious on Christmas and Easter, those who didn't believe at all but who smelt a great party in the making, the few Protestants in town, mostly members of Cynthia's family, and all the rest who wavered between some faith, a touch of faith, and those whose faith leaped into action when it suited them. In other words, every home, business, farm and residence in Kildunlee was vacant, and all the occupants were crowded into St. Paul's.

McGrath's two cousins from Boston, who had flown in the day before from Boston to Shannon with their husbands, were in the third pews, behind those reserved for the closest members of the wedding party.

Magnificent floral arrangements abounded every-where, and the rich scents of flowers and incense wafted throughout the Church. The ladies were in their holiday best and all the gentlemen had squeezed themselves into their finest suits. Surrounding barber shops and beauty salons had done a land office business, and the millinery approached Ireland's highest of fashion. Never, never, never had there been a "do" like this, what with the Commander, a rich Yank at that so rumor had it, running his own steamship company out of Boston, about to marry the beautiful gray-eyed, blond-haired Lady Cynthia FitzHugh, heiress to the very large estate, lands, farms and fortune of the FitzHugh family. It was a match Kildunlee, even most of Ireland, was the word at Niamh's pub, "...hadn't seen and wouldn't ever see again this side o' the end o' creation, an' the divil himself, the Lord rot him, forever smashed inter the pits o' hell..."

***

A sigh of appreciation went up as McGrath headed toward the altar.

"Oooo, the Commander looks so fine, he does.'

"Ah,'tis grand, 'tis grand."

Similar comments could be heard all over the nave. McGrath smiled at them all and went up to Father McDermott.

"Morning, Father McDermott, Father Tim. Eddie, you're looking all spruced up today."

"It's all Siobhan's doing. She helped me get ready this morning, otherwise, I'd look a sight."

"Are your parents here, yet?"

"Yes, they're in the middle of the right hand side with our friends, the Huestises. They have a cattle ranch near us and are old friends of my father and mother."

"Very good. Everyone's welcome today." McGrath turned to the two priests. "Are we ready to start?"

"We are. The bride is in the bride's room at the back of the Church. Eddie, you stand here just inside of the altar rail, and Commander, you're right beside him. Good.

Eddie, do you have the rings?"

"Yes, Father, right here in my pocket," and he took out the jewelry case from his pocket and opened it, displaying two exquisitely formed golden wedding rings. "Beautiful, aren't they?"

"Yes, they are," said Father Tim. "Let's set them here on the table and we'll bless them at the right time. Now, if everything's in order?" He queried Father McDermott.

"Yes, Father, we can begin. Edward, you'd best get to the back of the church to escort your wife, the Matron of Honor." And with that, Edward made haste to the rear of the church, and Father McDermott raised his right hand, and the St. Paul organist struck up the Kildunlee version of "Here Comes the Bride."

Three bridesmaids, cousins of Cynthia, resplendent in their pale yellow gowns, and three groomsmen, in dinner jacket and black tie, marched in a stately fashion down the aisle, followed by Edward in his formal tuxedo, escorting Siobhan, radiant in her white and gold gown. Behind them, a nurse wheeled John, Cynthia's war-injured brother, and he was placed to the bride's side of the altar in front of the altar rail, next to Lord FitzHugh himself, also in a wheelchair.

And finally, the anticipated moment: Lady Cynthia, magnificent in a blazing white gown and veil, bedecked with stitched white roses, escorted by her uncle, Sir Charles, whose decades with the Royal Army on parade, now showed in his supremely stately gait as he guided his beautiful niece to her waiting husband-to-be. They reached the altar rail, and after the customary handshake, he handed his niece to McGrath, who smiled a thank you, and held his arm for Cynthia to take. They smiled deeply at each other and Father Tim had to clear his throat to get their attention. They turned and knelt at the two kneelers specially placed for the bride and groom. The wedding

Mass began.

At last, the moment all were waiting for arrived. McGrath and Cynthia stood and faced the two priests. Edward moved closer to them, holding the ring tray, which Father Tim had just blessed. Reaching for the bride's ring, and placing it in McGrath's hand he said.

"Commander, please repeat after me. I, William Josiah McGrath, take thee, Cynthia FitzHugh, to be my lawfully wedded wife." McGrath repeated the solemn words.

"To have and to hold. To love, honor and protect, in sickness and in health till death do us part." McGrath again repeated Father Tim's words, and placed the ring on Cynthia's finger. Father Tim passed the ring tray to Father McDermott who addressed Cynthia.

"Your Ladyship, please repeat after me. I, Cynthia Catherine FitzHugh, take thee, William McGrath, to be my lawfully wedded husband." Cynthia then followed McGrath's example and repeated Father McDermott's words.

"To have and to hold. To love, honor and obey, in sickness and in health till death do us part." Cynthia again repeated Father McDermott's words, and placed the ring on McGrath's finger.

The two priests then spoke in unison. "By the power invested in us by the Roman Catholic Church and the Republic of Ireland, we now pronounce you man and wife."

The roar of hundreds of voices cheering, and many hundreds of hands clapping filled the church, as McGrath kissed his bride. The cheering only got louder as both priests, in great smiles and jubilation, tried vainly to calm the congregation down.

For a full three minutes–eternity it seemed to McGrath and Cynthia–the cheers and clapping resounded throughout the Church, as watery eyes were dabbed, empty stomachs grumbled and parched throats sounded in happiness.

Finally, the clamor died down, the Mass continued to its end, and McGrath and Cynthia, having completed the receiving line requirements, led everyone to Niamh's pub and the great outside heated tent for the non-stop festivities, which would surely go through the evening twilight till the small hours of tomorrow.

***

"Congratulations, Commander, ahhh, 'tis a fine lass you've got there."

"Oh, your Ladyship, what a handsome man he is. Watch, now, that the other girls don't steal him away."

"Here, Commander, yer'll take a drink with us, and no doubtin' it," and McGrath had to lift his glass yet again. Over the rim, his eyes met Cynthia's, and he winked as if to say, "Don't worry. I'll be fine tonight," and he smiled at her. She returned his smile and he felt his heart surge.

"And did I ever think I'd live ter see the day. Himself and her ladyship. Well, yer'll be eatin' Mrs. Lynch's meals now, and she's a fine cook, and I won't have ter make that bicycle trip in the mornin' no more. Here's luck," and Mrs. O'Shaunessy, together with her husband Mr. O'Shaunessy, and their five children toasted the newlyweds.

"Thank you, Mrs. O., Mr. O. We really appreciate your thoughts," Cynthia said to them.

Guests continued to come up to them and wish them well, sometimes several times over. The whisky, beer, champagne and fine wine flowed. Irish music, jigs, reels and slow tunes, filled the air. Buffet tables, laden with roasted beef, pork, lamb and more than two score varieties of salads and hot vegetable dishes caused the tables to warp and groan under their weight, and gaiety pervaded the pub and tent, where the heat had been turned off as the day grew unexpectedly warmer with the rising of the sun in a cloudless sky.

"Commander, let me introduce my friend, Bobbee Fuller. Bobbee, meet Commander McGrath and his new wife, Lady Cynthia FitzHugh."

"Afternoon, Bobbee, welcome to our reception."

"A lovely wedding it was," she smiled at them. "We arrived in time for the exchange of vows," Bobbee told them. "Really lovely."

Looking around the tent for someone, Lady Alice asked in general, "Has Sir Julian arrived, yet? We were to meet him here because I had to go to Galway to pick Bobbee up at the railway station. I haven't seen him."

"No," Cynthia said. "If he's not here, he should be here soon, though. It's only a few minutes' drive from his house to town. He's probably just wrapping up some last minute details for your trip to South Africa."

"Oh, South Africa," Bobbee beamed, "Alice, I wish I was going with you."

"Well, of course, you'll come to visit, won't you? And you, too, Commander and Cynthia. You'll both come to visit us when we're settled in South Africa, won't you?"

"Wild zebras wouldn't keep me away," he told her with a big smile. "But, I suspect that Sir Julian is probably next door in the pub chatting with Niamh, and he'll be here in a minute," McGrath told them.

"Commander, permit me to introduce my parents Ray and Beverly Hillaire, and their friends, John and Marcie Heustis. They arrived two days ago, just after the rehearsal, but, with all the excitement, I wasn't able to get all of you together. Folks, this is my former commanding officer, now retired from the navy, William McGrath"

"Pleased to meet you, Commander. Our son has told us so much about you and the adventures of the Detail here in Ireland," Edward's mother told him. "We've been looking forward to meeting you and your bride."

"We're glad you were able to make the trip. The trans-Atlantic flight is a long one. And please call me William."

"William it is, then. The flight is long, but I suppose someday they'll improve things and it'll be only a few hours across the North Atlantic," said Roy Hillaire, "We got to Galway two days ago and we've been resting up from our trip and getting ready for the wedding. We really haven't had much of a chance to see Eddie, Siobhan and our grandchildren."

"Don't worry, dad, there'll be plenty of time for visiting after the wedding."

"But this weather is so mild here in Ireland," Ray Hillaire told them. "It's great to experience it. It was forty below, not counting the wind, when we left home."

"I'm not sure I can handle that type of weather again," Eddie said, holding Siobhan close. "I've gotten used to Irish mildness."

Siobhan smiled up at "her Eddie" and snuggled even closer to him, and he welcomed her touch. Hillaire's parents beamed on their son and his bride, their first daughter-in-law. "Oh, Eddie, me own, I'm not sure I'd even let yer go back."

"Siobhan, I love listening to your marvelous, lilting Irish accent. So much more pleasant from our gruff voiced cowboys," Beverly said, her face wreathed in a radiant smile.

"Fear not, my dearest," Edward said to his wife, "I'm here to stay."

"Well, we would love to have you and our grand-children visit Montana. Perhaps during the summer when it's not so cold. It's a big, lovely piece of countryside and we have a large ranch. The kids would love the horses." And light, happy chatter continued among them.

McGrath felt a hand on his arm and he turned to see who it was. Livy, the Garda, had a dread look on his face as he leaned closer to him. "Commander," he said, in a voice just above a whisper, "Someone, I think it was Lady Alice, was just askin' fer Sir Julian."

"That's right. She's concerned that he's not here yet."

"Well, I know where he is, I do."

"Oh, do you really?" McGrath's eyebrows shot up, quizzically. "Where's that, Livy? McGrath asked.

Livy O'Toole, Senior Garda for Kildunlee and the environs dropped his voice even lower, so those around him should not hear. "He's at his desk in his study at his rented house. Dead."

14.

AT SIR JULIAN'S

"That's right, Commander, I seen him meself, didn't I. Dead as Brian Boru's corpse an' nary a drop o' red floatin' in his rigid body. Brains scattered all over the desk top blotter floatin' in blood an' soakin' in like a jar o' the pure outter the blue on barren barley fields dyin' o the ragin' douth, markin' yer pardon, me Lady," he said, with a nod toward her ladyship,

"That's all right, Livy. There has been worse around here, what with the war and all. Don't concern yourself with it."

"Thank yer fer understandin', me Lady. But, 'twere awrful ter see. An' the pistol there in his own hand.''''
"I don't understand, Livy. He was around town just three days ago for the rehearsal supper. I spoke with him in Niamh's pub when we were having a drink together and he seemed to be very happy and in good spirits. I can't imagine what happened to change all this."

"There ain't no tellin', Commander. Things happen ter people all the time. Some people hide their troubles real good till they can't hold it in no more, and then they do somethin' fierce. They taught us that in Garda School," Livy told them, nodding officiously. Livy O'Toole was one of the two local Garda. Livy's real name was Livius Severus Publius Francis O'Toole. He got his name from his father who had taught Classics at Trinity College in Dublin. His father had always claimed that he gave Livy the middle name of Francis to "…keep him in good graces with the Church." The elder O'Toole had wanted Livy to follow him into teaching, hoping Livy would gravitate toward the Classics and college-level teaching as well, but Livy chose to become a Garda. Livy and his number two, Fergal Hanlon, kept the peace in Kildunlee.

"I was makin' me rounds about the town and I thought I'd keep an eye out on the Manor and then Sir Julian's place, just ter be sure everything was all right and ter keep me conscience clear. I seen the front door ter Sir Julian's was wide open, an' I thought the wind had done it, so I stopped the police van and went ter close it. I called out ter the house and got no answer, but I thought it would be good ter take a proper look anyway 'cause there ain't no tellin' what clatter o' evil the divil himself, God rot him, may be getting' up ter. And there was himself, in the study. Sir Julian spread out on his desk, a pistol in his hand and his head shattered from the shot, again, pardonin' yerself, yer Ladyship. I was going ter stop at the Garda office but I came here right off, knowin' yer'd know what ter do. I hate ter bring bad news on yer weddin' day, Commander, but people hereabouts look up ter yer for all yer done during the war in these parts and here ye're back with us, and isn't it grand. I'll have ter send in me report ter Supervisor O'Meara, but we thought we should tell yer first since yer seem to know what might have ter be done."

"Thank you, Livy," McGrath said to the Garda, turning to Cynthia with an exasperated sigh, meaning, "My dear bride, what do I do now?" Cynthia took McGrath's elbow and gently led him a few feet away from where Livy, and a growing crowd of curious on-lookers, had gathered.

"William," she said in an undertone. "This is really inconvenient of Livy and an intrusion on our wedding day. But, I don't believe in portents, regardless of what

Cormac O'Callaghan said the other night."

"Neither do I," he answered her.

"Still, the people in Kildunlee look up to you as a leader, a world traveler and one who knows what's to be done. I think you should go with Livy and see what has happened. Sir Julian's house is only a mile from town. You can be there and back in no time, and the reception can continue as if nothing had happened. It'll be only a few minutes, and I'll be here waiting for you. Remember," she said, with a seductive smile, "We have business to attend to later."

William's face spread a bright grin. "In that case, neither Sir Julian nor wild horses can keep me away." And he kissed her gently and turned to Livy.

"Oh, and, William…" McGrath turned back to his bride. "I love you," she whispered in his ear, and kissed him gently in her turn. McGrath had to struggle to return his attention to Livy.

"Don't worry about telling me on our wedding day. It's just one of those things. It won't have any effect our marriage, will it," he said to his bride.

"No. Not a bit," she replied. "Why don't you go over and have a look, William, then get back as soon as you can. There are things to be attended to," and she gave him a rich smile.

He acknowledged her smile. "Back in twenty minutes."

***

It was barely a five minutes drive to Sir Julian's rented house, and McGrath saw, when they arrived, that the door had been left open and Sean Pierce, a young "Garda in Training" was on duty, keeping an eye on things.

"Arfternoon, ter yer, Livy and sir. 'Taint been a soul ter see since yer left ter fetch the Commander. Sir

Julian's still in there and he hain't moved so much as a muscle."

"Well, Garda Pierce, I wouldn't be expectin' him ter move, what with his brains all over his desk," Livy responded, with a wink to McGrath.

McGrath smiled and followed Livy into the well-appointed house. Sir Julian had luxurious tastes, and had furnished his residence in a deluxe manner. They turned in to the library, and saw Sir Julian sitting in his leather-bound chair, leaning over his desk with a very large hole in his right temple. His left cheek rested on the blotter, and blood oozed out from under his shattered head. Blood, brains and bone chips spread out on the other side of his desk, creating a scene of macabre color. A large-bore Smith & Wesson pistol was clasped in his right hand, and lay about a foot and a half away to his right.

"All in all, Commander, I guess there's no doubtin' he took his own life. But, why, I can't fer the life of me, figure out. He was headed ter South Africa with Lady Alice where they were goin' ter be married. They both had family there, too. It'd have been a fine weddin' may- be almost as fine as yours and her Ladyship's." Livy shook his head slowly. "Nope. Can't figure this one out."

"No. No, it doesn't seem reasonable," McGrath answered Livy, as he walked around the large oak desk and looked intently at the dead face of Sir Julian. His face was set in a grimace of sheer terror, with his mouth agape and his eyes staring wide open, in a state of extreme shock. His right temple had been crushed by the high powered bullet, which careened through the brain, and exploded out the left side of his head, spewing brains, bone and blood across the desk blotter, and the highly polished leather and dark oak. Blood trailed out of his nostrils and onto his dressing gown and the shiny oak, as if the bullet had also severed blood vessels in his head. Sir Julian's eyes, set in his lean, tanned face under a shock of straight gray-blond hair, wide open in a horrified glare, stared blankly into nowhere, but reflected an image of horror.

"For some reason or other, sir," Livy said to McGrath, "he must have been terrified o' takin' his own life, by the look o' him there. He was scared, but he did it anyway." McGrath, still studying Sir Julian's face, nodded absentmindedly to Livy and bent to sniff Sir Julian's hand.

"What are yer doin', sir, if I may be askin'?"

"Oh, just smelling for powder burns on his hand. You can see them here from when he fired the shot, and they smell like discharged gunpowder. He'll certainly pass a paraffin test. Here, see?" Livy bent over Sir Julian's hand, where McGrath indicated, and saw the powder burns along his fingers. He also sniffed Sir Julian's hand and smelled the discharged gunpowder McGrath had spoken about.

"You're right, sir. There's no doubtin' it, he took his own life, and I'm thinkin' that's what will be decided at the Inquest." McGrath nodded again.

"Look, Livy," McGrath said to the Garda, stooping over to point to a typed sheet of paper, "there's a typed letter here. It has a crest on it. It must be some type of official correspondence or document."

"Beggin' yer pardon, sir, I wouldn't touch it until Superintendent O'Meara and Dr. McHugh get here. Could be evidence fer something or other, yer know."

"I understand," McGrath said nodding once again absently to Livy and standing up. Moving closer to Sir Julian's terrifying face, McGrath sniffed the dead man's mouth.

"What are yer doin', sir, may I ask?"

"Nothing, really, Livy. Just satisfying my curiosity. Right. Well, if there's no further reason for me to be here, perhaps you'll give me a ride back to my bride," McGrath said, turning from Sir Julian's corpse and toward the door.

"O' course, sir, o' course, and thanks fer comin' over ter give yer opinion. People around here respect yer, as does meself, and yer opinions, I'm thankin' yer fer comin' over ter jest have a look. I'll be in touch with Superintendent O'Meara in a few minutes when I get back ter the station house, and no doubt he'll want to speak with you for a bit. Now, let me run yer over ter yer bride. Pierce, keep yer eyes open."

"Yes, Garda O'Toole," Pierce replied quietly, with a wincing glance toward the desk and its morbid occupant.

"Well, sir, it looks like Sir Julian took his own life, and was terrified of doin' so. Maybe that's why he has champagne jest before he pulled the trigger. Ter get his courage up, so ter speak?"

"We'll never know, Livy," McGrath said, getting into the patrol car, "We'll probably never know."

***

"William, how did it go? I felt so bad that Livy came to our wedding and asked you to go see Sir Julian. But you know how the townspeople feel about you."

"It went all right, Cynthia. Sir Julian's gone. Done in by his own hand, so to speak."

He addressed himself to all those crowded around him. "Sir Julian apparently took his own life. He's dead, God rest his soul. But, this is a day not for grieving, but for happiness, no matter what has happened," and his remarks were greeted by cheers. "So, with that said, Lady Cynthia and I will begin the festivities again, and we'll lead everyone in a merry waltz. Maestro, if you please." And Commander William McGrath took his bride, Lady Cynthia FitzHugh, exquisite in shimmering white brocade and veil, and tastefully bejeweled in diamond earrings and necklace, in his arms and led her on to the dance floor, motioning everyone else to follow, to the strains of Niamh Flaherty's brothers and cousins, the local Quinn band, supplemented by three additional musicians, doing their best to honor Strauss' "Blue Danube".

"William, this is wonderful. I don't care what's happened. I love you so much."

He leaned over and kissed his wife, to loud cheers, and said, "I don't think anyone else cares what's happened either. And I love you, too, my dear. I truly do." Melodies from the "Blue Danube" filled the evening air, as twilight approached.

15.

INQUEST

On the following Monday morning, in the small wooden building that served as a meeting house and court house, Francis O'Farrell, the Regional Magistrate for the western part of County Clare, which included Kildunlee, Doolan, Liscannor, Hag's Head and the other, smaller, surrounding towns, tapped his wooden gavel gently, but imperiously.

"This Inquest will now come to order," he declared. "Will the Clerk of the Court please read the details?"

"Thank yer, yer honor," replied Senan Neill. He held up a sheet of paper and recited dutifully, "On the mid afternoon of Saturday last, Sir Julian Brownlee was discovered slumped over his desk in his study. A Smith and Wesson revolver of large caliber was clutched in his right hand. Upon removal from his hand by the aut'orities, the pistol was dusted for fingerprints and only Sir Julian's were found on the revolver. There were naught other   fingerprints on the gun. A large bullet hole was displayed in his head, which the Ballistics and Forensics Department o' the County Clare Police Laboratory that had done the fingerprint dustin', also suspects ter have been caused by a bullet fired from the same revolver in Sir Julian's hand. A full report will be forthcoming this Friday. There were powder burns on his right temple. The bullet entered Sir Julian's right temple and exited slightly ter the rear o' his left temple, with part o' his skull an' brains splayed across the blotter on his desk. The discharged bullet rested on the desk two and a half feet ter the left o' Sir Julian's exit wound. Death were, evidently, instantaneous, and it is apparent that he had taken his own life. There were a typewritten sheet o' paper on his desk, with some blood stains on it from the gunshot wound. Sir Julian's signature was at the bottom of the paper."

"Thank you, Mr. Neill," Magistrate O'Farrell said. "Please call the first witness."

"Garda Livius O'Toole, ter the stand, please."

Livy approached the stand, raised his right hand, and with his left hand on the Bible, swore that he would tell the truth, the whole truth and, in his most serious demeanor, nothing but the truth, "So help me, God".

"Please ter be seated," the Clerk of the Court, Senan Neill, told him.

"Garda O'Toole," Magistrate O'Farrell said, "in your own words, please tell the Court of Inquest what you discovered when you went to visit Sir Julian's residence Saturday last."

"Yes, Yer Honor. I was doin' me rounds, as usual, keepin' me eye on things, before I went ter join the celebrations fer the Commander and Lady Cynthia's weddin'. I was passin' by Sir Julian's rented house an' I seen the door open, so I says to meself, I says, p'rhaps I'd better take a look. I went ter the front door and heard nothin', so I called out ter Sir Julian, and there be no answer. So, I entered the house, I did, lookin' fer Sir Julian, or what I might find, Yer Honor, and I turned in ter his study. What I seen caused me hair ter rise, me blood ter curdle and me heart ter stop," and Livy then gave an appropriate shudder.

"Yes, yes, of course, Garda. Please continue," Magistrate O'Farrell encouraged him.

"Well, yer Honor, there sat Sir Julian, slumped on his large desk, with a pistol in his right hand and the left part of his head spread across his desk. 'Twere a terrible sight ter see," said Livy, in his moment of glory, giving testimony in a Magistrate's Court at his first Inquest. He continued to regale the Court with the descriptions of Sir Julian, in exquisite and fine detail, reflecting the exact descriptions just read by the Clerk of the Court, Senan Neill.

"The pistol was in his right hand, and a sheet of paper lay just in front of him. It were typewritten and had his signature on it. The scene was just as the Clerk read it."

O'Farrell asked Livy, "Did you notice anything unusual about the crime scene, Garda?"

"No, yer Honor, I didn't. It seemed ter be a simple case of suicide ter me."

"Thank you, Garda, O'Toole. You may step down."

Evidence was given by Sean Pierce, the Garda in training, and his testimony reflected what Livy had told the Court.

"The Court calls Commander William McGrath to the stand," O'Farrell proclaimed.

"Commander William McGrath to the stand, please," Neill called, and McGrath was sworn in as a witness to the proceedings concerning the death of Sir Julian Brownlee.

"Commander, as a formality, please state your name and occupation for the Court."

"William McGrath, former Commander, US Navy, now discharged, Chief Executive Officer of McGrath Shipping Lines headquartered in Boston, Massachusetts and presently residing at the FitzHugh Manor here in Kildunlee."

"Thank you, Commander McGrath. Let me express my appreciation of your willingness to appear in Court at this Inquest. I understand that you and her Ladyship have just been married and wish to go to Boston for your honeymoon, and I apologize for any inconvenience these proceedings may have caused you," O'Farrell said to McGrath.

"Thank you, Your Honor, but my wife and I fully understand that the Law must take its course."

"Thank you. I appreciate your understanding," O'Farrell responded to McGrath."Now, Commander, will you please tell the Court exactly what you witnessed when you arrived at Sir Julian's house?"

"Your Honor, I can only state that what I saw is the same testimony as has been given by Garda O'Toole. He had approached me at my wedding reception and told me that Sir Julian was dead and would I come take a look. We then proceeded to Sir Julian's and viewed the scene together. Any testimony I have to produce would entirely support Garda O'Toole's previously stated facts."

"I believe that you and your opinions are held in high esteem by the people of Kildunlee, Commander, in light of your war experiences here and your contribution to Eisenhower's D-Day invasion. It would be natural for the Garda to seek you out to get your opinion."

"Thank you. And that's just what Livy did. We both went to Sir Julian's house and saw what has already been given in testimony. I can really add little else, except..." and McGrath hesitated here for an instant.

"Yes, Commander?" O'Farrell prompted.

"The only thing that struck me as being odd was the look of sheer horror on Sir Julian's face. As if he had some kind of premonition or frightening experience before the infliction of the gunshot wound. I can't explain it. But I have witnessed a suicide aboard ship in the Pacific toward the end of the war and the officer who shot himself had a calm look on his face, a look of resignation, not one of horror as with Sir Julian."

"Could it be possible that Sir Julian knew he was going to take his own life and that he was terrified of the probable pain?" O'Farrell asked him.

"Your Honor, I don't know. His expression just seemed to me to be unusual."

"Did you notice anything else out of the ordinary, Commander?"

"No, Your Honor, I didn't."

"Thank you, Commander, you may step down." And McGrath took his seat with the other witnesses.

Dr. Kieran McHugh was called, sworn in and asked to take the stand.

"Please state your name and occupation for the Court."

"Dr. Kieran McHugh, General Practitioner, with a concentration in Internal Medicine, for Kildunlee, Doolan, Liscannor and these parts."

"Thank you, Doctor," Magistrate O'Farrell said. "Now, will you please tell the Court, in the least technical terms possible, the condition of the deceased as you found him?" Dr. McHugh proceeded to describe, in thorough detail, but with attention to lay terms, the condition of Sir Julian at his first examination of Sir Julian in the library, and later in his medical examining room, before turning the corpse over to the mortician who would prepare the body for burial.

"Otherwise, there is little I can add to the testimony, your Honor, except that I agree with Garda O'Toole and Commander McGrath. Sir Julian's face was in an unusual and terrified stare. I don't know why, I'm really not a psychiatrist, but I have seen other suicides before and this one appeared to be strange, at least as regards Sir Julian's facial expression."

"Quite so," said O'Farrell. "Now, doctor, where is the corpse at this time and has there been an autopsy ordered?"

"The corpse is in Galway at the morgue, in a frozen state. It is awaiting the paperwork for forwarding to Sir Julian's homeland, Johannesburg, South Africa. That should take a week or two. No, there has been no order for an autopsy. I'm not sure Sir Julian's family or Lady Alice would approve of having one."

"I see," said O'Farrell. "In your medical offices, and, later, in the examining room of the Coroner, were intensive examinations made?"

"No, Your Honor. No request was made for these, and they are not done without a court order. So, we really only confirmed that there was a gunshot wound to the right temple which was the apparent cause of death."

"Doctor, for the record, and without betraying any doctor-patient confidentiality, will you please tell the Court the condition of Lady Alice Stronton, who is in your care."

"Yes, Your Honor. Just after Garda O'Toole told Commander McGrath about Sir Julian, and they had both visited the house and had seen Sir Julian's corpse, Garda O'Toole told me about the suicide, and that he thought that Lady Alice would take it very hard, which indeed she did. This was during the Commander's wedding reception when everyone was wondering where Sir Julian was and when would he get to the reception. I took Lady Alice outside, with her friend, Bobbee Fuller, and told her what had happened, as I knew it then. She took the news very difficultly and I had to drive her to my office where I administered a sedative to her. Later, with a prescription for sleep, I brought her to her house with Bobbee, who was to spend the night with Lady Alice. I stopped by the next day and, naturally, Lady Alice was very upset, but somewhat calmer. I think she'll be all right, given suffi-cient time in view of the shock to her system. She is now resting at home with Bobbee taking care of her. I'll stop in to see her after this Inquest."

"Of course. Thank you, Doctor. Your evidence substantiates the evidence of those who spoke before you. You may step down now," and Kieran McHugh joined

McGrath in the seating area.

Magistrate O'Farrell instructed Clerk Neill to call Superintendent O'Meara to the stand. O'Meara stated that he was the Supervisor of the Garda for Kildunlee, Liscannor, Doolan and the additional surrounding areas south of Galway and down to Hag's Head.

Superintendent O'Meara corroborated what had already been stated regarding the crime scene at Sir Julian's and the condition of the corpse, when he had seen it. He commended, officially, the work done by Garda O'Toole and the young Garda in Training, Sean Pierce, much to the satisfaction and pleasure of those in the court room.

His testimony backed up the evidence that had been given all along by the other witnesses: that Sir Julian had taken his own life, and further evidenced by the letter found under his head stating that his investments in South African gold mines had gone sour, that his fortune was reduced practically to zero and that now he had virtually nothing to offer Lady Alice. Simply stated, he had lost everything, was financially embarrassed and was a poor man, shamed through his investment folly. Some men cannot tolerate the fact that life had dealt them those cards, and considered the only honorable way out was to commit suicide. Such seemed to be the case here.

In the final moments of the Inquest, Magistrate O'Farrell instructed Clerk Neill to read the text of the note found lying next to Sir Julian's head.

"Yes, Your Honor," Neill replied, and he read the following note:

April 18, 1946

I solemnly declare that I am Sir Julian Brownlee and that I am of sound mind and being. I was shortly to relocate to Johannesburg, South Africa, with my fiancée,

Lady Alice Stronton, whom I love. We had been looking forward to a new and exciting life in South Africa, and it was my fondest desire to spend my years with my dearest love.

But alas, this is not to be. In recent months, based upon the advice of my Johannesburg broker, I had heavily invested my capital in South African gold mines, with the expectation of great returns. I was relying on these returns to increase my wealth considerably, so that I could give Lady Alice the life of luxury she so richly deserves.

Then, last week I received a letter from my broker informing me that the mines had run out, and that the veins of ore upon which I had placed high expectations were bereft of gold. I found myself a penniless man. I have lost all my wealth, and my honor, and I cannot bear to face my love, Lady Alice, knowing I have failed her. Nor can I bear to face all the others, not only in Kildunlee, but also in South Africa. I have decided to take the honorable route out.

So, I have done what I have done. I beg for your forgiveness and understanding.

Farewell,

Sir Julian Brownlee

Magistrate O'Farrell's eyes surveyed the Court. "Is there any one here who has additional evidence or further testimony to render to this Court, which might affect the outcome of this case?"

He continued to survey the Courtroom for several moments, eyebrows raised in anticipation. "Since it appears that there is no further evidence to be given, the jury will retire to the jury room and consider its verdict."

Clerk Neill led the jury to the deliberation room.

Fewer than fifteen minutes later, the jury filed back

into the court room, led by Senan Neill, and resumed their seats in the jury box, and delivered its verdict: Sir Julian Brownlee had discovered that his investments had left him a poor man and, because of this news, in light of his upcoming wedding to Lady Alice and the fact that he would be unable to provide her a satisfactory life, he took his own life.

Francis O'Farrell thanked the jury foreman, tapped his gavel once and declared, "Court adjourned."

16.

AFTERNOON AT NIAMH'S PUB,
A MYSTERIOUS PACKAGE

"Good afternoon, Doctor, what'll it be today? Nice pint o' Guinness?" Niamh said as she cheerfully greeted Doctor McHugh.

"No, no, too early, Niamh. Just a cup of your best coffee and a thick ham sandwich. I still have patients to see this afternoon," Doctor McHugh replied.

"Well, Doc, you're in luck. Brendan Rafferty brought in one of his best hams yesterday, all cut and cured, as they say. An' sure 'tis the finest in these parts. Shall I put some Swiss on it with a dab of your favorite Irish mustard? And the bread freshly baked this marnin'. Now, doesn't that sound tempting?" she asked.

"It does, Niamh, it does. An early lunch today because I'm seeing someone at twelve-thirty, so I have to be ready. Fed and fat."

"Ha! You fat? There can't be an extra ounce on yer skinny bones, Doc. You ought ter find yourself a nice wife that'll fatten you up. If you get any skinnier you'll be able ter hide behind a pencil," Niamh told him. He laughed at her comments and the others at the bar joined in.

"Argh, Doc, you'd best be findin' a nice girl for yerself, otherwise yer'll find yerself in old age with nothin' ter look at but yer stetherscope," Liam O'Banyon, the town's greengrocer, said, and the bar continued its chuckle. But Doctor Kieran McHugh was a gentle man who didn't take offense easily, and he knew that all the badinage at his expense was done with the very best of intentions and general humor, so all he did was to join in the merriment.

"Maybe I'll take on a female assistant, or a nurse. That'd give me possibilities," McHugh said.

"Well, yer'd best hurry up, Doc, before things rust away," Liam said, and the people at the bar had one more good laugh before returning to their conversations.

"One thick ham and Swiss sandwich, Doctor McHugh. With just a touch of mustard."

"Thanks, Niamh," and he turned his attention to his lunch.

The door to the pub opened and a medium-sized, slight man stepped in. The bar was long, about thirty feet, and it faced several windows, with small tables and four chairs at each table. Sunlight came through the yellow curtained windows and into the bar, brightening the whole place. The entry door was midway between two sets of three windows each, directly facing the bar. Into this cheerful place stepped the visitor.

"Well, now, if this place ain't turning inter a veritable League of Nations, what with yer an' the Spaniards over there. Good afternoon, Monsieur Gaspard," Niamh smiled at her new customer.

"*Bonjour, Madame.* A pleasure to see you again on such a magnificent day. I was of the, er, impression that the weather in Ireland always had the clouds with the rain, *Mais, non.* Today is beautiful. It reminds me very much of Provence."

"Sure'n it does, but I bet Provence is a bit warmer than here. I went there once on a tour and it was really hot, that bein' in July."

"Ah, yes, *Madame*, Provence in July is always hot. Better to go in May when it is a bit cooler and the mimosa are blooming."

"I'll remember that next time. Glass o' Pernod, Monsieur, or perhaps one o' yer favorite wines? I have Chablis, cold, Merlot, Cabernet Sauvignon, and, of course, port. What's your pleasure?"

"It is too early for port, so a glass of Merlot, the wine of love, *Madame*, would be just right for my palate."

"Comin' up."

The conversations around the bar continued and McHugh worked his way through his sandwich and Niamh's strong, black coffee. His eye caught two people at a table in a small alcove at the end of the bar. One he recognized as Joe Naughton, the town's handyman and jack of all trades, who was really a master at nothing at all, but could fix anything broken and did the dirty work nobody else wanted to do. With him was a girl McHugh thought he recognized, but his memory couldn't place her.

"Niamh, who is that girl with Joe Naughton at the table near the end of the bar?"

"Her? Oh, that's Bobbee Fuller, Lady Alice's friend. She's staying with her Ladyship since Sir Julian's death till the paperwork for Sir Julian's return to South Africa and hers are approved. She said Lady Alice was feeling a bit better today, so she came ter town fer a while."

"Right. I couldn't place her. She looks so different now, not in fancy wedding reception clothes."

The door opened again, letting more Irish sunlight into the room.

"Morning, Kieran, how's it going today? Early lunch?" McGrath asked him.

"Yes. I have patients to see this afternoon, in about a half hour actually, so I came in for some of Brendan's best ham."

"Looks good to me," McGrath said to him, smiling. "Just coffee, Niamh. I "walked down from the Manor to get a few things in town, and I'm going to have to hoof it back. I need the exercise; Mrs. Lynch has been feeding me as well as Mrs. O'Shaunessy did during the war. But now I have to get exercise or else I'll end up looking like the fatted calf in the Prodigal Son story."

"You look fine, William," Doctor McHugh told him. "Bit of exercise doesn't hurt, though." The doctor continued with his sandwich and McGrath sipped his coffee. Finally McGrath broke the silence between the two of them.

"Kieran, how did you like the way the Inquest went the other day?"

Doctor McHugh swallowed his bite of sandwich, took a large drink of coffee, and said, "I didn't like it. I didn't like the contortions on Sir Julian's face nor did I like the fact that there was no order for an autopsy. Given the fact that he seemed to be a happy man, despite his note, and was soon to be married, I just don't feel quite comfortable about his suicide, the look on his face and other things."

"What do you mean, 'other things'?"

Kieran McHugh was thoughtful for a moment, then, he replied. "Rigor mortis sets in shortly after death. It also stiffens the muscles of the body. But, to quite an extreme extent, Sir Julian's spine and back muscles seemed to have been affected by more than rigor mortis. Almost as if they had gone through a severe tightening, in a backwards direction, then were released after the body had slumped forward. But, without an order for an autopsy, I can't make a determination. It would be pure speculation and disregarded by the Court. That's the problem with the Law; nothing can be admitted into a court case without exacting proof, and speculation is unallowable in a Court of Law here in Ireland. Still, I think something else caused those facial contortions and the back muscles and spine to tighten. But, as I said, without an autopsy, nothing can be said."

McGrath thought about this for a moment before sharing his thoughts with his medical friend. "Kieran, I had some ideas along the same lines. I saw a suicide aboard ship during the last stages of the war. An officer had gotten a lot of bad news from home, Oklahoma, I think, over the course of several months, and he couldn't deal with it. He was a very excitable and nervous fellow, anyway. When we saw him, his face was placid despite the gunshot wound, almost happy, as if the problem was over and he was relieved of it. Not like Sir Julian."

"I know. Very curious," Doctor McHugh answered him. McGrath's gaze wandered to the far end of the room. "Looks like Lady Alice's girlfriend, Bobbee, is getting on well with Joe Naughton."

"They've been flirtin' since they came in here together almost two hours ago," Niamh told them, as she was passing down the bar to serve another customer.

"I don't know what we can do, if anything. There's only the facial expression and that probably wouldn't be enough to warrant a postmortem, would it?" McGrath asked him.

"No. It wouldn't. And, of course, we don't get much call for postmortems here in these parts. There'd have to be some a good deal more substantive reasons to ask for a postmortem, or a full autopsy. The difference here in Ireland, since you're probably wondering," McHugh, smiling, said to McGrath, "is that a postmortem merely verifies the cause of death and an autopsy does tests of the vital organs."

"Sounds like the same as in Boston. Incidentally, is Sir Julian still in the morgue in Galway? On ice?"

"Yes, and I'm beginning to see just what you're thinking. It'd be dangerous, though. But it might be conclusive."

"What am I thinking?" McGrath asked him.

The doctor finished his sandwich and coffee. "That you want me to contact my friends at the morgue to do a paraffin test on Sir Julian's hands, to see if there are any embedded traces of powder burns on them."

"You're reading my mind, Kieran. But what if Sir Julian didn't fire that shot? What if someone else did? Would there still be powder burns on the shooter's hands?"

"There would. They stay on the skin for several days, even a week, in some cases, after firing a shot. If he hadn't fired that shot, his hands would show no powder burns unless the shooter smeared it on, but they should still be on the shooter's hands because the action of the discharge would embed the powder traces into the skin. If Sir Julian had fired it, then the powder burns would show up there."

Laughter came from the far end of the bar, where Bobbee and Joe were sitting. They appeared to be having a good time and were holding hands. She was laughing at everything he said. The front door swung open and Jimmy Fallon came in carrying a small package.

"Hello, Jimmy," Niamh called. "What brings yer here at this hour o' the day?"

"Well, I be lookin' fer the Garda. Is Livy around?"

"Why do yer want Livy? Shouldn't yer be out deliverin' the post?"

"Well, I should. Yes, I should. But I have a problem here," and he showed them the package. "I have a delivery here fer a Mr. Harold Winthrop, care o' Sir Julian Brownlee, at his address here in town. It's from the Irish Passport Office in Dublin. Now, with Sir Julian gone, I don't know what ter do with it. It's registered post and so it has ter be signed for like. I thought I'd ask Livy what ter do. Return it, or give it ter someone in charge here."

"Excuse me, Monsieur. I could not help overhearing what you have just said. In France, undeliverable packages are returned to the post office of origin. *Peutetre* it is the same condition here and you should do the same."

"Oh, Jean-Luc. Forgive me. I haven't introduced you to these people yet. This is Doctor Kieran McHugh, our town physician, and Commander William McGrath, just recently married to Lady Cynthia, and of Boston, Massachusetts. This is Jean-Luc Gaspard of Paris, having a holiday here in the West Country, and what kind of business are you in, Jean-Luc?"

"Ah, *Madame*, you are so kind. My brothers and I have an art and picture framing shop in Montmartre, in Paris, not far from *Le Moulin Rouge*. I am pleased to meet you gentlemen." He shook hands with the doctor and McGrath and handed them his card. "In the event you are in Paris and buy an undiscovered Monet and desire to have it framed," he said with a smile. McGrath looked at the card which read:

Bernard Gaspard et Fils
Vendeurs des Belles Arts
268 Boulevard Clichy
Arrondissement XVIII
Paris, France
28-96-55-13

"Thank you, Monsieur Gaspard," he said to the Frenchman.

"*S'il vous plait, Monsieur*, Jean-Luc. *Oui, mon grandpere* started this art business and now my father has continued it to this day, and has made it, as you say, and become a wealthy man. Now, my brothers and I take care of it since *mon pere* does not go *tres bien*. The age, you comprehend."

"Yes. I understand, Jean-Luc," McGrath replied.

"Ah, *Monsieur Le Commandant*, permit me to express my joyous feelings at the wonderful time I had last Saturday at your wedding and the reception which followed. Apparently, here in Ireland, when there is a wedding, the whole town is invited, *les visiteurs, aussi*. I had *le temps merveilleux,* and your new wife, Madame McGrath, made a beautiful bride. *Merci pour tout*."

"I'm glad you enjoyed yourself and thank you for your very nice comments. And, please, call me William," McGrath answered Jean-Luc,

"An' yer've got it right there, Monsieur Jean-Luc. When there's a weddin' in an Irish village or town, like Kildunlee, everyone's invited and everyone goes."

"So, what am I ter do with this here package for Mr...." Jimmy, the postman checked the delivery address again, "Mr. Harold Winthrop?"

Jean-Luc shrugged his shoulders in the best Gallic fashion; McGrath looked at the doctor, and they both gave stares of "I don't know," then shrugged toward Jean-Luc. Nobody knew what to do with the package.

"Why don't you give it to Magistrate O'Farrell? He's still in town on business. He'd know what to do," Doctor McHugh offered.

"Well, I might just do that, Doctor. And thank yer fer the advice. It says here, it says, *NO RETURN, DO NOT FORWARD*. And that's official and from this here office. I'll be seein' the Magistrate right away, sure an' I will."

"Ah, *bien*, it has been a *grande* pleasure to meet you gentlemen, but now I feel the need for a bit of exercise. To keep the muscles young, you comprehend."

"If you're walking toward the cliffs, I'll take a stroll with you," McGrath said to Jean-Luc.

"*Mais oui*. By all means, William," and he turned toward the pub door. McGrath was about to follow him, but was detained by loud laughter in the rear of the pub. Joe and Bobbee were having a great time together. He sat close to the small table, enjoying his beer and being quite friendly with her. She smiled at him in a very seductive way, then picked up her brushes, palette, and oil paints and headed toward the door. Joe waved at her and called, "I'll be up to the Cliffs soon."

Bobbee smiled at him again and leaving the pub, turned and walked up to the Cliffs of Moher, overlooking the North Atlantic.

Getting up off his bar stool, with his lunch finished, and heading out to return to his office and his next patients, Doctor McHugh said, "William, I'll give my friend at the Galway Hospital Morgue a call and see what can be done as regards to Sir Julian."

"OK, good," McGrath said. "Maybe we're making more of this than there really is, but I'd really like to know, just to check all the possibilities."

"Right, but I will still have my doubts, anyway. Dr. Bryan Logan works at the Galway Hospital Morgue. I'll get in touch with him today. We went to medical school together and he's the Chief Coroner for County Clare. I'll ask him to try to find out what he can. But keep that under your hat."

"You've got my word," and McGrath turned to catch up with Jean-Luc who had struck out towards the Cliffs of Moher.

17.

JEAN-LUC AND BOBBEE

The following day began fine and clear, just the type of weather one would want for viewing the Cliffs and beyond. But a storm was brewing, visible in the distance, just above the horizon, and the winds from the north west, deviling in from the angry North Atlantic, that pit and cauldron of storm and feistiness, known well to McGrath and his Meteorological Staff, which had sent the many blasts had they lived through, during the war, here onto the Irish West Coast, seemed prepared to batter Kildunlee once more. But, unlike the usually calm Pacific, where they had been called to "Met" duty preparing the invasion forces for any upcoming storms, and eventually having to ride out typhoons Mary and Olive, the North Atlantic, a treacherous sea any time of year, was preparing to hurl a storm for a blast at the West Country of the green gem of Europe. But, that tempest was hours away, although the clouds, sliding in across the sky from the sea, low and black, forewarned that anyone near the Cliffs, with half an ounce of brains, should be prepared to hasten to the nearest pub, or other shelter. Pub was, of course, preferred, for it never rains in a pub!

"Well, my good French friend," Niamh scolded him lightheartedly, "Finished with yer Pernod already? Never seen a Frenchie drink his Pernod so fast. But," she said, smiling, "if yer like it, why not? Never had a taste fer licorice, myself, I can say."

"Ah, but, *Madame,* the taste of the Pernod, from a

bit of anise, with a, how do you *Anglais*, or pardon, *Les Irlandais*, say, an exquisite lunch, a nap, a *somme*, in the afternoon is the exquisite moment of repose. *Non?*"

"Jean-Luc, I can't say yer wrong. A snooze in the afternoon, after lunch, is a welcome treat fer the working class, and I'm one of them. That's why Rosie comes in about this time." And, as if to emphasize her situation, Niamh gave a great and vacuous yawn, and appeared ready to drop off to sleep. "Rosie should be here soon. Then I can take an afternoon nap," she smiled at Jean-Luc, "and be ready fer yer tonight. Yer'll be wantin' a good supper, then, right?"

"Of course, and I'll be interested to see what you will have on your famous menu, but now, *Madame*, a drop, a small drop, if you please. We Frenchmen love our aperitif. *Et, merci, Madame.*"

Niamh gave a short laugh and poured Jean-Luc a small Pernod.

He thanked her graciously, and turned to watch Bobbee, who briefly kissed Joe Naughton, then picked up her paints, a canvas and her easel and left the pub. She walked out the front way, waving goodbye to Niamh, and the other customers, with her painting apparatus tucked up under her arm.

Jean-Luc waited a few moments to let Bobbee get to her place on the Cliffs, quickly drank his Pernod, and, with an inquiring smile on his charming face, he followed Bobbee to her seat overlooking the Cliffs of Moher and the distant impending turbulence of the violent North Atlantic. Winds were beginning to freshen from the northwest, heading to Kildunlee. The air was fresh, clean and salt laden. But, it was dangerous. Jean-Luc felt a thrill in the wind, a penetrating breeze that warned, from his young days in Normandy, that the storm would strike in a few hours, certainly before dinner.

"*Bonjour, Mademoiselle.* And *Mademoiselle* has no

fear of the storm? You are very brave."

"Good afternoon, Jean-Luc. I thought you were still down at Niamh's."

"*Ah, non.* I have come up to the Cliffs to watch the storm approach. I think it won't be too long before it hits our coast."

"Looks like it. And no, I don't have any fear of the wind or our Irish storms. Actually, I welcome them. I love to paint the crashing surf and the bending trees. Can you imagine?"

"*Ah, bien, Mademoiselle,* I can, of course, feel the storm and the wind, but to stand here and be battered. It is not a good thing. Do you think?"

Bobbee laughed at his expression. "No, it's not a good thing, but we do have some time before it strikes, right?" she asked Jean-Luc. "And it's only a few minutes down to Niamh's for shelter."

"*Ah, oui, mademoiselle.* I should think at least an hour, perhaps a bit more. But it is not too good for you to stay here much longer. *Les tempetes* sometimes have a way of striking swiftly, and we would not want to see you get all wet and have your painting ruined."

Bobbee smiled at his concern, adjusted her easel, and a small folding table for her brushes and a miniature palette displaying her paints.

"*Alors,* so you are going to paint the rising sea as the clouds gather and the storm gets closer?" he asked her.

"I am. I'm going to try to get the darkness of the clouds contrasted with the white of the sea caps. You deal in art in Paris, don't you," she asked, turning towards him.

"*Oui, mademoiselle,* I do a bit of art deals, but it is my brother, Charles-Francois, who is the real expert. He has been called in many times by the *Surete* to discern the differences between a real painting and an imitation. I really know so little, only what I've learned, but I continue to study *l'art*," he told her.

Bobbee nodded while she concentrated on swabbing broad, thick background streaks upon her canvas. Her colors took on a bright hue and her strokes were long and curling.

"Perhaps, *mademoiselle*, I am mistaken, but are you not using the mezzotint method?" Jean-Luc asked her as he examined her canvas with a critical eye.

Bobbee nodded vigorously, "Yes, I am. You recognized it right away. You appear to know more about art than you let on."

"*Non, mademoiselle*. It is just that I have seen the mezzotint method before, in Charles-Francois' shop and I recognized it here. He is an expert on mezzotint and he taught me about it. I noticed immediately that you are using it, so I commented."

"Yes, this is mezzotint, a mode of painting I've used for years," she told him, as she continued to add broad brush strokes. He watched her style for a few moments.

"*Mademoiselle*, I think you try the technique of *pointillisme*, added to your mezzotint. I don't recall, but I think it was developed by one of my countrymen, but whether it was Cezanne or Lautrec I can't remember."

Bobbee chuckled for a moment. "Really, Jean-Luc, you should know your French Art History better than that. Cezanne, of course, developed the *pointillisme* method." She used the French pronunciation of the word. "Shame on you Jean-Luc," she said with a smile.

"*Oui, vous avez raison*. I should have known better. After all, the entire school of *l'impressionisme* comes from France. I had better speak with Charles-Francois when I return to Paris. My knowledge of *l'art*, I am afraid, is lacking. Thank you for pointing this out to me."

Bobbee dismissed his concern with a brief wave of

her hand. "Oh, here comes Joe," she said. "He said he'd be up here once he finished some work in town."

Joe Naughton, the handyman about town, walked briskly toward Bobbee and Jean-Luc. The expression on his face showed that he wasn't pleased that someone was speaking with his girlfriend.

"Well, Frenchie, are yer up here ter see Bobbee's painting or watch the storm?" His attitude and tone were belligerent, showing no trace of pleasantry.

"*Ah bien, monsieur*, I am here only to see the ocean and the gathering clouds. I noticed *mademoiselle* here doing her painting and so I stopped to admire her work. It is *tres jolie* as you can see." Joe's attitude softened a bit as he listened to the older man.

"It is. It is. I like ter watch her paint. So," he addressed Bobbee, "will yer be paintin' me in that picture, me darlin'"? Joe asked her with a leering grin.

"Sure will, Joe, you know that. I'll put you in the foreground, watching the oncoming storm."

Jean-Luc scanned the skies, taking a deep breath of the freshening salty air. "*Ah, bien, mes amis*, I have to return to town. I have some letters to write and it is almost time for a pleasant nap before one of Niamh's magnificent *repas de soiree*. So, I bid you both *au revoir*," and he turned toward Kildunlee.

"So long," Joe said, and Bobbee smiled briefly at Jean-Luc's retreating back.

"Nothin' funny goin' on here with the Frenchie and yer is there?"

"No. You've nothing to fear from that old man. He just happened to stop by to chat while he walked along the Cliffs. Now, sit down and be a good boy, for a change," she teased him, with a lascivious smile. He stretched out next to her chair, anticipating later events.

18.

SUSPICIOUS CIRCUMSTANCES

The large grandfather clock in the study that had by now become McGrath's manorial headquarters had just finished striking the four o'clock hour. Dark clouds now covered the skies and the green landscape outside the tall windows took on a foreboding glare. McGrath smiled to himself, dwelling on the days when he had to report on and analyze these types of meteorological phenomena. No more, now. He had a shipping line to run and the weather had become just a passing hobby, something to notice and remember, but nothing to concern himself with.

"Excuse me, sir," Patrick Riordan, the FitzHugh Manor butler addressed his new master. "There is a telephone call for you in the hall. Shall I tell the caller you are available? I believe it is Dr. McHugh."

McGrath nodded and smiled at Riordan. "Yes, please tell him I'm here and I'll take the call in a moment. We really have to have an extension installed here in the study."

"His Lordship never wanted one here, sir. He felt it would disturb his peace."

"Right," McGrath answered him. "But I don't want to run to the hall every time I get a call. Will you please contact Irish Telephone and let them know that we want at least one extension installed here at the Manor?"

"Yes, sir. It should take only a few weeks." And Riordan turned to let Dr. McHugh know that McGrath was on his way to the telephone.

A few weeks, McGrath thought to himself and smiled. *By that time I'll probably be back in Boston.* He picked up the receiver of the heavy black desk telephone, neatly tucked into a niche in the wall of the hall.

"McGrath here."

"William, Kieran McHugh."

"Afternoon, Doc. What's going on?"

"Well, William, I've had one heck of a day. A surgery full of patients, and more crying kids that I ever want to see in the next five years. Simple stuff, though, bloody noses, scraped knees, head bumps. The poor kids were more frightened than injured. I must have quite a reputation."

"Comes with the job, Kieran, comes with the job. But I can't imagine that you called me to tell me about a slew of screaming kids."

"No, William, I didn't. On the other side of things, I've had some interesting news. In fact, two pieces of news that put my poor head in a twist. I got a call from my friend, Bryan Logan. You remember, the coroner, up at the Galway mortuary?"

McGrath's face puckered in interest, and his brow furrowed. "Right. You said you were going to get in touch with him. What did he have to say?"

"You remember, William, that the facial expression on Sir Julian was one of almost sheer terror, and we all put it to his last moment's fear of taking his own life with his pistol?"

"That's right. It came out in Court like that."

"Well, never mind his last moment's fear of his pistol. What had happened to him was that there were severe facial contractions from what was inside his body, not what was outside."

"What do you mean, inside not outside?"

"Listen to this, William. The coroner took small blood samples from three different parts of his corpse, and he tested them all. He found a foreign element present in Sir Julian's corpse. And, he tells me, that, if this element is in these three parts of his corpse, then it's definitely all through his body."

"Kieran, what are we talking about here?"

"What we're talking about, William, is a massive dose of strychnine. Enough to kill five men, maybe more, but certainly enough to do away with Sir Julian Brownlee, and any amount of other men as well."

"But, this changes everything. It was assumed that Sir Julian shot himself and that fear caused his face to contort."

"Right, William. But that's not the case here. When Dr. Logan had a good look at Sir Julian, he found that the muscles in his back and thighs had been torn. This is a definite symptom of ingesting strychnine. It causes severe muscle spasms. His back and thigh muscles showed evidence of rigid contractions and knotting. He must have been in terrible pain. That's why his facial features were so contorted; the poison caused his cheek and forehead muscles to contract violently. It wasn't the anticipation of a gunshot. "

"Kieran, can your friend be mistaken? Could he have made an error?"

"No, William, Bryan Logan is the most exacting medical person I have ever met. Nothing escapes his exams and his conclusions have always been correct. There's no mistake here, at least not on his part. Sir Julian didn't commit suicide by shooting himself. William, he was murdered with a large dose of strychnine. And he wouldn't have administered it to himself, then shot himself with his pistol. Self poisoning doesn't make sense here, not with a gunshot to the head."

"Good Lord, this puts the whole case in a new light. What do we do now?"

"We'll have to apply to the Court, to Magistrate

O'Farrell, to have a complete autopsy, and see what the results are."

"Are you sure you can get one, just based on these tests results?"

"Bryan Logan can get one ordered if anyone can. He has a lot of scientific pull here in the West Country and I'm sure that he can convince the magistrate to order an autopsy."

"You'd better get him on it, then."

"I've already started the procedure. I'm way ahead of you," Dr. McHugh said chuckling. "But, there's more, and it involves Magistrate O'Farrell. You remember when we were in Niamh's pub the other day and the postman came by with a package from the Irish Passport office addressed to Sir Julian?"

"I remember," McGrath answered him.

"Well, it seems that there is a part of Irish Law which states if a piece of Official Irish Postal material is undeliverable, and is a registered post, and especially if it states on the front, *DO NOT RETURN TO SENDER*, for whatsoever reason, then it has to be turned over to the local Magistrate to be opened, not returned to the sender. Recall that this was sent from the Irish Passport Office and it was very official."

"Exactly. I remember. Kieran, now you've got my curiosity flying. What was in the package?"

"Jimmy, the postman, took the package back to the post office and the head clerk knew about this section of Irish Law, and he telephoned Magistrate O'Farrell, who sent a Garda over to collect it. Then, in front of his Clerk of the Court, he opened it, and lo and behold what do you think was there?"

"Kieran, you're killing me. I haven't a clue. What was in it?"

"A passport, of course. What else would be there?"

"Well... all right... fine. But why are you telling

me this? It must have been a new passport for this Harold Winthrop and maybe someone else we don't know. Right?"

"Yes and no."

"Kieran, if I were there, I'd hit you over the head with a North Atlantic cod. Now, what's going on here?" William said with a chuckle in his voice."

"What's going on here, William," Kieran McHugh responded, with his own voice in a bit of a humor, "is that the passport was certainly for Harold Winthrop and there was only one passport in the package. But the photo on the passport was none other than Sir Julian Brownlee, himself."

"Brownlee? But, he must already have had his South African passport. Why would he want an Irish passport in a fictitious name?"

"Your guess is as good as mine, as the saying goes. But, that, coupled with the strychnine discovery certainly points to strange goings-on."

"Yes. Yes, definitely. I think we'd better pursue this with O'Farrell. Is there anything I can do now?"

"No. Just keep this quiet until we hear from the Magistrate. Then we'll see where we have to go next."

"OK. I'll do that. I'll keep this under my hat," McGrath told McHugh. Then, after saying goodbye and that he would wait to hear from him, and the outcome of his conversation with the Magistrate, McGrath went back to his study in complete bewilderment.

19.

FIGHT AT THE PUB

The little town of Kildunlee sits just under a half
mile to the east of the Cliffs of Moher, on the Galway
Road. It is to the north of Liscannor and Doolan and the
walk to the Cliffs, at least when the weather is fine, is
quite pleasant, through green meadows, some pine woods
and amongst the ever-present stones that seem to populate
the landscape of Ireland, like those along the Burren and
which contribute to the many thousands of miles of stone
walls that surround houses and farmland. When the
weather is fair, the farmers, who thrive in this rich, green
land, bring their cattle and sheep to graze in the verdant
meadows that lead to the Cliffs. The Irish government had
placed a wall, made of slabs of slate, all along the Cliffs,
twenty feet from the edge, so the farmers can have a good
gossip without worrying that their animals will fall over
the brink.

The town has one main road running through it, St.
Paul's Street, which also happens to be the name of the
local Catholic Church, and which also happens to be part
of the seemingly never ending Galway Road. St. Paul's
Street leads straight to Galway, but it is frequently in dis-
repair and its surface is not kept up, so the travel is hard.
It's also very winding and difficult to navigate, so not
many Kildunlee residents travel often to Galway, and
when they do, it's always for something important, such
as a wedding. Kildunlee boasts a population of just over
400 souls, and it has the necessary stores and shops to

serve these souls, so that travel to Galway is usually unnecessary. O'Banyon, the greengrocer, Deegan, the iron monger, or hardware store, O'Connell's clothing and dry goods store, Driscoll's animal feed and grain, with the Irish Post Office next to the required pub, owned by Niamh Flaherty, a widow since the late 1930s. The pub has no special name and everyone refers to it as simply, "the pub". The countryside which surrounds Kildunlee is entirely farmland: sheep, dairy and beef cattle, and pig farms like the one owned by Siobhan's father, Brendan Rafferty.

But the pub is the center of town and that's where everybody goes to find out the latest news, and perhaps even bring some news of their own. Gossip is swapped and traded like a commodity, here at the pub, and everything worth knowing is known at the pub and primarily by the publican, Niamh herself. She is a veritable fountain of knowledge concerning the goings on in Kildunlee.

Lunch was long over and most of her customers had returned to their jobs, farms and gardens, had resumed work in their shops, were toiling in their fields, or had gotten involved with one thing and another. The afternoon, climbing into the later hours, found Niamh at work, polishing glasses at the bar. The two visiting Spaniards, enjoying their vacation, were having an early aperitif, just before the four o'clock hour, and conversing quietly in their native language, not a word of which Niamh understood. In the back of the pub, where the sunlight and lamplight didn't quite reach, Bobbee and Joe Naughton were flirting, as usual, making complete idiots out of themselves. The more than occasional kiss could be heard, if Niamh bent her ear in their direction. Low, satisfied laughter followed now and again, and it was clear to Niamh, and anyone else who noticed them, that Bobbee and Joe couldn't care less about anybody who knew they were there. The only fly in the ointment was when Tim

Kearney came in at four o'clock for his late-afternoon, pre-supper pint of Guinness.

"Those two still at it?" he asked Niamh. "Joe's goin' ter lose his job if he don't get back ter work. Me, I got more'n I can handle, especially wit' cuttin' Eddie Hillaire an' his portion of Brendan's acreage in shape for plantin' and piggin'. Must be nice to sit around and fuss wit' a girl."

"Easy now, Tim. Watch what you say. They may take offense," Niamh warned him. "They aren't doing any harm, just keeping ter themselves and it ain't harmin' a soul this side o' the grave."

At that moment, silence was heard from the couple. No laughing, no kissing and no soft talk. Only silence. The two Spaniards halted their conversation and watched the proceedings with interest. One grinned at the other and said something to his companion, which probably meant that some action was about to occur, and wouldn't it be funny to watch a fight in this sleepy little Irish town.

"Yer got somethin' ter say ter me, Tim Kearney? Speak yer mind!"

"Nah. I got nothin' ter say ter yer. Just talkin' to Niamh, that's all. We was wonderin' how yer got time ter sit here drinkin' and bein' wit' yer girlfriend and the rest of us got work ter do an' a livin' ter make. Ain't you supposed ter be over at Eddie Hillaire's farm, gettin' the stalls ready for the piggin' an' puttin' up the fences ter keep them in?"

Joe Naughton stood up, stepping around Bobbee's chair as he did. "And what's it to yer what I'm doin' on me off time," he said in a very belligerent tone.

"Easy, Joe," said Naimh. "Tim didn't mean anything, did you, Tim?"

"Nah. I ain't lookin' ter start trouble. An' I got a lot of work ter do." He downed his pint and headed to the door and out to Hillaire's farm, still wearing a scowl on his face.

"He'd better not be sayin' anything ter me, not in front of Bobbee," Joe stated.

"Joe, he didn't mean anything. Forget about it," Bobbee told him, with a broad, seductive smile on her face. "Come on, let's take a walk," and she took Joe's hand and led him out the side door and up to the Cliffs.

***

Niamh continued to polish the bar glasses, but heaved a sigh of relief that there had been no real trouble between Joe Naughton and Tim Kearney. Both of the men were large, strong, and had a wild streak in their genes. Her bar would have sustained considerable damage if they got to beating each other up, and she was glad that nothing like that had happened.

The two Spaniards finished their aperitifs, Spanish Sherry, especially requested by them, in a letter to Niamh before leaving Spain, and prepared to drive to Lough Rae. They had heard of a fine dining establishment there and they were eager to try it.

"Thank you, Niamh," one of them said in stilted English. "We see you more later tonight, w'en dinner done. *Muchas gracias*."

Niamh smiled in her incomparably pleasant way. "Sure, I'll be here. Hope ter see yer tonight fer a nightcap. Should be a good crowd here."

***

Edward and Timmy were the grounds men for the FitzHughs and they kept the estate lawns and gardens looking their finest, resplendent in that magnificent hundred shades of green, produced only by that hallowed Irish soil. And every imaginable flower and bush the earth could support, glorious in their blazing colors throughout the treasured summer months, were the charge of Edward and Timmy. They worked under the piercing and watchful eye of old Jonah, the chief gardener, who, the young men said, must have been tending the shrubbery shortly after St. Patrick landed from Britain.

But, although the younger men teased old Jonah, they really admired him for his botanical knowledge and awareness, and they respected him for it. Still, when the long day had come to an end, the garden tools had been put away, and the sheds locked up for the night, both Edward and Timmy felt the yearning for a tall draft of Guinness. Usually, their comrade, Brian, the tack room keeper, would have joined them, but he pleaded that he had another pressing engagement. It seems, he had met a "young lass" from over Liscannor way, and he was to take the bus for a "...brief visit."

"Ah, let him go, Edward. He'll be sorry he's missin' a well pulled point," using the Irish "oi" for the letter "i".

"Aye, an' I can see the foam sloshin' down into the glass now. If yer up for a point, Timmy, let's get ter Niamh's before I die o' the parch." And the two young gents made haste from their quarters behind the manor house towards Kildunlee, and Niamh's pub.

***

Naimh's was really crowded that evening, it being Thursday night and the weekend almost upon everyone. Farmers from the area were in for their evening "points" after a long day in the fields, slaking their thirst, lest they die "...o' the parch." Niamh and her assistant, Sheila, were kept very busy filling glasses, stoking conversations and making sure of a jolly evening for all their guests. The last thing Niamh wanted was another scene between Tim Kearney and Joe Naughton. The action during that late afternoon was bad enough and she didn't want any more threats now, with the evening's imbibing in full swing. She had sent a message to Livy O'Toole to stay handy and keep an eye on the goings on, and Livy had shown up just after seven o'clock. People were happy and no one was getting out of hand.

"Sure, Livy, I think it'll be a fine night, and no doubt. Joe and his Bobbee are in the back, drinkin' and talkin' and God knows what else they have on their minds, but Tim Kearney hasn't stopped by yet. If he does, I'll send Sheila to the Garda station ter fetch yer if things seem ter be heatin' up."

"Fine, Naimh. I'll be around. Not much happenin' out in the countryside, so I can stay in town tonight."

"That makes me feel better, Livy," and with that, he grinned at her and left her pub for the Garda station to get some paper work done.

The evening wore on and all was well till about eight-thirty when Tim Kearney came into the pub. Conversations didn't stop and activity didn't cease as Tim came to the bar. Niamh could see that he'd had some drink, but served him anyway when he asked for a "point" of Guinness. He was in a sullen mood and appeared to be angry about something or other, staring toward the rear of the pub, the area where Joe and Bobbee always sat. Tim said nothing, but something was grating on him. He downed his "point" and ordered another. Sheila served him, knowing nothing about the afternoon's adventures.

"Having a good evenin', Mr. Kearney?" She asked him in a merry tone.

"Argh. A good evenin'? An' what's it ter yer? Some of us have ter work ter get ourselves through this life an' others can loaf the day drinkin' an' kissin'. Ain't fair. Same again." Sheila pulled another pint for Tim, and after she had put the glass in front of him, went to speak with Niamh.

"Niamh, I think Tim Kearney's had enough. He seems pretty angered up, too."

Niamh pressed her lips together, taking in a deep breath. "Get Garda O'Toole. And hurry."

Sheila went out the door in a near run.

"Well, Tim, it looks as if yer've had quite a bit o' the drink tonight," Niamh said to Kearney. "I think that's all I can serve yer."

"Argh. A man works hard all day, and he's got a right ter a point or two," Kearney answered her, his voice rising. "I ain't got toime fer kissin' like some o' these people around here." This time, his voice carried clear to the back of the pub, and it was heard by Joe and Bobbee.

"Tim Kearney," Joe called out, "What are yer on about now? Is it trouble that yer lookin' fer? I'll give yer plenty. Ye're drunk. Never could hold yer beer."

Silence came over the bar, and the patrons looked from Joe, who had come to the main section of the pub to face Tim, to Tim himself, waiting for a fight to start. The visiting Spaniards, who had been nursing their Spanish Sherry, had returned from their dinner excursion at Lough Rae, and were smiling at the events, finding this scene all quite amusing.

"Did yer even do a lick o' work t'day, Joe Naughton? Or have yer been lollygagging with that Limey doxy o' yours?"

No one moved a muscle at Tim's charge, and yet lightning flashed throughout the pub, striking everyone, causing fear of an imminent fight.

"Yer'll take that back, Tim Kearney, or I'll beat yer senseless, not that it'd take much doin', yer with only half a brain ter yer name," Joe yelled at him.

"It'll take a lot more than you ter try ter beat me, Joe Naughton," Tim hollered back, and threw his glass at Joe.

Edward, the FitzHughs' grounds man was putting on his jacket and the glass hit him, falling to the floor and shattering into scores of slivers. A brief intake of breath swept through the crowd, but they knew this wasn't the last of it.

"I'll beat yer till yer dead, Tim Kearney!" Joe screamed at his antagonist, and he strode toward Kearney. Several of the men tried to block his path, but he, like Kearney, was a large, strong man, and he broke through, determined to beat Tim Kearney to death.

"Stop right there! Don't move forward," the voice of Livy, the Garda, commanded. He'd spoken with Sheila and had rushed to the pub, hoping to avert a fight. "Don't move, Joe Naughton, and yer stay put, Tim Kearney. There'll be no fightin' in our pub!"

20.

AFTERMATH

McGrath caressed his wife's fair hair and ran his hands down her immaculate cheek. He smiled at her.

"I'm going to town for an hour or so. Some errands. Want to come?

"William, I'd love to go, but there is some estate business I have to tend to. Why don't you go ahead and be back in time for lunch? Mrs. Lynch's got a great meal planned, I've heard."

"I can imagine. Glad I walk to town, otherwise I'd get fatter than one of Brendan Rafferty's pigs."

She smiled up at him and kissed his lips. His arms went around her and held her for a moment.

"You are beautiful, my dear. So glad you're mine."

"No one else's, William, no one else's," and she kissed him once more. "Now, get thee gone! I have work to do and you're distracting me."

"That's why I'm here," and he turned to leave the room.

***

"Argh, good marnin', and if it isn't himself. How are yer this fine marning'?" Niamh asked him.

"Sounds like you're getting more and more Irish each day with your accent, Niamh," McGrath answered her. "But I'm fine."

"We haven't seen yer fer a couple o' days. Been busy up ter the Manor?"

"Actually, yes. Seems there's quite a lot of business involved in running a manor. Almost as much as in running a shipping company."

"Well, I'm sure you've been busy. Whiskey?"

"Not today. I'll have a coffee, hot and black. As usual. I have to keep a clear head."

Niamh poured him some coffee. "Have yer heard about the ruckus last night?"

"Ruckus? No, I haven't heard a single thing. What happened?"

"There was some trouble between Joe Naughton and Tim Kearney. They had some bad words here in the afternoon, then again later in the evenin'."

"Over this Bobbee?"

"Yes, her." Niamh told McGrath about how Joe and Tim almost got into a fight shortly before the supper hour, but Bobbee prevented it by getting Joe out of the pub. Then she told him about the events later in the evening, when Joe and Tim had more bad words and she had to send Sheila for Livy, the Garda. "Argh, Commander, 't'was awrful. Bad things they said ter each other. Bad things. But Livy made them get out o' here and go their separate ways. I thought they'd get inter it here, or even in the street, but Livy sent them in opposite directions."

"Well, I guess certain women and booze will cause these things. But it's over now?"

Niamh continued to polish a glass, almost ignoring him.

A frown rested on McGrath's forehead. "Niamh, what happened? Was there more? Where are those two and the girl Bobbee?"

"Well, we know where the two are, but this Bobbee has disappeared. Vanished. Clean out o' sight."

"Really? No sign of her?"

"Nope. Her baggage is gone from her room. But we know where Joe and Tim are."

"And where's that?" McGrath asked innocently.

"Tim is in jail and Joe is in Galway hospital, shot through the chest three times and they don't know if he's gonna make it. If he don't, Tim'll be up on a murder charge. He's probably gonna get jail time fer assault anyway."

"I'm sure you're not joking about all this, Niamh, but I find it hard to believe. In a small town like this, can there really be such bad feelings?" McGrath sipped the hot, black liquid which brought his mind to bear on the trouble of last night.

"We really don't get much trouble around here, Commander, but sometimes these things happen. As you said, when the proper, or maybe the improper, girl comes along. One like that Bobbee."

'"But where is she, now that it seems that she had started this mess?"

"No one knows. But Livy thinks she must be the key to the whole problem. But no one can find her. I hope she's not dead, like Joe may soon be."

McGrath finished his coffee. "Well," he said, setting down his cup, "I'd better talk to Livy and see what he can tell me." He put some money on the counter and turned toward the door. "I'll see you sometime later, Niamh. Hopefully, no more trouble will happen again here."

"I'm hopin', Commander, I'm hopin'," she said with a large concerned grin on her face.

***

Commander William McGrath sat in his favorite chair in the study at the Manor House, a large, overstuffed armchair which molded around him and brought much comfort. Dinner was long over and he was sipping a late night Irish Mist, to settle Mrs. Lynch's wonderful roast lamb, roasted Irish potatoes and rich, brown gravy. His eyes were far away, not from the brandy, but from the news of the day about the previous night's fight and all that it entailed. *Why did Joe and Tim get so angry at each other? Why did Tim shoot Joe?* They were friendly enough whenever he had seen them in town. Some good natured antagonism, but nothing serious. And, most of all, where was this Bobbee? How could she just disappear? Bag and baggage? These thoughts drifted through his mind and he didn't notice Cynthia glide into the room, looking amazingly beautiful in a snug light blue dress. She sat in a large arm chair, crossing her magnificent legs, but the song of nylon, which was always noticed by McGrath, failed to pierce his occupied mind.

"A penny for your thoughts, Commander?" She said smiling.

"Mmmmm," he responded, staring into the middle distance. "Still trying to make sense of this fight and the, apparently, attempted murder of Joe Naughton. Or, at least, his being shot by Tim Kearney. Can't figure it out. And this Bobbee. She's vanished like smoke in a gale. Makes no sense." He took another sip of his Irish Mist, and let the fragrant, mellow liquor titillate his senses and drift through his lean, muscular body, settling the splendid roast lamb.

"Well, William, there's not a thing you can do about it tonight. You may as well put it out of your mind till the morning. Besides, there are other things that have to be seen to."

"Mmmm? What's that?" He asked, distractedly.

"It is time for bed. It is getting late."

"Time for bed?" He glanced at his watch. "Oh. You're right. It is getting late."

"As I said," Cynthia whispered huskily, "Time for bed."

McGrath smiled up at her exquisite face, "Is that an order or a suggestion?"

Her lips formed a perfect O with the word "Both."

William McGrath, former rugged sea dog, almost spilled his Irish Mist in his haste to join his wife.

21.

THE GARDA CALLS

The pounding inside of Joe Naughton's head was unrelenting, as if a dozen leprechauns with large sledge hammers were trying to crush his skull. Never in his life had he ever had such a bad hangover. *Only from some Jameson's?* he asked himself. But the continual pain, throbbing, and dull ache were splitting his head, sending waves of nausea through his entire frame. His stomach was ready to empty its contents all over his small cabin. The pounding became louder, sending bright, yellow, sunlight piercing flashes across his vision, making death a welcome and viable option.

"Open up, Joe Naughton. 'Tis Livy O'Toole, Garda of the Irish Constabulary, wantin' to speak with yer!"

Lord, thought Joe, *'tisn't me head alone tryin' ter get me ter the other side, 'tis the Garda.* He glanced at the old round alarm clock, ticking away on the sideboard that his Ma had left him ten years ago when she exhaled her last breath. Eight-fifteen. The day was gray and seemed to have a gentle mist falling. *Marnin',* he thought to himself. The pounding in his head joined the pounding from Garda O'Toole.

"Open up, Joe Naughton. Tis the law wants ter speak with yer!" Livy called again, followed by several more raps.

"All right, Livy, I'm on me way. Stop the noise or yer'll wake the saints in their holy graves."

"It'll be a grave yer'll be in soon, but I don't know how holy 'twill be!" Livy shouted back.

Joe heaved his large body out of the soft easy chair in his living room, and the furniture and windows started to spin. His head throbbed worse than before, when Livy had begun the racket on his front door. Joe's stomach gave full notice of relieving itself of its contents, and he made straight for the front door, and hauled it wide, almost knocking Livy to the ground in his dash to get outside. A few steps toward the bushes and the awful sounds of retching and belching filled the air, much to Livy and his companions' disgust. Joe fell down on his knees, far from his mess, and had a difficult time getting on his feet.

Livy and Fergal Hanlon, the assistant Garda, pulled him to his feet and half dragged him back into the small cabin, depositing him back in his chair. The third person in the room was Colonel Charles O'Meara, Supervisor of the Local Garda and the Garda for all of County Clare. They all regarded Joe with utter disgust. Livy took a paper out of his side pocket.

"Joe Naughton," he read, "I hereby arrest you on suspicion of the shootin' o' Tim Kearney last night. Anything yer have ter say may be used against yer and may be admitted in a court o' law. Please gather yer belongings and come with me ter the Garda Station."

Joe stared at Livy, suddenly feeling very sober, but only for the moment that the Garda's words sunk into his be-sotted brain. "What're yer sayin'? I ain't shot no one. I come here ter me own house arter I left the pub. I ain't done nothin' wrong!"

Livy stepped over to where Joe kept his rifle, a great beast with a large caliber bore. "Well, we'll be seein' if yer've done something or not." Livy smelled the muzzle of the rifle. "This weapon's been fired, and recently, too, by the smell o' it. Yer'll have ter have a paraffin test, Joe, and no mistake. It ain't lookin' too good fer yer. Now, get yer things and come with us ter the Garda Station before we have ter drag yer."

"I ain't done nothin'"," Joe shouted. "I ain't done nothin'! I come here right arter yer threw me outta the pub. Tim went one way with his doxy and I went the other. We didn't see each other arter that. Yer ain't got no right ter take me ter jail fer something I ain't done!" Fear showed through in his voice and sweat appeared on his face.

"Joe, yer can come quiet as a mouse in a haystack or we can put the bracelets on yer. What'll yer have?"

"Am I not just arter tellin' yer, I come here right arter yer tossed me outta Niamh's pub, into the freezin' night. I come right here and treated meself ter a drop. Right here in me chair," Joe said indicating the large easy chair in the corner of the untidy room. And I didn't go nowhere arter that, sure 'n' I didn't."

"That's yer story, is it?"

"Aye, an' no mistake. I stayed here all night, didn't go nowhere, didn't see anyone, except that Lady from South Africa stopped by an' we shared a jar or two. Said she saw the lights on and could use a bit of warmin' up."

"Warmin' up?" Livy queried.

"It was cold out, and she said she'd been walkin' the woods trying ter get over Sir Julian's death. She just wanted to sit before the fire, that's all, an' no mistake. She stayed only about twenty minutes or so"

"We'll have ter check on this. But it don't sound likely, Joe, since Lady Alice Stronton ain't been seen in Kildunlee fer two days an' more. So, get yer things an' let's go."

"I told yer, Livy, she were here last night. Maybe twenty minutes. Just ter warm up an' have a jar." Joe started to feel sick again. His head was beating like a bass drum on Saint Paddy's day. He turned and staggered to the door, threw it open wide and retched violently. Livy, Fergal and the Colonel looked at each other.

"Mr. Jameson makes fine whiskey and it usually

don't make yer sick like this. How many jars did yer have, Joe? Yer makin' a spectacle o' yerself and all o' us sick."

"I don't know, Livy," Joe responded, wiping his mouth on his shirt cuff, "I had only a few jars o' poitín, an' it never hit me like this. I don't know," and he wiped his mouth again with a filthy, stained rag he used as a handkerchief. "I wouldn't be knowin' what happened ter me." For a moment he looked at Livy, almost sorrowfully. "I wouldn't really hurt Tim. We was mates, though we had a few words here an' there. How is he doin' an' where is he?" He asked Livy. The other two watched Joe in the event he tried to make a break for it, even though his sad demeanor and physical state seemed to prevent that.

"Tim is in Galway Hospital. An' he's critical. He's got three shots in his chest, one real close to his heart. He might not make it, Joe. Yer rifle's been recently fired and it looks like it's the same caliber o' what's been used on him. Course, we'll have ter do some f'rensics on the rifle and, like I'm just after tellin' yer, do a paraffin test on yer hands. Fingerprints, too. An' I had ter break up the fight between the two o' yer last night, an' fer sure yer both were cursing the high heavens ter each other and threatenin' ter beat the other so badly that it'd make cement look like tapioca puddin'. But, Joe, it ain't lookin' good and things might go a damn-sight badly fer yer. There'll be an Inquest and the law takes over from here on in. Now, come on, an' no tricks or I'll be forced ter put the bracelets on yer, I will."

Joe gathered up a few things and put them into a canvas bag. "All right, I'm ready. But I didn't shoot Tim. He were my friend an' 't'is true as the sun rises each marn," he said, and swung the canvas bag over his arm.

22.

THE WEST MEETS THE WEST COUNTRY

The dining room table was a spread of beer and Jameson's bottles with plenty of soda for the young ones. Plates of specialty snacking items were half empty and the conversation was pleasant and convivial.

"Edward, Siobhan, now that we've been here over a week, and comfortably settled in, we were wondering. Does this type of thing with someone getting shot in the middle of the night, happen all the time here? Especially in light of the fact that this Sir Julian, the South African gentleman, did himself in," Ray Hillaire asked his son and his daughter-in-law.

"Sure 'n' it doesn't, Mr. Hillaire," Siobhan quickly answered her father-in-law. "'Tis true we've never had such a thing goin' on here before. There's been little shootin' since the Free State became a republic in 1926. But, like this, no, nary a time," Siobhan answered.

"It's true, dad," Edward said. "This is such a quiet, easy-going place that you would never suspect any hard feelings to arise between two of the townsmen. And they were, in general, cordial to each other. But, tomorrow, in the little office building that doubles as a meeting house and the court house, the local Magistrate will hold an Inquest, and it will probably be determined that Joe Naughton shot Tim Kearney in a frenzy of anger and, after Livy brought him in, he was remanded into custody in Galway jail."

"Yes," Edward's father replied, "That's what I've

heard in Niamh's pub. That's a pity, but I guess that these things happen, even here in the West Country." Then, turning to Siobhan, he smiled, and said to her, "Please, Siobhan, call me Ray."

"For sure, I will. So I will," she answered Ray Hillaire, smiling graciously at her father-in-law.

"And that goes for the rest of us. I'm Marcie and these other two Montanans are George and Beverly," and everyone smiled and chuckled at the building camaraderie of this extended family.

***

Edward's father and mother, together with their friends, George and Beverly Heustis, had arrived from New York's Idlewild International Airport a week and a half ago, in time for McGrath and Cynthia's wedding, having flown across the North Atlantic in a large, four-engine propeller-driven airplane. Pan American World Airways provided the service and it was a sixteen hour flight. Arriving at Shannon International Airport, not too far from Galway, they had spent the first day at a plush hotel in Galway City, recuperating from the long flight. Once rested and back on their feet, and having shed the grogginess of flying, which, at a later date would be called jet-lag, they made their phone call to Kildunlee. Living on a large horse ranch in Montana, and enjoying a healthy income, they had their own telephones scattered throughout the house. But, that wasn't the case in Kildunlee, or in most of Ireland. Few people had telephones, and those that did were either an important business person or were among the wealthy.

There was one phone at the Manor House, of course, and at Niamh's pub, O'Banyon's grocery store and at St. Paul's Catholic Church's Rectory. The only other phone in town, and one that was used by all the townsfolk was at the Post Office. For a fee, any person in need of communication could use the Postal Service tele-phone, in a quiet and private, small, closet-sized room. So, the only way that the Hillaires could get in touch with their son, Edward, was to place a call to Kildunlee from the Hotel in Galway, get a message to the postal clerk to say that they would like to speak to Edward, and would the clerk send a message to Edward at his home that they would call back in two hours for a chat. The postal clerk, Maureen Shea, called Jimmy Fallon from his sorting of the mail and told him to race like a March hare to Edward Hillaire's place and tell him that his folks would call back at eleven, and that was two hours from now. Jimmy took off on his bicycle like a starving hound after a fox and made great speed in getting to Edward's house.

As always, after delivering his message to Edward, he was offered a jar of Jameson's for his troubles and to make certain that Jimmy didn't "...up 'n' keel over o' the parch."

Edward left his farm for the village of Kildunlee at about ten-thirty and got to the post office some ten minutes early. He chatted with Maureen till the phone call came through from Galway. His parents said they, and the Huestises, would be there late in the afternoon, probably around four, that they were driving down from Galway, and that Ray, his father, hoped he could manage driving on the left hand side of the road.

"And be careful, Dad," Edward warned him, "These Irish roads aren't like the roads in Montana. They're real-ly awful. Potholes, ruts, twisty and very narrow."

"Thanks for the warning," his father chuckled, "but we can't wait for the bus. Your mother, and me, too, are eager to see you again and, of course, Siobhan and our new granddaughter."

His parents and the Huestises drove into downtown Kildunlee shortly before four thirty, and were immediate-ly directed to Edward's small farm. Although it was small, even by Irish standards, with an acre and a half, sporting a whitewashed, thatched cottage with a tiny vegetable   garden behind the house, it was really a parcel of a larger farm, owned by Brendan Rafferty, Siobhan's father's. Brendan's farm had a much bigger farmhouse, where he and Siobhan's siblings, Donal, Kathleen and Deirdre, lived, and over a dozen acres where pigs and sheep roamed, and vegetable plots flourished.

A cheerful and warm welcome greeted them, with introductions all around. After the gleefulness calmed down, and they felt they were ready to find their lodgings, Edward and Siobhan took them to a large Irish thatched cottage, where the four would spend their three weeks before returning to Montana, again on a Pan American airliner. Fourteen more hours of gazing at the blue North Atlantic.

But they were all settled in nicely now for their visit to Ireland and Siobhan had invited them for an afternoon Tea. Tea for the ladies, beer and Jameson's for the gents. But there was also a tall bottle of Gilbey's and Cinzano, since Edward's mother, and Beverly as well, liked their martinis. Cookies, small cakes, neatly cut sandwiches and bottles of ginger ale for the gossoons covered the dark oak dining table in Siobhan's dining room.

"Edward," Marcie began, "Tell us about this former commanding officer of yours, and your adventures. Is he still intending to stay here in this part of Ireland, the way you are?" And her son again spun several stories of the meteorological teams taking weather observations leading up to D-Day, of their return to the United States aboard a Canadian Corvette, and being transferred to the Pacific to do the same work again till the end of the war.

It had given the town a high reputation among all Irishmen and in all the surrounding towns and villages. The town folk were proud of that fact, and it gave them great pride in letting it be known, at the neighboring village pubs, that they were from Kildunlee, and it was not uncommon, over a pint or two in the local, for them to say, "Argh, I come from Kildunlee, yer know, the town where McGrath and his sailors helped Eisenhower plan D-Day, an' let me tell yer about the Commander." And the beer flowed into the storyteller's glass with nary a farthing leaving his pocket.

He had told his parents this story a dozen times and his mother never tired of hearing it. Yes, he told her, Commander McGrath was, for now, still in these parts, was married now to Lady Cynthia FitzHugh as you know from having attended their wedding recently, living up at the Manor and they both hoped and expected to leave for Boston quite soon, possibly within a only few days of tomorrow's Inquest. They had already had one delay in their honeymoon plans because of the Inquest relating to Sir Julian's death. Eddie thought that McGrath, or the Commander, as the townspeople called him, would have to return to Boston on a regular basis to keep an eye on his shipping line.

"McGrath's Shipping has expanded considerably in the last year or so and his presence is called for at headquarters," Edward told them. "And you will all meet Commander McGrath and his wife Lady Cynthia again tomorrow. We've all been invited to the Manor House for dinner."

"That sounds wonderful," said Beverly, "I've never been to a Manor House before."

"Argh, sure 'tis lovely, and no mistakin'," Siobhan told her.

Ray Hillaire smiled at the beautiful, charming west-country Irish accent of his daughter-in-law. "'Tis a grand house, an' 'tis fit for a king, although his lordship is only an earl."

There was general nodding and an agreement that dinner the following evening at the Manor House would be a highlight of the visit, second only to McGrath's and Cynthia's wedding several days previously, and they all looked forward to it, with great relish.

"Well, Siobhan," Ray Hillaire began, "there's more than one reason why we came all this way to meet you and the kiddies. And let me say that we are very pleased with our son's choice of a wife, and that Margaret is a beautiful child."

"Aye, that she is," Brendan Rafferty, Siobhan's father, said. "She is, aye, she is, an' no mistake. They've made a beautiful little colleen, they have," he said with pride in his voice.

"You're right, Brendan," Marcie told them all. "She's a treasure, with all those raven locks. She must have gotten them from you, Siobhan," Marcie said to her daughter-in-law.

"Aye, sure 'n' 'tis true. Eddie's dark blond hair had nothin' ter do with it," and they all laughed at her comment.

"But to get back to the other topic," Ray continued, "we'd like all of you to come over to Montana, as a wedding gift from us to the bride and groom. And, Brendan," Ray said, turning to Siobhan's father, "we include you in the invitation. It wouldn't be right if you weren't with the family for a visit. And, Edward, your mother and I were thinking about this coming July. It'll be warm enough for a visit with no piercing wind tearing down on us out of Saskatchewan."

At the mention of the Canadian winter winds, screaming down from the arctic and the Yukon, into his parents' ranch, Edward gave an involuntary shudder. "Don't remind me, Dad, I'd almost forgotten. The wind here is soft and gentle, like a calm breeze, and only in the worst winter storm does it get sharp, but nothing like the wind in Montana."

Brendan insisted that he couldn't take advantage of

the Hillaires' generosity, and that he had to stay in Kildunlee and "...take care o' me livestock and fields, an' I don't know anyone I'd trust ter take care o' me pigs and sheep as well as I do."

But Ray wouldn't take no for an answer, and he tried to persuade Brendan to accompany them, and with Siobhan, Edward and the kids to come to Montana. He told Brendan he could use his own money for air fare if he wanted to. Ray told them that this was a wedding present for Edward and Siobhan, and that Brendan was included to act as overseer of the "gossoons" as they were called.

"Brendan, we really would love to have you come, and we'd need your help with the kids, so please say 'yes'."

"Oh, Da, yer've never been off this island, except for that long fishing trip ter Scotland, an' yer deserve a good long rest. Yer've worked all yer life and yer need a break," his daughter told him.

"There, Brendan," Marcie told him. "Even your daughter wants you to come along. You have no excuse not to come, now. And, besides, we're all part of the same family."

"All right, all right," Brendan said with a large grin on his face. "I know when I'm beaten. I'm goin'. But, it'll be me first flight and God only knows what'll happen."

"Brendan, you're going to love it!" Ray told him.

"So, now that that's settled," Edward began, "we have a surprise for you. Tomorrow, before we go to the Manor House for dinner, and that's about seven o'clock, Siobhan and I are taking you up to see the Cliffs of Moher to watch, as the song goes...'the sun go down on Galway Bay', and to see where it all began for Siobhan and me. There's also O'Brien's Tower and a nice amble through the thick woods between the Cliffs and town."

They agreed that this was a wonderful idea, to see some of the spectacular Irish countryside, and especially the Cliffs, and the parents decided to meet at Niamh's pub at one for lunch, then, when Edward and Siobhan joined them, take a long stroll to the Cliffs before it got too dark for walking in the woods. That would leave them time after their return to the village to freshen up for dinner with McGrath and Cynthia.

"The Commander sends his best wishes and regrets that he and Cynthia can't accompany us to the Cliffs, but he has to attend the Inquest tomorrow. It's got to do with the recent shooting and it might drag on," Edward told them.

"Argh, sure 'n' 'tis a terrible thing, but the good Commander has seen the Cliffs a hundred times," Siobhan told them, "And he said he'll see all of you at dinner in the evening."

The Hillaires and the Huestises got ready to leave, and Siobhan started getting the "…gossoons ready for bed before they fall asleep on the floor." With the weather predictions on the bright side, the following day promised to be quite memorable and enjoyable.

23.

ANOTHER INQUEST

The Honorable Francis O'Farrell gaveled his court. "This court will come to order. Will the Clerk of the Court please read the indictment?" He said, turning to Senan Neill.

"Yes, yer Honor." And, clearing his voice, in a very important manner, Senan Neill began to read.

"Sometime during the night hours o' April 21st, 1946, it is alleged that a local resident o' the town o' Kildunlee, County Clare, Ireland, a certain Joe Naughton, after a furious argument with Tim Kearney, also a local resident o' said town of Kildunlee, at the local pub, owned by Niamh Flaherty, did willingly and intentionally fire three shots at the aforesaid Tim Kearney and did cause him ter be critically wounded from these three shots ter the chest and shoulder area. Tim Kearney was removed ter Galway University Hospital where the medical staff is desperately attempting ter save his life."

Senan put his papers down on the desk and resumed his seat.

The Regional Magistrate looked straight at Joe Naughton. "How do you plead?"

"Yer Honor, sir, I didn't do nothin' ter Tim. We was friends o' the sort that had a jar now an' then, a few words here an' there but we'd never have such a battle. I'd never do a thing like this ter Tim." Joe was on the verge of tears in his throbbing emotion. "I ain't done nothin' ter Tim, yer Honor, I ain't."

"Thank you. You can resume your seat, Mr. Naughton," said O'Farrell. Then, turning to Senan, he instructed him, "Will the clerk of the Court please call Garda Livius O'Toole?"

"Yes, yer honor. Will Livius O'Toole, Garda for Kildunlee and its surroundings, please take the stand," and Livy was sworn in.

"Garda O'Toole," said O'Farrell, "Will you please tell the court what report you have received from the Forensics Department of County Clare and the results of their analyses?"

"Yes, yer Honor," and Livy took a sheaf of papers out of his Garda jacket pocket and began to read.

"It is reported in the Forensics' Department statement that the alleged murder weapon, a rifle of large caliber, with a muzzle opening measured at one half an inch, matches the size of the bullets taken from the chest and shoulder areas o' Tim Kearney. It is reported that the caliber o' the rifle matches exactly the caliber o' the bullets. It is reported that the rifle of Joe Naughton was found ter have been fired as recently as the evening in question. Furthermore, yer Honor, it is also noted in the report, that, as a result of a paraffin test, Joe Naughton's hands show traces of powder burns, verifying that he had, indeed, recently fired a weapon, and that the test showed that the powder burns o' Joe Naughton's hands were fresh."

"Thank you, Garda O'Toole." Again, turning to Joe Naughton, the judge asked him, "Do you have any statement against these allegations?"

"No, yer Honor, I ain't. All I know is that I ain't done nothin' ter hurt Tim. I ain't done nothin' ter him."

"Thank you, Mr. Naughton." Francis O'Farrell turned to the jury foreman, Martin McBride, a local beef and vegetable farmer, and instructed him and his jury members to adjourn to the jury room for deliberations. Senan Neill, striding out importantly, led the jury out of the court room and down a short, dusky hall to a small makeshift jury room with a dozen rickety wooden chairs and a wobbly wooden table in it. It took only ten minutes for them to send a signal to the Sergeant-At-Arms, with Senan filling in for that position as well, that they had arrived at a decision. The jury was then led by Senan back into the courtroom and they filed into the jury box where all twelve of them resumed their respective seats.

"Has the jury reached an Inquest verdict," O'Farrell asked McBride, who thoughtlessly remained seated.

"Please stand when addressin' His Honor," Senan reminded McBride, who immediately jumped to his most rigid and proud stance in his towering five feet three inches.

"Yes, yer clerkship," McBride answered him. And, facing O'Farrell, his cloth cap in his left hand and the verdict paper in his right, "Aye, yer Honor, the jury has. It finds the defendant, Jon Naughton, of Kildunlee, County Clare, Ireland, based upon the testimony and f'rensics reports, clearly guilty o' the shootin' o' Tim Kearney."

The foreman sat down and two sounds could be heard throughout the court: a collective sigh that it was almost over and that Joe Naughton would get his, and a sob from Joe himself.

"I tol' yer, yer Honor, I ain't done nothin' ter hurt Tim. We was mates," and the choking sobs could be heard in his words.

"This court does not have the authority to decide your guilt or innocence, Mr. Naughton, it can only make recommendations. Therefore you are remanded to County Clare Jail to await a trial by jury, at County Clare Criminal Court, as to your guilt or innocence of the shooting, and, if he dies, the possible murder of Tim Kearney. This court is now adjourned," and, as O'Farrell rapped his gavel once and rose to leave the bench, the onlookers also rose, and many of them immediately made haste to Niamh's to discuss the events of the morning.

As he was led from the court room back to County Clare Jail to await his appearance in the Galway Criminal

Court, Joe Naughton realized that he would soon be on trial for his life, for a crime he truly believed he did not commit.

The Inquest had been over for an hour and people were still standing in front of the tiny building that served as a courthouse, Inquest house and whatever other legal necessity or general meetings that might arise.

The discussions, in front of the courthouse and in the pub, centered around how Joe Naughton, who had been a friend of sorts, when they were both sober, of Tim Kearney, and how could Joe even think of shooting Tim. Even when they had had several jars of the pure, they only had a bit of fun teasing each other, and during their sober moments, they never had a battle between themselves. It was so unlikely, everyone wondered how it could happen. Joe wasn't like that, and, for that matter, neither was Tim. And where was that girl, what was her name, oh yes, Bobbee. Hadn't seen her in days. Where'd she go? She was a friend of Lady Alice Stronton, the woman from South Africa. She hadn't been seen in a while either. Didn't even bother to come to the Inquest, although the whole town was here, and standing room only. Things didn't make sense.

The conversations continued until Garda O'Toole ushered the Kildunlee philosophers away from the front of the court house.

"All right," Livy said in his most imperious, "Yer'll be getting' along now. Don't block the court house door. His Honor will be leavin' shortly. On wit' yer now, on wit' yer." And he did it with such a smile on his freckled face, that no one took any offense and they all gravitated over to Niamh's, "...fer a point or two ter think things over," or "...a drop o' the pure ter get things straight." At any rate, whatever the excuse to grease one's throat, Niamh was doing a land office business as if she were in Juneau during the northern gold rush.

"A Pernod?" McGrath asked Jean-Luc, who was just entering Niamh's establishment. "I'm having a short whisky but I'd be glad to stand you a drink."

"*Ah bien, mais oui*, I'll join you, Commander. *Et merci*," Jean-Luc said, constantly mixing his French with his English as if he found it impossible to refrain from his native language even here in Ireland.

"This is very unusual, *mon ami*, very unusual. I don't understand it at all."

"No, neither do I," McGrath replied as Niamh's serving girl, Sheila, poured a large Pernod for Jean-Luc and a short "drop o' the pure" for McGrath. "It makes no sense. Everyone's saying Joe would never intentionally hurt Tim, but there it is. He apparently took his rifle and shot his friend, evidently over this Bobbee, who's been missing for days, now. No one's seen her in ages."

"*Mon ami*, you are correct. She is long gone and I don't believe we will ever see her again. She has vanished like the, how do you say, will o' the whisk?"

"Wisp," McGrath corrected him.

"*Ah, oui*. Wisp. I shall have to remember that. But, tell me, Commander, have you seen Lady Alice lately? I was in here yesterday, since this is the place where every scrap of the information seems to congregate, and I heard someone talking that he had seen the Lady the day before and she did not look well."

"Yes," McGrath said, sipping his whisky, "I ran into her early yesterday at O'Banyon's buying groceries and she didn't look well. Worried, maybe, or just upset might be the words to describe her. She certainly didn't look well. But, I guess, when your fiancé takes his own life, there's reason to be upset."

"I agree with you, Commander, she must have been upset, and, without the doubt, bearing the sorrow. *Ah, bien*, what can we do? Only offer what comfort we may have."

"Right," McGrath agreed, still thinking about Lady Alice, and especially her friend, this Bobbee. Where had she gotten to? "I still can't see how this girl Bobbee fits into this whole thing. There's no pattern here. She arrives, a friend of Lady Alice's, causes trouble between Joe and Tim, then disappears into thin air. I wonder where she's gotten to?"

"*Mon ami*, I don't think we'll ever know, and that is probably the thing for the best. She is gone, who knows where. But, she is gone."

McGrath nodded his head in agreement, but the idea of Bobbee still troubled him. *What part did she play in this fiasco?* Then his face cleared and a smile crossed his chin.

"Jean-Luc, I almost forgot. In a couple of days, this Saturday, actually, Cynthia is having a birthday party for her father, Earl FitzHugh. We'd like you to come. Edward and Siobhan, and his parents and friends from Montana, will be there plus several others. Think you can make it? It should be a good party, but a bit on the hushed side when the Earl is present. He's not well and will stay for only a few minutes."

"Ah, *mon ami*, the wild horses could not keep me away from such a *soiree*, and I shall be honored to attend. *Mais oui*, I shall be there, and *merci tres bien* for the invitation."

McGrath raised his glass to Jean-Luc's, and they drank to the health, poor as it was, of the Earl. "See you then. Have to run. Cynthia's expecting me."

"*Au revoir, mon ami*, and my best wishes to your bride," Jean-Luc called to McGrath as he turned and left the pub.

24.

AN EXCURSION TO THE CLIFFS

With the Inquest over, and the tacit promise of a wonderful dinner later that evening at the Manor, Edward and Siobhan, the Hillaires and the Huestises all met at Niamh's pub for a typically fortifying four course Irish lunch, "… ter help keep yer strength up so yer'll not be laggin' in getting' ter the Cliffs," Niamh told them. The morning sun had risen over the eastern horizon from the Irish Sea, bringing promised warmth for the afternoon, although the early morning still had temperatures in the low forties. Perhaps the party climbing to the Cliffs would see sixty degrees by mid-afternoon. And with a warm and pleasant day before them, the splendid panorama of the majestic North Atlantic, from the edge of the ruggedly beautiful Cliffs of Moher to the ocean's distant horizon, stretching to the coasts of Newfoundland and Quebec, would give testament to the magnificence of creation. White caps pirouetted on the deep blue ocean, still tinted by the almost clear sky, and swells rolled merrily across the surface of the sea. The view was nothing less than spectacularly breathtaking.

"Oh, George, I'm so excited. This is my first time being so far from Montana, and in Europe, no less. What with the dinner at the Manor House tonight with the Commander McGrath and his wife, and, you may not know this, but there's a birthday party for his Lordship, Cynthia's father, this coming Saturday. Oh, it makes me so excited. I feel like I'm being treated like royalty."

George smiled broadly and looked lovingly at his wife. "Now, Beverly, don't get carried away. I'm excited, too. And this has been quite a fling – with the shootings aside, I mean," and he chuckled at that. "And it looks like we're getting the Cook's Tour, and it's great. But, you're right, I didn't hear about the birthday party. When did that come about?" He asked his wife.

"Well, Siobhan, and don't you just love that name, and her accent is so lovely, told Marcie and me when we were at the Hillaires' yesterday afternoon. At Eddie and Siobhan's, I mean."

"I know who you mean. I was there also, remember. So, what's it all about. Fill me in on the details."

"Well, the old fellow, His Lordship, is quite old and infirm. But, it's his birthday and Cynthia, she insists we call her that, wants to have a shindig for him so she's throwing a party and we Yanks are invited."

"First I've heard of it, but I love a party so I guess we're going," George Heustis said, as he picked up his heavy, wool jacket, and slung it over his shoulder. "We'd better get to the pub, lunch'll be ready soon."

***

From the thatched cottage where they and Edward's parents were staying was only a ten minute walk to Niamh's pub. The two couples met in the sitting room of the cottage and started off for Niamh's. The air still held a touch of crispness in it, but as the sun rose higher in the cobalt blue sky, warmth continued to radiate from the ground, the roadway and the walkway till their stroll became quite pleasant and they slowed their gait to admire the beauty of the verdant Irish country side.

"None of our harsh winters here," Beverly told the group. "I could almost live here myself. Then I wouldn't have to put up with fifty-below days, packed in ten layers of wool to keep myself warm," she said smiling.

"Beverly, I expect we'll be coming here, and on to the Continent, quite a bit from now on. Travers and his crew run the ranch quite well without us, so we might as well come over to see our grandchildren. I believe we'll be fairly permanent fixtures here in Kildunlee, and in other parts of Ireland."

"Oh, Ray, I'm so glad you said that. I just love little Margaret, don't you?"

"Of course," he said, "but I'm prejudiced, after all she is our granddaughter," and, at that, they arrived at Niamh's and went inside.

"Well, good arternoon ' ter yer! And how are all o' yer on this fine day? Yer lunch is all ready since it's just gone one." Niamh's smile beamed at them, her ruddy face a picture of welcoming. "An' 'tis a fine lunch we've laid out fer yer today, and no mistake. Yer'll not be wantin' ter eat till much later at yer dinner at the Manor tonight."

"How'd you hear about that, Niamh?" Beverly asked.

"Argh, nothin' escapes me here. 'Tis where all the latest gossip and news passes through. Sure'n if yer'll be wantin' ter know somethin' yer better stop in at Niamh's ter get the latest, an' no mistake."

"Must be the Kildunlee information exchange," George said, smiling, and they all joined in a good laugh, with Niamh's hearty chuckle well above the rest.

"Now, sit yerselves down over here, next ter the window so yer can see all the traffic, and Sheila'll be bringing out the first course in a minute." She turned to Ray Hillaire, saying, "And what will himself be havin'?"

"What would you suggest? I don't know what kind of lunch you've prepared."

"Ah, 'tis a bit of ham and cabbage and a well pulled point o' Guinness wouldn't come amiss."

"Niamh, make that two," George said.

"Argh, 'tis a fine decision. Two well pulled points. And the ladies?"

"I'm game if you are," Marcie said to Beverly. "Make that four well pulled pints."

"Argh, an' a fine one for the ladies, I'm here ter tell yer. I'll send Sheila out with the first course. An' a fine ham and cabbage yer'll be havin'."

"I'm sure of it, Niamh, I'm sure of it," Beverly told her, and they settled in for a bountiful Irish lunch.

***

Edward and Siobhan showed up at the pub just as the clock was chiming the half hour after one. They smiled when they entered the pub and saw all four of the Montanans beaming with pleasure at the tail end of their meal.

"Did yer get enough ter eat?" Siobhan asked them.

"Enough to eat?" Marcie asked in mock horror. "We could feed half of Montana on what Niamh fed us today. It was magnificent, but, now, I think we need a bit of a walk."

They all agreed to that. The gentlemen paid the tab, leaving a healthy tip for Sheila, and then they joined Edward, Siobhan and their wives on the walkway outside the pub.

"It's about a half mile to the Cliffs, over glorious countryside, and through the pine woods up on the hill, there," Edward told them, and he pointed to a slight hill rising to the Cliffs of Moher.

"'Tis a lovely jaunt, and sometimes you'll see a rabbit or two. I'm sure yer're going ter like it," Siobhan said. "It might get a bit tricky walkin' through the pine woods, because of the thick branches an' all, but the air is a heady fragrance," she told them, "like a well pulled point."

"My heavens, any more well pulled pints and we

won't be able to go anywhere this afternoon," George said, and they all laughed.

"Well, Eddie and me figured we would all spend the afternoon at the Cliffs, and come home just as the sun was settin', before it got too dark. That way, yer can get back ter the cottage and freshen up fer dinner tonight. Besides, we'll have ter be checkin' on the kiddies. Deirdre is watchin' them today, an' she's good, but I like ter keep an eye on things. So, if yer ready off we go." And they began the slow journey up the gentle rise to the Cliffs.

The climb wasn't straining, and it gave them the exercise they craved after Niamh's satisfying lunch at the pub. And the pine forest, heady with a lovely perfumed fragrance scent, was almost dizzying.

"This is delightful," Beverly said to George. "Really delightful," and she filled her being with the fresh, Irish forest redolence.

"I'd have to agree with you. Beats the hell out of sagebrush, anytime."

Edward heard this exchange and he smiled at the recollection of the odor of steamy, dust coated sagebrush in summer, and the subzero, frigid, ice-laden air of a Montana winter. It wasn't that he didn't love his parents or his childhood home, he reminded himself, but his home was here, his love was Siobhan and Margaret, and the other children. Oh, he and Siobhan would visit Montana, and, he was sure they would get a king's welcome, he expected nothing less, and he could tell his friends from younger years all about his adventures during the war in Ireland. But, Ireland, that was his home now. No place else.

"A penny fer yer thoughts, me love?"

"My thoughts are of you and what we have here in Ireland. And, yes, I am your love."

Siobhan reached up and kissed him tenderly on the lips.

"Will you two love birds get a move on? We want to get to the Cliffs. At this rate, we'll get there at breakfast time," Ray called to them.

And Edward Hillaire, a very happy young man, indeed, with his beautiful wife, made haste to join the others.

"If you look ter the north, you can see O'Brien's Tower. It's a small cylinder, perched on the edge of the Cliffs," Siobhan informed them.

"What was it used for?" Marcie asked her.

"Well, Marcie, it was used by the ancient Celts ter keep a lookout fer the Vikings who loved ter raid this part of Ireland," Siobhan told them. "When a Viking sail, or, more likely, several sails were seen, then a raid was about ter happen, and the lookout ran ter tell the town so they could hide their valuables and get ter cover. Not a soul was lost after the tunnel was built," Siobhan continued.

"What tunnel was that," Beverly asked.

"The escape tunnel on the other side of the pine woods. See, there's a monument near ter commemorate its use."

"It was the tunnel we used to get away on the night before D-Day, dad. The one I told you about."

"Can we go there and climb down the tunnel?" George asked.

Edward raised his gaze to the sky. The sun had peaked and was sliding down towards the distant west to grace the Canadian Provinces. Twilight was beginning to arrive and light was fading fast. They had been walking for two hours, admiring the scenery, and, especially the Aran Islands off the West Coast of Ireland. His mother was quite amazed when Edward told her that there were basking sharks in the Aran waters, and that they sometimes reached twenty-five feet in length. She swore that she would never go near them.

"Don't worry, Mom, they eat only plankton, tiny

sea creatures. So you're safe."

"Well, that's a relief," she told them.

But Edward brought them back to the moment. "I don't think we can go to the tunnel, do you, Siobhan? It's getting dark." And his thoughts went back to that terrible stormy night, a year and more ago, when he had to say goodbye and he thought they were finished.

Siobhan saw the thought in her love's mind, and she reached out her hand and squeezed his. There would be no parting for them now. Or ever.

"That's right, and we still have ter wend our way back through the pine woods, and that can be a bit o' a walk in the dark. We'd better go back down ter the village now," Siobhan told them, and they started on their way back to Kildunlee.

***

The going was easy, all downhill, and no climbing. But the woods, thick with trees and bushes along the darkened path, presented a challenge, and they had to walk slowly, and be careful.

"You know, Ray," Marcie said to her husband, "this walk hit the spot. I thought I'd put on ten pounds at lunch, but this walk has given me an appetite for dinner with the Commander and Cynthia tonight."

"Me, too," he told her as he picked his way through the pine trees. He almost stumbled on a large, protruding root. They were two abreast in their march. Edward and Siobhan leading; his parents were next, then the Huestises. They chatted unceasingly, as they made their way amongst the trees, in the falling shadows, their route dim but not totally obscure. Not a care in the world at the present, surrounded by the forest's arboreal aroma and the enchanting magic of Ireland.

***

"Ah! Ah!" George called out and spun around, clutching his left shoulder. "Ah! Lord!"

"George!" Beverly called to her husband. "George, what is it?"

"Oh, my Lord," cried Ray, "not his heart!"

George had halfway spun around in the twilight and had fallen to the ground, clutching his left shoulder. Blood seeped through his clenched fingers.

"Oh, Lord, the pain," he yelled, lying on his side, clutching his shoulder with his right hand.

"What is it, George? Your heart, again?" Beverly asked, running to her husband. "Oh, my God, there's blood all over his shoulder! It's not his heart. He's been injured!" Beverly cried, her voice in a panic.

Edward, Siobhan, Ray and Marcie all rushed to Beverly's side to see George's injury.

"That's a gunshot wound. Straight into the left shoulder," Ray told them, while hoisting George up to a sitting position, despite all his verbal protests. "A few more inches to the right and it would have hit his chest dead center."

"You're right, Dad," Edward said. "We didn't have much firearms use in the Naval Weather Service, but we did have training in first aid and this is certainly a gunshot wound."

"But I didn't hear a sound," Marcie said. "And I didn't see any flash." She put her arms around her dearest friend, trying to console her, to bring her some comfort. "It's only a shoulder wound, Beverly, it's not serious. Maybe a hunter's shot gone wild."

"I hope you're right, Marcie, I hope you're right," Beverly said through her tears, sobbing.

"Aye," Siobhan told them. "Sure an' 'tis dark enough ter see a flash from a shot, but there was none."

"Perhaps a silencer?" Edward asked them. "Aren't they illegal?"

"They are in Montana and in all the other states, but I don't know about Ireland."

"They are," Siobhan said, "Aye, they are. They were outlawed some years ago and no one uses them now fer fear o' going ter jail."

"Whoever used it on a rifle—and this wound is large so it must have been a rifle shot—certainly knew what he was doing."

"Come on, now, we don't have time to talk about gunshot holes. We have to get George down to Doctor McHugh. Dad, we can make a cradle and join hands under his knees and shoulders and carry him to town. It's less than half a mile." Edward and his father shrugged George up into their arms, grasping each other's hands for support and trundled George, swiftly, but gently, down the path toward Kildunlee. His groans and murmurs could be heard by all of them. The three women went in front and bent back bushes and tree branches to make the way easier to navigate, trying to console Marcie all the while.

Ray looked with pride at his son, thinking him a fine man who can make decisions and then carry them out successfully. For a minute, he felt a touch of wistfulness, knowing that this son of his would surely never return permanently to Montana and run the Hillaire Horse Ranch. That would be left to his two younger brothers and one sister. *They can manage*, he thought, *and they know horses well and have good business sense, but the three of them together don't have the determination and drive of Edward. Still*, he told himself, *it will all work out,* and he turned his mind to carrying George out of the woods, the edge of which they were rapidly approaching, and towards Doctor McHugh's office, surrounded by the early evening lights of Kildunlee, just a quarter of a mile away, gleaming beacons in the fast fading Irish light. A soft Irish mist began to fall, almost a drizzle, but lighter. Drops floating in the early evening air, not soaking them, and barely wetting their cheeks and hair.

"This is a pleasant and cooling drizzle," George managed to say, smiling through his discomfort.

"George, I've seen these Irish mists turn into strong thunderous showers in a half hour," Edward told him, smiling back in the growing darkness. "I haven't seen a weather map lately, so I really don't know what's coming. Let's hope we get you patched up and all of us at the Commander's dinner table before the rain gods let loose."

They all chuckled at that and it made carrying George all the easier. Siobhan ran ahead and knocked briskly at Dr. McHugh's surgery door. Beverly continued to comfort Marcie who was beginning to calm herself now.

25.

DINNER AT THE MANOR

Rain pelted against the windows, beating a staccato rhythm, driven by the stout west wind that seemed to have arisen from nowhere. But McGrath and Edward both shared the secret that the west and north winds attacked the West Coast of Ireland at their whim, and frequently drove to the Galway area in ever maddening frenzies. Tonight was such a night. After George had been cared for by Doctor McHugh, who had reported that the wound was really superficial, with no bones broken or arteries severed and that, whoever had fired the shot had made a clumsy error, or that he was such a crack shot and had cleverly chosen his target, George's fleshy shoulder, with clear deliberation, so as to inflict more fear than injury.

They were all greatly relieved at the comparatively minor status of the wound. So, the Hillaires and Huestises returned to their cottage and Edward and Siobhan went back to the farm. It was after dark, nearing seven o'clock, and the light drizzle that had begun just after George had been shot and the gentle mist had turned into a light rain.

The six of them had rested and were now prepared to go to the Manor House to join McGrath and Cynthia for dinner. Cars had been sent to the Kildunlee cottage for the Hillaires and Huestises and to the farm for Edward and Siobhan. Sherry was then served by Riordan, the butler, assisted by the two housemaids, Edna and Lizzie.

The mood of the company was upbeat because of the slightness of George's gunshot wound, and, although the bullet had torn through the outer part of his shoulder, the arm itself didn't require a sling, just a large amount of bandaging.

"You say you never heard a shot or saw a flash in the dark?" McGrath asked them, concern showing on his brow.

"No. Nothing at all, Commander," Ray answered him. "Not a noise or any kind of a flash. We've done a lot of target practice in Montana, and lots of it at night, so we're all familiar with nighttime shooting and the light and sound effects it causes. But tonight... nothing."

"Hmmm," mused McGrath, "Sounds as if whoever did the shooting must have used a silencer. I wonder why. Livy isn't going to like this. He's going to have more reports to write up, and even call Colonel O'Meara again. And to think," McGrath said with a broad smile, "all he ever wanted was a backwater small Irish village with little for a Garda to do except rustle up the occasional 'bowseys'."

"Someone mentioned the silencer right after George got hit," Marcie Hillaire said, "But we couldn't imagine why anyone would want to shoot George. And with a silencer, as if he wanted to cover it up for some strange reason. I don't understand."

Riordan and the maids served the several elaborate courses in a very slow, leisurely and stately manner, according to McGrath's explicit instructions, beginning with fruit compote; then reshly caught brook trout, roast beef with Mrs. Lynch's specially roasted potatoes, with sparkling green beans and lasciviously rich, thick brown gravy. Cynthia had instructed Riordan to decant several bottles of His Lordship's finest Burgundy, with the Earl's blessing and a requested glass sent to his room, and this extremely flavorful red highly complimented Mrs. Lynch's roast beef. McGrath resisted the temptation to compare Mrs. Lynch's culinary endeavors with Mrs.

O'Shaunessy's. There was danger in this thought, he told himself, and McGrath, with a secret smile, dismissed the idea. *All I have to do*, he reminded himself, *is to watch my waistline,* and he returned his attention to the conversation at the table.

***

Siobhan moved uneasily in her chair. They were all sitting around a well laid dinner table, set with the finest silver, Waterford Crystal and sparkling, snow white linen. A large gleaming Waterford vase held a large burst of chrysanthemums, roses, marigolds and rich greenery from the FitzHugh greenhouses, and the table setting added support to the magnificence of the repast. The centerpiece made a splendidly colorful oasis in a sea of shining silver and white. But Siobhan was uncomfortable and Edward noticed his wife's discomfort.

"What is it, me own," he asked her under his breath. She took the napkin and dabbed her eyes. The general conversation immediately stopped.

"Siobhan, what's wrong?" Cynthia queried.

"I... I don't know. With Eddie's parents and the Huestises here... ter visit... I wanted everything ter be so nice. Ter show you our lovely island. Now, everything's gone wrong. I can't explain it. I'm so ashamed. There's not been anything like this since way before we got our independence. Now, there's strange trouble and I feel so ashamed and embarrassed." Tears were coursing down her cheeks, and her breath came in gasps.

"No, Siobhan, it's not your fault or your worry," Marcie got up from her place at the table and put her arm around her daughter-in-law, and, for the second time that evening, was comforting a loved one and holding her close. "It's nothing to do with you or Ireland. It must be some deranged individual with a grudge making trouble for us all."

Cynthia and Beverly came to Siobhan as well, both trying to comfort the young wife of Edward, whom they had come to love as had Marcie.

"The Garda will find out who is causing all this trouble and have them put away. Don't you worry. I bet it'll be over real soon," Beverly told her, and then gave Siobhan a big hug.

"Come, you've barely touched your dinner. We can't send it back to Mrs. Lynch. She'd be just furious," Cynthia told her, with a pleasant smile. That comment brought a similar smile to Siobhan's pretty face, and she looked up at the three women standing by her. "Thank you. I just feel so upset because I wanted things ter be nice fer all of yer," she told them.

"You have," Marcie answered her. "You have. You've made our Edward very happy and given us a beautiful granddaughter. You have, Siobhan, and we love you very much." Marcie leaned down and kissed Siobhan on the cheek. "Now, have your dinner. We mustn't upset Mrs. Lynch." And with that, and a great hug from Marcie, the ladies returned to their seats, dinner resumed to a satisfactory conclusion.

***

"We hadn't had the time to tell you of the party this Saturday night," Cynthia announced to Ray and George.

"Yes, the party," McGrath said with a great, beaming smile on his ruggedly, seafaring, handsome face.

"William and I have talked about this, as you may have heard, and next Saturday actually, three days from now, is my father's birthday and I've been planning to have a party for him. He's not well, as you all know, but I think he would enjoy having a birthday party thrown for him. Doctor McHugh thinks it may be his last. He is a very sick man."

"I know," said McGrath, "And I was sorry when I

first heard of it," he told the group around the dining table. "A party for him would be a nice gesture, but," he said turning to his wife, "are you sure it wouldn't be too much for him? His heart is terribly weak, you know."

"William, no one knows that better than I do," she said to him, "but Doctor McHugh, and the heart specialist in Dublin, thought that if he were at the party for a little while, and we kept things subdued, he'd be fine, or OK, as you are accustomed to saying in Boston," she added smiling at her husband, and gently touching his fingers. McGrath returned her smile, again admiring her beautiful gray eyes.

"Well, if we keep it down to a dull roar on Saturday, we hope you will all be able to attend my father's birthday party. I'm sure he'll just make a brief appearance for some cake and ice cream, perhaps a glass of champagne, then he will return to bed. So, can we count on everyone coming this Saturday? Seven in the evening, and we hope the weather will be a bit better. William, can't you do something about this hideous weather?" Cynthia said to her husband, with a grand smile on her face.

"My dear lady, all I can do is to analyze and report on it. I can't change it," he chuckled. "If I could, we've have sun and blue skies six days a week and rain every Tuesday to keep the landscape green."

Cynthia laughed at McGrath's proclamation, as did the others. "Good then. We'll see everyone here next Saturday. Father Joseph and Father Tim, as well as Doctor McHugh, and several others will be here. It should be quite a hooley."

26.

McGRATH AND JEAN-LUC

"It is not good, *Monsieur*, I do not understand many aspects of this whole case. There are so many things missing," Jean-Luc took a sip of his ever loved Merlot, savored the flavor, and gave McGrath a smile of satisfaction. "I cannot at all account for the disappearance of *Mademoiselle* Bobbee. No one seems to know where she has gone to, *Eh, Monsieur Le Commandant?*" He asked McGrath, "Have you any idea where she has gone? She seems to hold a large clue as to what happened here." Jean-Luc took the small knife Niamh had given him, and he applied more *fromage au bleu* to his cracker.

It seemed to McGrath that Jean-Luc could sit and eat blue cheese, or, as the French called it, Roquefort, all day, and he would wash it down with a litre or two of French red Merlot. Then he would get up and walk a straight line to the nearest restaurant for another savored French meal. *Ah well*, thought, McGrath, *each to his own. I prefer a good Jameson and a bag of potato chips, or*, as he reminded himself, *here in Ireland these were called crisps. Gads!* He thought to himself. *Why can't we all talk the same language?* But, still, his mind recalled the several French restaurants he and his Boston friends and family had happily frequented in times past, and he could feel the hunger pangs beginning. Mrs. Lynch was an excellent cook, but she was not Chef Alain at *Le Cerf Blanc* just off State Street in Beacon Hill, where only the famous, or the extremely rich, went for meals. And, with a clientele of about fifty families, Chef Alain did very well, and his *Coq Au Vin* was extraordinary. McGrath wondered where Jean-Luc could take him to in Paris for a comparable meal.

"*Monsieur* is quiet this morning. *La chat Amercaine* has got your tongue?" Jean-Luc asked, with a broad smile.

"No. Not really, Jean-Luc. I'm of the same opinion as you. I can't see where this Bobbee came from and where she's gotten to. I ran into Lady Alice the day before yesterday and she seemed really down and out. I suppose if I had lost my betrothed, I'd be quite sad also. But she really seemed terribly distressed; way down in the dumps. I didn't know what to say to be something of a comfort so I just wished her a good morning and told her that if was there was anything Cynthia or I could to help that she should call upon us. I asked her about Bobbee, and she only shook her head and shrugged her shoulders. I have to suppose that she's all upset about the death of Sir Julian and the Joe Naughton shooting. Can't be anything else, and I'm sure it can't be helped, of course. It's a very sad situation," he said and took a small sip of his treasured Jameson's.

Jean-Luc looked at McGrath intently, and then gave him one of his beautiful broad and glittering Gallic smiles. "I am sure you are on the right track, as you say. But, I am convinced that this girl, Bobbee, would lead us to the essence of the case. Don't you think so, *mon ami*? But, she has taken to the winds and now has completely disappeared. No one knows where she has gone."

"I agree. I really do think she is the answer to all of this, or, at least, a large part of the problem," he said with emphasis, helping himself to some more of Mr. Jameson's finest Irish whiskey, with Niamh's blessing, and leaving several coins on the bar to cover his bill. "I'm sure she has a lot of light to shed on this case. But, what bothers

me, Jean-Luc, is *where* has she gone? Or, is she a figment
of our collective imaginations. Did she really exist?"

"Ah, *mon ami*, of course, these thoughts always
come up. We always wonder if we have seen events as
they seem to have appeared. But, *oui*, she exists. For if
she did not, then there would not be a dead body, a critical body in the hospital almost dead, a great fight between
Monsieur Naughton and *Monsieur* Kearney, and *Monsieur* Heustis wounded. *Oui, Monsieur Le Commandant*,
Bobbee did, in fact, exist. But, where she is now, we do
not have the idea, *non?*" Jean-Luc took another cracker
laced with Rocquefort and drowned it in a large swallow
of Merlot.

"But, *Monsieur le Commandant*, I can tell you one
item of absolute truth."

"What's that?" McGrath asked him, his curiousity
suddenly aroused.

"This *Madamoiselle* Bobbee, or whoever she is,
knows nothing of art and has never been to an art school,
with or without Lady Alice. I know this as a fact."

McGrath gaped at Jean-Luc. "Well... how... how
do you know this?" he stammered.

"It is simple, *Monsieur*. The day we were here in
the pub and Bobbee went to the Cliffs to paint, do you
remember?"

McGrath nodded to Jean-Luc.

"You went back to the Manor and I went to the
Cliffs after Bobbee had started up for there. When I first
arrived, she had begun doing some work, what she called,
painting. It was abysmal. It was not painting. It was trash.
I asked her about her style and questioned her about
whether she used the mezzotint method and she said yes
she did. Her method was not mezzotint, *Monsieur*. As I
said, it was trash, and not even some type of modern ab-
stract school. I said she ought to try *pointillisme*, and then
suggested that it was invented by either Cezanne or

Lautrec. She immediately corrected me that it had been started by Cezanne, which, as I'm sure you know, is completely false. It was invented by another Frenchman, Georges Seurat. *Monsieur le Commandant*, she knows nothing about art and is entirely incapable of painting. She is false, a phony artist, which makes everything more complex." Jean-Luc took another large swallow of his beloved Merlot.

McGrath was shaking his head, stopping only to massage his temples. Thoughts raced through his mind, all leaving him completely befuddled. "Jean-Luc, from what you tell me, Bobbee had no knowledge of art. Then why was she posing as an artist? Why did Lady Alice pan her off as her roommate at the Sorbonne and as a fellow art student? I don't see any reason for any of this. It's a sham! But, why go through all the trouble of this charade?"

"*Ah, bien, Monsieur*, you may have hit our nail on its head, but we may never know."

"I remember some of what you just said about the great French painters from my Intro to Art course at college."

"Ah, yes, you went to the MIT, *n'est-ce-pas*? A good school, a very good school. *Moi*, I went to the *Polytechnique Francaise*, our equivalent of your MIT. But, I am not a scientist as you are so I left and transferred to the *Ecole Normal Superior* to study *l'art* so I could work with my father and my brothers. So, *Monsieur le Commandant*, I know art, and I know it *tres bien*! As I said, *Mademoiselle* Bobbee is not the *artiste*, and she has no knowledge of art. And, *comme j'ai dit*, this makes the matters very complicated, very complicated indeed," and Jean-Luc returned his attention to his Merlot.

"Jean-Luc, I don't know where we go from here. I haven't the slightest idea."

"Nor do I, *Monsieur*, nor do I."

McGrath took another sip of his whiskey. He had to drive back to the Manor in a little while, and he always adhered to the severe strictures from Great Grandfather Josiah, the founder of McGrath Shipping Lines, to never have more whiskey than was good for the moment. And one large glass was enough for McGrath. He had to get himself and his new Land Rover, which he had recently purchased, back to the Manor. Besides, there would be lunch with Cynthia and Magistrate O'Farrell, and that would be a bit of a lavish affair, for Cynthia always turned out Mrs. Lynch's best for important and special guests. This was not even to mention the preparations for Lord Fitzhugh's birthday party this evening.

"Another whiskey, *monsieur?*" asked Jean-Luc, as he spread a large swath of Roquefort on another cracker. This was followed by a large swallow of Merlot.

"No. No thanks, Jean-Luc. I have to be heading back to the Manor in a few minutes. The Magistrate is coming for lunch and I have to be bright-eyed and bushy-tailed. One is my limit this morning." McGrath took a sip, and then stared into his glass, in a deepening mood. His thoughts were lost for several moments, as he watched the traces of whiskey drain down the sides of his glass.

"A penny for your thoughts, *monsieur?*" Jean-Luc asked, smiling. "Perhaps a franc? I would not want to disrupt the plans of *Madame* McGrath, so perhaps one whiskey is sufficient this morning."

McGrath laughed out loud at Jean-Luc's proposal, and several regulars at the bar, including the two vacationing Spaniards, looked at him, wondering what the funny topic was.

"What really bothers me, Jean-Luc, is that this guy, Sir Julian, apparently blew his brains out in his study. They were all over his desk blotter, and he'd made a mess of it, too. We both saw that. But, if that's so, and the Inquest seems to have accepted suicide by pistol shot as a cause of death, then where did the strychnine come from? Dr. McHugh had his friend from the Galway Hospital Morgue run some tests on Sir Julian's blood samples and they were loaded with strychnine. Where did that come from? I've seen a suicide when I was aboard ship in the Pacific Fleet, just before the bombs were dropped on Hiroshima and Nagasaki, and this dead guy had a look of pure bliss on his face, if you can call suicide bliss. It was as if he was relieved of his earthly problems, whatever they were. But the point I'm making is, if Sir Julian shot himself, why did he also take poison? There seems to be no sense to it," McGrath said to Jean-Luc, shaking his head.

"*Non, ce n'est pas* I agree with you, *mon ami*. I, too, have seen a suicide and the person who had done away with himself had a pleasant appearance on his face. I cannot tell you why this Sir Julian had such an appearance of sheer terror on his face."

"And look at it this way. If he had shot himself, then there would be no reason for a much slower, and at best agonizing, death from strychnine. A shot would take only a second or two, and it would have left him in a relatively calm condition. But strychnine? This causes attacks to the central nervous system. It makes the victim's arms and legs spasm until he is almost in an arched back position, like a drawn bow, ready to loose an arrow. And, normally, when strychnine is taken the victim's face is in a grimaced image, with contortions from pain the way Sir Julian's was, showing muscular contractions from the inherent physical suffering and agony. But, this poses the question, if he blew his brains out, why did he take the strychnine? It can't be that someone had administered the poison to him, because there were no glasses in the study. All the glasses in the study cabinets and the hall display cases were analyzed and checked for usage and poison residue. There was nothing. It makes no sense," McGrath said to the Frenchman, as he finished his whiskey.

A little silence settled between them, as they both considered the question of the pistol and the poison. Why should both be used if one would be enough to do away with Sir Julian? Why would Sir Julian himself use both methods when he knew the pistol would be quite fast and efficient, and extinguish his life in a flash? And as for the strychnine, would he even subject himself to the pain and agonizing torment of taking the poison, just to put a bullet through his head only moments later, that is, if he was able to manage the use of a pistol amid all the poison's evil work? Why did Sir Julian kill himself, anyway? Regardless of his suicide note, he apparently was still an extremely wealthy man, with business interests in many parts of the world: South Africa, Europe and South America.

Why would he want to give all this up and eliminate his life, especially in light of the fact that he was about to marry a wealthy and attractive woman like Lady Alice, with untold connections who could magnify his fortune several times over? It made no sense to McGrath. Apparently, it made no sense to Jean-Luc either. His brow was as furrowed as deeply as McGrath's.

"I have no answers more than you have. It is, as you say, a great puzzle and I am confounded and confused. My mind is lost in the wilderness. I deal in art, the finer things of life. I do not often come upon these problems of death and suicide. I do not know how to help you. *C'est un mystere, Monsieur Le Commandant,*" the art dealer said, shaking his head, "c*'est un mystere.*"

27.

LORD FITZHUGH'S BIRTHDAY PARTY

The skies had finally cleared and the sun was providing its marvelously colorful setting over the western Atlantic. Filtered rays spread their majestic sheen of gold, purple, silver and pink hues across the sky, rivaling that of Monet's palette. Rain showers of the past two days chose to meander to the southeast, and had left Kildunlee to dry out. Many of the guests who were invited to Lord FitzHugh's birthday party – he had turned seventy-two this year – had already arrived, and Riordan, the maids and the footmen, all arrayed in their best sartorial livery, were bustling back and forth among the guests offering champagne and Mrs. Lynch's finest canapés to the new arrivals, with freshly squeezed lemonade prepared for the abstemious teetotalers.

The cream of the crop of Kildunlee's residents were at Lord FitzHugh's party this evening: both American families from Montana, Edward and Siobhan, Jean-Luc the art critic, Dr. McHugh, the vacationing Spaniards, Francis O'Farrell, the Resident Magistrate, Brendan Rafferty and the O'Banyons, the two Garda, and a number of other prominent Kildunlee locals, not to mention Niamh and Sheila. Niamh's sister, Annie, who was taking care of Niamh's son, who she had had with the "Boats", was covering the pub this evening for those few "unfortunates" who hadn't been invited to the Manor.

The same band of musicians which had played at the wedding reception of McGrath and Cynthia had been commissioned to play for Lord FitzHugh's party, and play they did. Not only did they render the liveliest of Irish reels, but "The Blue Danube", a touch of "String of Pearls", "In The Mood", and other current melodies were performed. And added to that marvelous program was the best they could do with a soft presentation of one of Mozart's string quartets, only one movement, of course. Mozart's music was His Lordship's favorite.

Brendan was speaking to his son and daughter-in-law, each with a glass of champagne in hand.

"Well, now, what would yer think? Here we are, in the middle o' the Manor House, brought together by an American an' a Protestant turned Catholic, Glory be ter God, an' everybody happy as a sow in a foot o' mud wit' ten piglets. 'Tis fine, I'll be tellin' yer, 'tis fine."

"Oh, Da, with the war over an' Eddie, me own, back wit' the babe, it can't get any better. 'Tis lovely, isn't it?" And she reached up, again, to kiss her Eddie's lips, which received and returned her love.

"Siobhan, we've got to stop this public displaying of our love, otherwise people will start to talk."

She stretched her arms around his neck. "Eddie, me own, yer don't know what extra weight I'm carryin' tonight. 'Twill appear soon."

Edward almost dropped his glass. "Don't tell me! Margaret's going to have a brother?"

"Hush, me love. We'll talk tomorrer," and her eyes sparkled at him.

"Are you two at it again? Doesn't love ever stop between you two?" Marcie said, laughing.

"Never," Edward told his mother, "Never."

***

"Ah, *Madame*, may I compliment you on a *tres bonne soiree* this evening. A very lovely party, *Madame*. My highest compliments," Jean-Luc said to Cynthia.

"Thank you very much, Jean-Luc," she answered him. "William and I are very glad you were able to come."

"*Enchante, Madame,*" Jean-Luc responded, gallantly kissing Cynthia's hand, and turning, he nodded to the two Spaniards, who were enjoying the music and the delicious Fundador, ordered especially for their taste.

At the moment the music stopped, a respectful silence descended upon the company, and the door from the hall opened. His Lordship, a glorious smile on his aged and wrinkled face and wheeled by his valet, O'Grady, entered the room. Applause, in muted and respectful tones, sounded throughout the dining room. Compliments were given to Earl Trevor FitzHugh, and many good wishes on his birthday.

"Congratulations, your Lordship."

"Happy birthday, Earl Trevor."

"Splendid party, Lord FitzHugh."

And on and on. Lord FitzHugh accepted his glass of champagne from Riordan, who was honored to serve his old and revered Master, a Protestant nobleman renowned to be extremely loving toward his tenants, his servants and the inhabitants of Kildunlee. His generosity was praised through the county.

"Thank you, Riordan. Thank you, all" his old voice squeaked out. "I can stay only a few minutes, you know. Old Doc McHugh's orders, quack as he is," he said with a gentle smile, and everyone chuckled at his humor.

"But, don't stop your good times on my account. I'll be heading for bed in a few minutes, as soon as I've had my evening champagne," and he raised his glass in an aged, and time-worn hand. "Let us drink a toast to my daughter, Cynthia, and her navy man, William. I approve of this marriage and I praise my daughter for finding such a fine man, although he comes from the colonies," he said with a mischievous smile, and all the guests joined his humor. His hand, beginning to tremble from the slight, but taxing, overwork, and his heart straining to maintain the moment, he said one final phrase. "And may Cynthia and William bring forth wonderful children to play in these grounds and follow us in our good footsteps while showing charity to all of the Kildunlee people. God bless all," and the old, ill man raised his flute and drank fitfully from the sculptured Waterford glass.

"Hear! Hear!" was heard throughout the hall and dining room, and several teeming eyes meet with dry handkerchiefs which were no longer dry when they went back into the owners' pockets.

"So, let the party continue! I must get to bed. McHugh's orders," His Lordship said."And a merry night to all," he said with a wave of his withered and old hand, as O'Grady wheeled him back to his chambers and his longed-for bed, to the sound of appreciative applause.

***

McGrath was speaking to Jean-Luc in front of the mantle atop the dining room hearth, where blazed a cheery fire against the late spring evening chill, when their conversation was interrupted by a sharp report. Their conversation immediately stopped, although the other conversations in the room continued. McGrath put down his champagne glass on the white marble mantle.

"I don't believe that was a car's backfire, Jean-Luc."

"*Non*, nor do I *Monsieur*. It sounds as if came from the direction of the Library."

Both men hastily left the large dining room where most of the guests had assembled. As they went into the hall, they were followed by the eyes of everyone who were assembled there. Curiosity began to build, until the rest of the guests started to follow McGrath and Jean-Luc out of the dining room and down the short hall to the

Library. McGrath opened the door wide and he and Jean-Luc went in. What greeted them was a shock; completely unexpected.

In a large leather armchair sat Lady Alice Stronton. Her forehead had one bullet hole in it and blood was tricking down past her eyes and nose to her chin. Her blanched face was in a seemingly relaxed position. Her left hand, now resting in her lap, held an automatic pistol of high caliber, and the rear of her head, including much of the interior, was spread across the red leather back of the chair. In her right hand, her thumb and forefinger clasped a large white business size envelope.

McGrath and Jean-Luc stood by the chair. The two Garda joined them, accompanied by the Regional Magistrate.

"Glory be ter God," Livy exclaimed. "It's another suicide. Or is this another murther? I can't keep up with all this murtherin'."

"Look at the envelope, won't you, Commander," the Magistrate said. "It has your name on it."

McGrath extended his hand to retrieve the envelope, but stopped, looking at the Magistrate and the two Garda. "Go ahead, Commander. Open it. You are amongst friendly witnesses here and there is absolutely no question of duplicity," the Magistrate said. The two Garda nodded in agreement. McGrath picked the envelope from the dead fingers of Lady Alice and read the inscription.

"It's certainly addressed to me. Shall I open it and read the contents?" McGrath asked the Magistrate.

"By all means," he replied.

McGrath gently forced the envelope flap open, straightened the several pages inside and began to read the typewritten letter.

My Dear Commander McGrath;

I am addressing this letter to you because I believe that you have considerable standing, influence and also prestige in the village of Kildunlee. Many others also have standing, but, because of your service to Ireland and the Allied cause during the war years, it seems to me that you are an honorable and upright man. Hence, I address this letter to you.

Commander McGrath. I can no longer bear the burden of my guilt. My heart is over-laden with guilt and torn apart with regret and grief for what I have done, and I cannot continue through this life without a complete confession of my deeds. I appointed myself as my own judge and jury some days ago, and it is to this end, that of absolving myself of guilt and acrimony, that I write this letter. If there is a life beyond this trial of pain within which we have to spend our years, and through which we have to walk and suffer, then I trust that whoever is in charge, whether we call him God or not, will understand all the suffering and pain I have had to endure and perhaps find an ounce of mercy for me. I can only admit my guilt and place myself on the mercy of the court: myself. I find myself guilty as I have been charged and have recommended that I be executed. Therefore, I am at once the accused, the judge, the jury and the executioner. I have finally carried out the sentence which my conscience has demanded: summary execution of Lady Alice Marie Stronton, late of Pretoria, South Africa, for the murder of Sir Julian Brownlee. Yes, Commander, I murdered Sir Julian in cold blood, and, at the time, I rejoiced in his death throes. For Sir Julian did not shoot himself in the head. I did. But first, I poisoned him with strychnine; enough, as we say in South Africa, to kill ten wildebeests.

It is not a thing I took lightly, the killing of Julian, for that is what I called him. We were engaged to be married in Pretoria in a month's time. But I race far ahead of myself, and the events as they unfolded. In my haste to get this letter composed and written, I am out of the correct sequence of events. Let me start at the beginning of this whole romantic fiasco.

I met Julian in Pretoria last summer, in late August, shortly after the war ended in the Pacific. We were all ecstatic that the war had ended in Europe and we were waiting for the end in the Pacific. Finally, it came, and South Africa, along with the rest of the world, threw party after party to celebrate the end of this madness of bloodshed.

Pretoria, if you do not know, has a penchant for having parties, and we had more than our share after what they called VJ day.

I was invited to one of these evening soirees, since my family is quite prominent in South African political and social circles, my grandfather and father having made their fortunes in the gold mining industry. At any rate, I was at one of these gatherings and I happened to be introduced to Julian, or Sir Julian Brownlee, as he was referred to at the time. No one ever called into question where and how he had gotten his title, we just accepted it. Nor did we question his wealth, for it was considerable, and we knew only that he had been in the 'armaments trade' during the war. No other information was known about him.

We got along well, and really became attached. He took me to the finest restaurants and balls that Pretoria had to offer, and the only thing he ever asked me for in return was the occasional introduction to people who were interested in the armaments or import trade. I did this and Julian made a number of acquaintances and many contacts resulting in several quite profitable trade deals. At length, in the middle of last autumn, he asked me to marry him and to settle in South Africa with him, perhaps even to help him with his trade business. I, of course, accepted, announced the engagement to my family, who made it public to South African society, and we went from there. The wedding for Julian and me was to have been four weeks after you read this letter. Obviously, nothing of the like is to happen. Time passed and plans were set for our marriage. Julian made several trips on business and I thought nothing of these. The only thing that I noticed about him was that, every time he returned to Pretoria, he was in excellent spirits. I had assumed that it was because of a successful trade, or armaments, deal.

The months rolled by and he told me that he had to come to Ireland to see some very important people, who wanted to do a deal in a remote part of the world and to 'stay out of the limelight', regarding some importing and arms shipments. I had agreed to wait for him while he traveled to Ireland, and told him that I wished him well in his plans. Julian left for Ireland, taking the trains north from Pretoria to Cairo, then by ship to Rome and by airplane from Rome to London. To get to Ireland was a simple matter from London, and he was soon in the Galway area. In the meantime, I started to miss him and wanted to be with him, so I got the idea to follow him to Galway, which I did. However, in order to surprise him, I stayed in the small Kildunlee house, near Niamh's pub. I had rented a car in Galway, and, the day after I arrived in Kildunlee, I motored over to the house Julian was renting with the intention of surprising him. His man, Singleton, let me in with great gushes of greetings and good wishes, for he knew Julian's and my plans. Julian's greeting was a bit odd. He was entirely overtaken by my arrival, having no idea that I was on route to Ireland to be with him, and he was quite taken aback, even a bit brusque. I chalked this up to his surprise at my appearance, and, nevertheless, he became his old self and we had a marvelous visit. I told him that I was still writing little articles for the South African Rifle and Gun Club *magazine, and I asked him whether it would be all right for me to borrow his typewriter to dash off an article or two. He agreed, and said that I could stop by any time to use, or even take, his typewriter, and that he would inform Singleton of our arrangements. I stayed on for dinner that evening, and later returned to my rented house to edit my articles, Julian saying that he had meetings in Galway for the next day or two with some business contacts.*

It was the next day, on a Tuesday, I believe, that I finished my handwritten articles and was in need of Julian's typewriter, so I motored over to his house and asked Singleton for the use of the machine, since I had some work to type up. He, of course, said that his master had informed him that I would be using the machine and that it was quite all right that I go through to the study, where Julian kept the typewriter and his personal writing implements. I put my handwritten articles on the writing desk, to the left of the typewriter, rolled a sheet of paper under the platen and got ready to type my papers. It was at this time that I noticed a letter written to a certain Felicity Howarth, dated the previous evening, and signed by Julian.

The letter was a love letter, and its contents crushed me. In effect, it said that he would be taking the next ship, within seven days, from Southampton for Halifax, Nova Scotia, and from there he would either train, or if it were possible, fly to San Francisco. From San Francisco, there was a flight to Honolulu, and, from there, either flights or ships to Sydney, Australia. He vowed his love to this

Felicity Howarth, and told her that he looked forward to their life together in Sydney.

As I said, I was crushed. I just couldn't believe that Julian would do such a thing and cheat on me, totally disregarding my feelings and playing with my emotions. I had placed him among a great many prominent people in Pretoria and Johannesburg to make lucrative business deals, after which he asked me to marry him. Then, with barely a thought about me, he scrubbed me from his life and intended to head to Sydney with this Felicity Howarth.

Needless to say, I couldn't write my articles in the devastated mood I was in, so I packed up my things in my valise, bade goodbye to Singleton, and went back to my rented house. I cried for the next twenty-four hours. The pain I had to bear from Julian's betrayal was impossible to carry, but I fortified myself to confront him about it and to get to the truth. This I did the day after he returned from Galway, and all he did was to laugh at me and ask if I really thought he would marry an old woman like me.

This, as you can see, only served to further destroy my plans and hopes of reconciliation and happiness, and it increased my pain and emotional torment. He had the audacity to laugh at my pleadings and crying, which only made the situation more dire. At the end, I left and returned to my hotel. But my mind would not leave the situation alone, and emotions left me and logic began to arise. I required justice, if not full revenge. For a full day and a half, I hatched a plot to do away with Julian, and to make it look as if he had killed himself. I had to get away to prepare.

I took the steamer from Dublin to Liverpool where I

*acquired some strychnine from a black market merchant
who specializes in selling such oddments. After all, anything can be bought for the right price. All I needed now
was a girl, any girl, who wanted to make a bit of money,
who wouldn't ask too many questions, and who would be
able to vanish when things were done. I was introduced,
by this unscrupulous merchant, to a certain Audrey, and
both she and the go-between merchant assured me that
whatever was required of her, she would produce, again,
for the correct price. My family being very wealthy, money was no object, though, of course, I didn't tell this to
Audrey. We agreed upon a certain sum for Audrey's services, and, naturally, she became Bobbee, my old school
friend, come to visit from Johannesburg.*

At this last, a collective intake of air went up from
all gathered in the library. The identity of Bobbee was
finally uncovered, as much as it could be.

"So, this Bobbee came from Liverpool, eh? Never
did trust that lot over there," Sir Charles grunted.

"Commander, please go on with reading the letter,"
Magistrate O'Farrell said. McGrath continued his narra-
tive.

*Bobbee came to Kildunlee shortly before your
wedding, Commander. I wasn't sure how I would use her,
but I knew I would have need of her. I had my final plans
set. I called Julian two days before the wedding and asked
him if I could stop by, just to have a glass or two, and to
let bygones be bygones. He hastily agreed and I made
ready for our meeting in two days. I drove to his house
very early the morning of the wedding – and here, Commander, I must apologize for committing a murder on
your wedding day, but my mind was frantic for revenge,
and I wanted a dramatic effect in payment for what Julian
had just put me through.*

So, I went to Julian's house, knowing full well that Singleton would be away getting ready for the wedding and the celebrations afterward. He was seeing a young lady in Doolan, and he would have to pick her up, so I knew Julian would be alone. Leaving this Bobbee waiting in the rented car, I went into his study, where he was working, and saw a bottle of champagne chilling in an ice bucket. He greeted me cordially, saying, "So splendid of you to come, Alice. I'm really glad to see that you've accepted things. Good of you, and all that."

He was really cavalier about it all. So, I uncorked the champagne, got two flutes from the cabinet in his study and filled the glasses, while he kept busy at his desk. It was very easy to spill a full ounce of strychnine into his glass. It was colorless, odorless and tasteless, and he was so preoccupied that he never noticed.

"Here, Julian," I said as I handed him the flute. "To great things to come." He toasted me and drank half the glass down in one gulp. It didn't take long for the strychnine to work. His face turned red and contorted. He gasped for air; his muscles twitched and became rigid. His face had a terrifying grimace to it, as if he was in deep, excruciating pain. And he was. Julian thrashed in his chair several times, trying to accuse me of poisoning him, but strychnine acts fast, and his life fled from him within minutes. He fell down on his desk and died. For some reason or other, I laughed, as heavily as he laughed at me when I came to him to reconcile only days before.

But I knew that he couldn't be found poisoned. That would obviously be murder. So, I went to the adjoining room, where he kept his gun case, since everyone from South Africa keeps guns, and I took a large caliber pistol and loaded it. At this time, Julian's hands still could be moved, before rigor mortis set in, so I placed the pistol in his right hand, put the muzzle to his temple and forced his finger to pull the trigger. In this way, I felt that he had shot himself and that I was absolved of all guilt. That feeling was not to last.

But, for the moment, I washed the glasses and then returned them to the cabinet, and Bobbee, who had come with me but had stayed in the rented car, with my instructions not to enter the house till she heard a shot, helped with the tidying up. I poured the remaining champagne outside onto the flower beds where it was quickly absorbed and gone, dumped the ice, cleaned, dried and returned the bucket to its place behind glass in a study display case, and put the empty bottle in the car to be disposed of later.

While I was doing this Bobbee washed the glasses, dried them and returned them to a cabinet. Apparently, my Bobbee had seen this type of scenario before, many times, for whatever I did to enhance the apparent suicide of Julian fazed her not a whit. Truth to tell, she chuckled several times at my ministrations, even admiring my heinous planning. She told me she had seen this, and worse before, and knowing what I had in store for her as payment for her services, she relished the idea of being involved in such a complicated and devious plot.

Then, I used his typewriter to compose his "death note" which was read in court. From there, I went to your wedding, Commander, bringing Bobbee along as my university roommate whom I had just picked up at the train station in Galway, feeling completely at ease, free of guilt and resolved that I had taken the correct action. Bobbee played her part to perfection, although, by this time, you must know that she is not an artist, nor has she any knowledge of art. She is simply a greedy whore who is willing to do anything for money.

However, Commander, you suspected murder and not suicide, regardless of the forged note. You had seen suicide aboard ship, as you had told us, and the man who had killed himself showed a relaxed face, almost as if he was relieved of his problems. Not with Julian. His face was still contorted, as if in agony, but the court wrote that off to fear of the pain of the pistol shot. It seemed obvious to me, however, that the Commander was not a man to let go of his suspicions, regardless of the verdict of the Inquest. I felt that something must be done to ensure that those suspicions did not lead him to me. The only way I could do that was to produce another victim, and to serve up the "murderer" on a platter – for surely not even the clever Commander McGrath would think that there could possibly be two *murderers about in the simple town of Kildunlee.*

I got Bobbee to start making up to Joe, urging him to have an affair, then leave him to go to Tim to help ignite indignation and thereby cause bad feelings between the two Irishmen and to cause a fight to break out. This happened and Bobbee did a fine job at her acting. That one night when the two men got into a fight, and Livy had to break them up, I had arranged, with Bobbee, to put a narcotic into Joe's whiskey, so that by the time he got home he would sleep for hours. While he was at the pub, getting into trouble with Tim, I went to his house and took his rifle.

When Tim was on his way home, I shot him, trying not to kill him, but I fear I did. I know he ended up in Galway Hospital and I don't know his state at this time. I waited until Joe got home and started to fall into a deep, drunken, drugged sleep. I went in to his house, talked to him for a few minutes to give him an un-provable alibi, waited till he was completely asleep, then, putting the rifle into his hands, I fired it into a stack of cloths, practically silencing the report, yet getting powder burns on Joe's hands. I later burned the cloths far away, Thus, it seemed obvious that he had shot Tim in his drunken and angry state. You know the rest.

I thought that I had all of this mélange straightened out, but that was not to be. The pangs of guilt that I had sent Tim to Galway Hospital and Joe to Galway prison weighed down upon me unbearably. I had to make things right for these two innocent Irishmen. By this time, Bobbee, with a very hefty sum in her purse from me, had taken the train from Galway to Dublin where she would take ship to Liverpool and then train on to London to get lost in the East End crowds. She has enough money to go and live very well in South America if she chooses. I have not seen her since. I am sure none of us will. I began the last part of my planning to show that the "murderer" was still loose, and that Joe should be released from prison.

One fine evening, several days ago, I followed the Americans up to the Cliffs, and on their way back, I shot George Huestis. It was not my intent to kill him, just to wound him. I did this to convince the authorities that Joe Naughton was innocent and to alleviate some of the pain I had caused and to ease my own guilt feelings. Also, I wanted to demonstrate that the "murderer" was still at large. Remember, we South Africans are brought up with guns and we use them very well. I have been shooting since I was six years old, Commander, and I handle a gun quite well.

That's the end of my story, Commander. There is nothing more to tell. I killed Julian Brownlee. I caused the trouble between Tim Kearney and Joe Naughton. Bobbee was my invention and she is long gone, never to be found again. No one else is guilty. It is only me that has caused this series of events. I am the accused; I am the judge; I have found myself guilty; I have carried out the sentence.

And, Commander, as you read this letter, which I composed, in the name of poetic justice, on Julian's own typewriter, I shall have shot myself in the head, and, with my brains sprayed all over this marvelous chair, I shall bleed to death and die.

I regret all I have done.

May God forgive me.

Lady Alice Marie Stronton

28.

JEAN-LUC EXPLAINS ALL

"Glory be ter God, an' the saints an' all the angels," exclaimed Livy. "If that don't beat all. A murther that might be a suicide, another murther, an attempted murther and now a full fledged suicide. Nothin' the likes o' this has happened in Kildunlee before." He shook his head and dried his forehead with a very large, and colorful, handkerchief. "They sent me ter Garda school ter look fer fingerprints, ter look fer tyre tracks an' the like, ter run the Saturday night stocious bowseys in, but they never taught me how ter deal with the likes o' this. Glory be ter God!"

Cynthia gently placed her hand in McGrath's. He responded by giving her a gentle squeeze.

"William, I'm afraid. This has never happened in these parts before. People are scared, even though they put a brave face on things. But, murder and suicide? Perhaps Livy's right. There's something evil going on here."

"I don't know, Cynthia, I don't know. It all seems strange to me. There's too much of a coincidence here. I haven't got all the pieces together yet, but there's bound to be some logical answer."

"William's absolutely right," said Sir Charles, Lord FitzHugh's brother, "There has to be a reasonable answer to all these goings on. And, bloody hell, they just can't happen willy-nilly. Yet, Cynthia's right. Nothing like this has ever happened here before. Even though I live in London, I've spent quite a considerable amount of time here and I've never heard of this type of thing. Damned unimaginable! Preposterous!"

"I'm just wondering if there's going to be any more of this stuff," said Eddie, "I don't want our kids to be raised in a town where murder and suicide are commonplace."

"Ah, Eddie, me love, 'tis not like that at all here, it isn't," Siobhan told her husband. "There's bound ter be a why an' a wherefore."

The guests, all of Kildunlee's cream of the crop, invited to Lord FitzHugh's birthday party, stood around in small clutches, speaking in low tones about the latest mortal event.

"We have trouble in Montana, and there are all sorts of goings on, but it's only to be expected in a state where there are no large cities, no entertainments or attractions, where everyone has at least a sidearm or a .3030 in a saddle holster and where desolation and loneliness are frequently the rule. The outdoor, empty expanses and too much liquor can get to you sometimes and there's just no telling what someone might do."

"Now, Ray, it's not as bad as all that. After all, there are many sane, if that's the right word to use, people, who go about their daily business just trying to make a living, and trying to get through the day. This must be some type of aberration," Marcie Hillaire told her husband.

Still, the people spoke in low tones, offering their opinions to their neighbors, venting their frustrations as to the suicide of Lady Alice Stronton, wondering what, if anything would happen next. And can the Garda, so under-trained for this type of occurrence, deal with the complexities of this death, self-inflicted or not? Will the Garda, and Livy's Supervisor, Colonel Charles O'Meara, and all his lab specialists, inspectors and forensic experts have to be called in? That would put Kildunlee on the map all right, and being on the map in such a light, possibly known as the "Town of Death", is not something the residents of this small, sleepy West Country Irish town wanted. They wanted only to be left alone; to work their farms and crops, tend to their shops and businesses, have a pint at Niamh's, when the parch was upon them, to attend Mass, and other services, on Sunday, and to live their days in peace and whatever comfort they could manage in this hardscrabble, but agriculturally fertile, and productive, land. They didn't really want every curious tourist, from Europe and North America, to come traipsing down their main street looking for the next victim in some form of mortal act, so they could send a postcard home telling the "folks back home" how they saw the victim and the perpetrator on the same day, and wasn't that exciting. And, bloody hell, weren't there enough ruddy English passing through on tourist passports without having their numbers double?

And, now that the Yanks from Montana had arrived – and all of Kildunlee knew that they were more accepted than the English with their overbearing ways – a few more to sample Niamh's ale, beer, poitin, midday and evening feasts that passed for lunch and supper, wouldn't come amiss, but not by the hundreds!

The party guests continued their low tones buzz, in separate groups of three and four. The two Spaniards conversing in a distant corner.

"Commander," said Livy, "What do yer think we, I, should do? Call Colonel O'Meara again?"

"We may have to, Livy. I don't intend to be at all offensive, but, as you said a few moments ago, this may be out of your realm. It might be a good idea to put a call through to the Colonel as soon as possible. He may have to call the CID in on this one. We do have a very strange situation on our hands."

"Aye," answered Livy, "I can call Colonel O'Meara first thing in the marnin'. The post office's closed now."

"Don't be silly, Livy. You can use our telephone. It's right out there in the hall," said Lady Cynthia. "I don't think the Colonel will be happy if you wait 'til morning."

"Thank you, yer Ladyship. Yes. Yer're right. The Colonel would want to be informed as soon as possible," said Livy. He started to make for the hall, grabbing his Garda hat, since he was about to perform an official duty. Livy was always in uniform, especially at events at the Manor, although he did, when he was off duty, wander about in his old corduroys and wool shirt.

"What I'm concerned about is when is this going to end. We can't go on having murder after murder, with a suicide thrown in here in Kildunlee," Dr. McHugh said. "This has got to stop sometime."

Jean-Luc had been talking to the two Spaniards for the last few minutes, swirling his Beaujolais in a large belled wine glass. He stepped forward and raised his hand to prevent Livy from leaving the room. Livy stopped in his tracks and McGrath frowned, wondering what Jean-Luc was about to say.

"What is it, Jean-Luc? Why have you stopped Livy?" Cynthia asked.

Jean-Luc took several paces to the center of the room and stopped next to the large brown armchair where Lady Alice had shot herself, and he began to speak.

"Ah, *Messieurs et madames, mes bons amis,* it is not the problem as to when will all this killing stop, for, *mes amis,* there will be no more killings. *Enfin,* they have ended. It is the problem as to what shall we do with all the evidence that has accumulated since it began."

This brought a gasp from the guests. Evidence? Since the beginning? What was Jean-Luc talking about?

"What evidence do you mean, Jean-Luc? There

have been several killings here and they all seem to be related to Lady Alice alone. She's admitted to it in her note. What else is there to find out? How can you say that the killings have stopped?" Cynthia asked her friend.

"Ah, *Madame*, there is evidence that has arisen like the whale from the sea, it shows itself everywhere, but it is known to only a few of us. Is that not correct, José?"

José, one of the two vacationing Spaniards who evidently spoke very little English, stepped forward toward Jean-Luc.

"Yes, it is true," he began in fluent, and perfectly flawless, English. "Señor José Luis Valenzuela at your service, together with my esteemed compatriot..." and José waved his hand at the other Spaniard who stepped beside him.

"Señor Alejandro Basilio Arellano. I think that my parents wanted me to be a king, hence the middle name," he said with a broad smile, perfect teeth gleaming in his Mediterranean complexion.

"But... but, you guys just don't speak English. We barely could get an idea across to you," Ray Hillaire said.

"*Oui, Monsieur*. That was all part of the plan. The best way for José and Alejandro to find out information was to pretend that they didn't speak much English. Whiskey, beer, beef supper, thank you, and very few other words. And it worked, for they picked up several bits of information from the girl Bobbee, and the fellow, Joe."

"Yes," said Alejandro, "It was a ploy and it worked, for we found out some of the things she was planning to do, and both Luis and I hate fishing," he said with a broad smile. "But, perhaps, Jean-Luc, you would be so kind as to explain why you and we are here."

"Permit me to introduce myself, *messieurs et madames*. Jean-Luc Gaspard of the *Deuxieme Bureau*, the French equivalent of the British MI-6. And my two Spanish friends here..." and Jean-Luc gestured to José to explain.

"José Luis Valenzuela and my compatriot, Alejandro Basilio Arellano, both of the CNI, or the *Centro Nacional de Inteligencia*, also Spain's counterpart to England's MI-6, or its Secret Intelligence Services. The same could be said for the United States, the OSS, the Office of Strategic Services. We are all in the same business: looking for spies, looking for traitors and finding despicable characters like Sir Julian Brownlee. All of us, at your service."

"The OSS?" McGrath exclaimed. "Wild Bill Donovan's outfit?"

"One and the same, *Monsieur Le Commandant*, I assure you."

"I have never met Donovan, but he has a heck of a reputation."

"*Si, Senor* McGrath. As do you, but in another direction. Yours is mild and good. *Senor* Donovan is, well... let's just say that he gets dirty jobs done."

"And where did you two Spaniards learn to speak such beautiful English?" Edward Hillaire asked them.

"Of course, *Senor* Hillaire. To get into the CNI, one must attend two years at Cambridge or Oxford. Both Jose and I went to Oxford. We now speak English quite well, and have done so for a long time, since about nineteen thirty seven, at the time of the beginning of the Spanish Civil War."

"I can't believe what it is I'm hearing," Father McDermott said. "This isn't happening, is it, Father O'Neill? Tell me I'm dreaming."

"Sorry, Father, you're not dreaming. It's for real. Remember I was involved with MI-6 during the war as well. Wasn't I, Commander?"

"You were, Father, you were. But, I'll tell you. I'm confused, and I want someone to tell me what's going on around here." McGrath's statement, though spoken with a level voice and in control, took on the demeanor of authority, not so much as a command, but a firm request for information.

"*Mais oui, monsieur.* That job will fall to me. And, as Luis has just told you, we have finally found one of the most, if not the most, despicable persons who ever walked the earth. Sir Julian Brownlee."

Silence pervaded the room, and everyone, all the birthday party guests looked toward Jean-Luc for his explanation.

"Let me give you the honor, Luis, of beginning the story."

"Thank you, Jean-Luc. Sir Julian Brownlee, for a number of reasons, is the worst criminal we have ever uncovered. He claims to be from South Africa, and, indeed, all his paperwork, passports, ID photos and the like, seem to substantiate that claim. But, this has never been proven, and, in fact, he has no real roots in South Africa. My colleague here, Alejandro," Alejandro made a slight nod of affirmation, "has made a number of discreet inquiries about Sir Julian, and none of these have proven that he was born, raised or lived for any length of time in South Africa, and these discrete inquiries were made in Johannesburg and Pretoria, and the smaller cities in the area. The results? No records of a Sir Julian Brownlee, or even a Julian Brownlee, exist. So, where did he come from, and how did he come to such criminal prominence? Jean-Luc, this is your story, so please continue."

"*Merci,* Luis. As my good friend has just said, there is no trace of a Julian Brownlee in all of South Africa. But, some evidence has been unearthed that he had roots in Eastern Europe, just where we don't really know, but perhaps in Romania. *Mais oui,* but that has never been proven. And as to his identity, his passports, photo IDs and so on, these, *certainement,* can be purchased, for a price. *Enfin, mes amis,* as we all know, everything has a price, and to get what he wanted, Sir Julian – and we will call him that since that was the name he went by – was willing to pay whatever the price was. He dealt in small crime in the beginning of his career, drug smuggling, trafficking and the like. Then, in the late nineteen-twenties, the opportunity came up to do some small arms sales, and this was to a set of rebels in South America. So, Sir Julian, seeing a chance to make money got himself involved and, apparently, made, as the Commander would say, quite a bundle. But still he was never satisfied. He wanted to be rich. So, he started arms dealing on larger and larger scales. No one was able to stop his rise since he was ruthless and simply did away with anyone who got in his way. Murder was as common for him as fishing is for us today." Jean-Luc took a small sip of his Beaujolais.

"*Continuer, mes amis,* Sir Julian established himself as the premier arms dealer in all of Europe, with side transactions to other parts of the world, as well as in South America, as I have just said. As the luck would have it, the war started with the invasion of Poland in 1939, and the Spanish Civil War had begun in 1937. Sir Julian saw these two events as great opportunities to make a vast amount of money, then to retire, under some type of false identification, although all his identifications were false, to someplace where he would not have been known and where he could lead a life of respectability amid all his acquired wealth. He had Australia in mind." This last statement brought gasps all around.

"Australia? Why would he want to go there? How do you know?" Edward asked Jean-Luc.

"*C'est tres simple, mon ami.* Sir Julian had made sufficient money, certainly in the tens of millions of pound sterling, to keep him in luxury for the remaining part of his life, perhaps for another thirty years and more. And he wanted anonymity, a new persona, free from his past dealings, so he could be a pillar of the community, and to salve whatever conscience he may have had."

"But, Jean-Luc, how did you know he was headed for Australia? Other than what was in Lady's Alice's death note?" Cynthia asked him.

"It was also very simple, *Madame*. You remember, shortly after his death, which we all thought was suicide, although my Spanish friends and I, as well as the good Commander, were not convinced of it. *Non*, we believed otherwise. Then, when the registered parcel arrived at the Kildunlee post office, addressed to Sir Julian, and sent from the official Irish Passport Office, he was dead and so unable to open the parcel. However, with thanks to an obscure Irish law, similar to one we have in France, which requires an Irish Judge to open a parcel destined for a deceased person, we discovered that the passport contained inside was under an unknown name, but had Sir Julian's photo on it, with travel plans for Australia. *Monsieur Le Juge*," Jean-Luc said this with a nod to Francis O'Farrell, the Regional Magistrate, who returned his acknowledgement with a nod and a slight smile to the Frenchman, "made the discovery. But, *helas*, it was too late to do anything, since Sir Julian already was dead.

"This is all well and fine, Jean-Luc, but how did Sir Julian make all this money, and how did he get on the wrong side of the law?" McGrath asked him.

"Ah. *Maintenant*, we come to the crux, as you say, of the matter and the reasons why Luis, Alejandro and I are here in Ireland, ostensibly on holiday, but truly to apprehend one of the most heinous criminals we have ever sought." José and Alejandro both nodded their heads.

"That's true, Jean-Luc, very true," said Alejandro. "The reason why we were seeking to find Sir Julian, is not only that he was an arms dealer, which might be bad enough in itself, but *because he cheated all those who did business with him, and caused many good men to die needlessly!*"

Again, gasps, blank stares and several "Oh, my Gods", "Glory bes," and "I don't believe its" sounded throughout the room.

"*Oui, mes amis*, he cheated all those who gave him money for arms and let countless die for his profit. He took the money, apparently bought the arms, shipped the arms to the purchasers, but seldom, if ever, did the rifles, pistols, machine guns and other weapons arrive in good order. They were always damaged, unready for use and badly cared for, and always was there the excuse from Sir Julian's front man that the weapons' caravans had been attacked by the opposition, many were destroyed, many were rendered useless and the rest, though somewhat operable, got through to the purchaser. And what he did was to keep the money from the sale of the arms, send the damaged weapons to the recipients, claiming that he could not prevent hostile attacks, and then he would take the remaining well kept rifles, pistols and so forth and sell them to others on the black market, thereby making twice and more the profit with only one packet of arms. It was ingenious, making twice the profit, and his prices were high, and he always covered himself with the excuses that he could not guarantee the safety of the shipments, if they had to travel through a dangerous countryside, which he made sure of. Hence, *mes amis*, he bought good arms and used, broken arms. He sent some of the good arms plus the broken ones to the purchaser and refused to assume responsibility for safety of the shipment. Then, with the money he had left over, he bought arms in excellent condition and sold them to someone else, easily making a double profit. *Enfin, mes amis*, it was how he made his millions, and how he then planned to go to Australia and settle." Jean-Luc turned to Alejandro. "*Mon ami*, you wished a few words to help explain this situation."

"*Si, gracias*, Jean-Luc. We experienced the same things which Jean-Luc described about Sir Julian just a few minutes ago. The Spanish Civil War was in full tilt, and Luis and I were on the side of the Nationalists, those allied with Generalissimo Franco. There was to be a great push to take two principal cities: Madrid and Bilbao, both of which were under control of the Republicans. That included the International Brigade, with Hemingway, who wrote about blowing up a bridge, his friends and many others from other lands in sympathy against Franco. Anyway, plans had been made for the great assaults against Bilbao and Madrid. Certain lieutenants, trusted men, had made arrangements with Sir Julian's go-betweens, to buy a very large amount of arms for these two assaults. It was at this point that Sir Julian saw another way to make an extremely large double profit. He took the money from the Nationalist representatives and bought arms on behalf of the Franco army, from where we still don't know. And, as Jean-Luc said, the arms arrived in bad condition, so that when the assault began, the Franco forces were outgunned and had to withdraw from the two battles they were supposed to have won. The weapons were mostly useless, and the excuse, coming down from Sir Julian's man was that the Republicans had launched a major attack on the supply lines and destroyed many of the guns. Little did we know at the time it was all a lie and a sham."

"Yes, and more than that, even though the arms were in bad condition, the Franco forces had to order more, just in order to keep militarily current with the Republicans," Luis offered.

"So you see, *mes amis*, how rotten Sir Julian was. He let many Franco troops die because of faulty arms, and he could not have cared less. Unfortunately, the same happened to my compatriots during the war."

"Just how did you come to have dealings with Sir Julian," Father McDermott asked.

"*Monsieur le Cure*, it was from the very utmost of necessity. You've heard of Jean Moulin, *oui*?"

"Yes, wasn't he the head of *La Resistance Francais?*"

"*Mais oui, monsieur le Cure*, you are right. Moulin needed arms for his troops to have skirmishes with the *Boche*, the German occupiers. The Germans had excellent arms, well made and delivered from the Krupp Works. There was never a problem with German arms. But *la resistance* had only old target rifles, World War I pistols, ancient hunting rifles and so on. They needed new and up-to-date armament. So, Moulin, through a subordinate, made an arms deal with Sir Julian, and the same thing happened. Hundreds of thousands of pounds sterling were lost on poor weapons with the same weak excuses of betrayal and attacks by German troops which destroyed the arms and left the remainder almost useless. Then, *sans un doute*, Sir Julian sold the good arms to another purchaser, again doubling his income, and letting Moulin's *resistance* soldiers die for nothing. It is a sad story, this. How one man can make double profits, let men die because they can't defend themselves, and then have no conscience about it. A terrible situation."

"But, Jean-Luc, how did you finally know what Sir Julian was doing? And why did he decide to get out of the business, so to speak, and head to Australia?" George Heustis asked him.

"*Ah bien*, with all bad business dealings, there is someone who has a conscience, and one of Sir Julian's subordinates began to have bad feelings about the way things were done. This was, apparently, a secretary of some sort, we still don't know. But the person, man or woman, it is still unknown, but we believe it to be a woman, perhaps one of his lovers, made several letters available to the Franco and Moulin regimes, outlining what Sir Julian had done, and just how he could be apprehended. That person is probably long gone. I don't mean dead for there has been no body discovered, but simply vanished, possibly to Switzerland in retirement and in disguise, never to be uncovered. We have no idea who it is, but we are greatly in his or her debt. Still, word gets around and Sir Julian got wind of this 'betrayal', as he might have called it, and he set about acquiring new passports, new photo IDs and a completely new identity. Sir Julian would vanish from the face of the earth and Mr. Harold Winthrop, the name on the new passports that arrived from Dublin, would arrive in Sydney to live a comfortable life as a pillar of society with his new bride, Felicity Howarth. It didn't work out, as you know; Lady Alice killed him in his study here in Kildunlee. And that is the end of the life and career of Sir Julian Brownlee, which is why I can say that the murders and suicides in this little sleepy Irish coastal town are done and there will be no more."

Looks of amazement radiated from the faces of all of the guests in the room. The FitzHugh Butler, Riordan, had carefully and respectfully draped a sheet over Lady Alice's form, and, although blood seeped through her clothing onto the sheet, it was not noticed by the guests because of the evening's revelations. The details were too much to take in and digest for anyone to be concerned about a bit of blood on the shroud of a corpse.

"I guess, Jean-Luc, the only question I would have," Siobhan asked the Frenchman, "is why did Sir Julian ignore Lady Alice and latch on ter Felicity Howarth?"

"There is a simple answer here, *Madame* Hillaire. Both ladies were prominent in South African society and both had many connections. Lady Alice helped Sir Julian to gain more money by some almost honest transactions. But she was not the beauty that Felicity is. Sir Julian used Lady Alice just to make more profit from his business dealings, mostly honest this time, but not always, and he promised her that, after the war, they would both set up a large farm near Pretoria. This would have been ideal for a wealthy Lady Alice, married to a rich man, overseeing a large prosperous farm and moving in the highest circles of South African society. Sir Julian had no intention of doing this. He wanted to be with Felicity Howarth in Sydney, in a totally new life. Besides, *Mademoiselle* Howarth was also a very rich lady in her own right. How had she made her fortune, well into the millions by age thirty-eight, three years younger than Sir Julian? *By doing the same arms trading, but in the Pacific*! And she was as ruthless and cunning as he was. She had an office in Jakarta, with all the necessary operations for making arms deals, and she sold guns all over the Pacific, mostly to rebels and those fighting against the Japanese invaders. Some of the time her weapons were useable, but she dabbled in the same double profit tactics as Sir Julian. Each one was unknown to the other until they met in Pretoria at an engagement party for Lady Alice and Sir Julian. *Ah bien*, an incredible stroke of fate, *non*? They gravitated toward each other, and they needed each other for protection in their new lives in Sydney. It was a perfect, although evil, match. But now, as we can see, their plans for living in Australia are lost. Sir Julian is dead and gone, and all his money with him. It is lost, somewhere in hidden Swiss accounts and will most probably revert back to the Swiss Government, given time."

"Jean-Luc, what about this Felicity Howarth, then" Livy asked.

"Ah *helas*, she is gone, too. She was to have changed her identity in order to join Sir Julian. We know this from the letter Sir Julian wrote and which Lady Alice found that day when she went to Sir Julian's study to borrow his typewriter. So, who she is now, or what she looks like, no one has any idea. She had to protect herself from any person looking for any information about arms sales during and after the war. She may be any place, living a quiet, but wealthy life, and we will never know where. But, as I have just said, the murders and the suicides here are finished."

Niamh stepped forward to address the party.

"Aye, what Jean-Luc says is true, sure 'n' it is. I got a written message from him this marnin' before we even opened the doors o' the pub, wasn't it so. An' Cormac O'Callaghan has seen that the troubles are over an' done wit'. An' he tells me, he says, he'll be back in a month's time ter tell a story or two, he says. The troubles are done, and what Jean-Luc says bears truth, since the *seanachie's* comin' back."

Siobhan gave a small gasp, and her hand flew to her mouth. "Oh, me God," she exclaimed. "Oh, me God! I see it all now. I see it!"

"What do you see, my love," Edward asked her, rushing to her side, concern for his wife showing on his face.

"I see it. Don't yer all? 'Twas Cormac, the *seanachie*, who told us that this was goin' ter happen. Sure an' didn't the evil o' Killian O'Donnell get reflected in Sir Julian himself? Didn't they both show the spit o' the divil himself tryin' ter steal from good folk, with no thought o' the results, but only profit fer themselves? Didn't they, now? An', truth ter tell, didn't each one get his just desserts? Killian tried ter steal from the greatest athlete o' all Ireland over a thousand years ago, an' Sir Julian stole from everyone he did business with. Isn't there a parallel here? Yes, I see it. I see it, I do. An' each man got his reward. Killian went into forced labor and Sir Julian was shot. The seanachie was tryin' ter tell us that the evil was comin', but it would be dealt with, and justice served, as in a thousand years ago. He said he wouldn't be back till the deeds were all done, an' now they have, haven't they?" Siobhan turned to her husband. "Oh, Eddie, me love, Jean-Luc is right. 'Tis all done. There won't be anymore killin' an' shootin'. It's all gone." She reached her arms up to her husband's neck to embrace him, and to seek solace and comfort in him.

"I believe you're right, my love, I really believe that you're right. We're all safe, now, and Kildunlee has once again become a good place to bring up kids." He kissed her gently on her forehead, and held her close.

A dumbfounded silence settled on the room; no one spoke out loud, though a few whispers were heard here and there. An incredible story; one that would be hard for anyone to comprehend, or even believe. It seemed a fiction. Evil gravitating to evil, at the expense of good people. But, it seems that the good people, at least this time, had, indeed, triumphed in the end.

McGrath broke the silence. "Well, Livy, I guess you can make that call to Colonel O'Meara now. He'll surely want the details of this beaut of a yarn. I haven't quite got it straight myself. Looks like people will try to make a profit at anything – good, bad or indifferent. I thought I'd seen a lot during the war, but this takes the cake."

"Right, Commander. I'll be makin' that call this minute, with yer Ladyship's permission. I only wish I could see the Colonel's face when I start ter tell him about Sir Julian."

Heads nodded and voices could be heard expressing their incredulity at the tale Jean-Luc, Luis and Alejandro had told.

"Can't believe this," Sir Charles said. "Most extraordinary! Most extraordinary! Anyone join me in a drink? Bung ho, and damn all!" Sir Charles bellowed, pouring himself a rather large whiskey.

"I'll take one," Ray Hillaire answered him, and Sir Charles placed a beautifully cut glass Waterford crystal rock glass in Ray Hillaire's hand, with at least six ounces of Mr. Jameson's best in it.

"Good grief, Sir Charles, you expect me to drink all

of this tonight?"

"Bloody hell and forward the British army!" Sir Charles bellowed, and downed two ounces of his preferred ambrosia, only to be copied by the American.

"Riordan, please show Garda Livy to the telephone. Then perhaps you could bring in another tray with some drinks for everyone. We'd appreciate it," McGrath told the butler.

"Right away, sir," Riordan answered, and he rushed to carry out his new master's wishes.

"William, what will happen now? I mean when this story hits the papers? I really don't want people coming here to snoop at Kildunlee as the town of murder and suicide," Cynthia said to her husband.

"Cynthia, I don't think that will happen. There will be a flurry in the press at the beginning, of course, but it will die down. After all, everything's over and done with. There's nothing to see anymore." He put his arm around his beautiful wife and gave her a gentle hug. "Don't you worry, my dear. It's all over and we're all safe."

"*Mais oui, Madame*, what *Monsieur le Commandant* says is quite correct. It is all over and there is nothing to see. Kildunlee will again return to being a sleepy West Country Irish village, as, I believe, it wants to be. Mostly paperwork for *Monsieur Le Juge* O'Farrell and *Monsieur Le Colonel* O'Meara and the burying of Sir Julian, which the Irish government will have to do. It is their responsibility since Sir Julian has no country, nor does Lady Alice. There is no more to say, and, as has been said, you are all quite safe, now."

Magistrate O'Farrell took another long pull at his Jameson's. "It will probably fall to me to dispose of the paper work and the body, as Jean-Luc has just said. For my part, I intend to recommend a burial at sea, with no honors, and a ton of rocks to keep the bleeding rotten corpses on the floor of the ocean."

29.

AT THE CLIFFS

McGrath brought the car to a halt about 500 feet away from the edge of the Cliffs of Moher in the little circular parking area the Irish National Park Service had provided for visitors. The air was heavy, portending rain in a few hours and he noticed a threatening line of low clouds moving in from the northeast. Cynthia got out of the car and took a deep breath.

"I used to come here when I was out riding, just to watch the ocean and get some fresh air. Even when I was a little girl, I loved coming here. Don't you like it, William?"

"Well, you know I do, but to come here for fresh air? The air in Ireland is so fresh all over the countryside that here can't make a difference."

"Oh, but it does. The sea makes it special. Smell the tang, the sweet freshness!" And she took another deep breath again.

"I know you love this place, but wouldn't it have been nicer to ride up here together, on Warrior and Sassy? We haven't been horseback riding in weeks, now."

"Oh, we'll be riding again, but not today. I just wanted a few minutes alone with you. The activity of our getting married, and then the troubles with Sir Julian and Lady Alice have been awfully time-consuming and just a bit upsetting, don't you think? And especially since you had to go to Court,"

"I do, Cynthia, and I am glad for these few minutes.

But, there's something I have to talk to you about along those lines."

He reached down and picked up a flat, gray stone and hefted it in his hand for a moment. They walked a little closer to the edge of the Cliffs, noticing the warning signs that the visitor should not get too close to the edge. There was a wall of upright flagstones vainly trying to prevent people from approaching too near the edge. But, thankfully, no one had gone over in recent years. The threat of smashing onto rocks, 700 feet below, and being hurled about by the angry North Atlantic tides were warnings enough, apparently.

He tossed the stone over the cliff and watched it arc downward till it was out of sight.

"Cynthia, there's something we have to talk about."

"Yes, there is, William." She said, smiling at him.

"I've been here since March, over eleven weeks, because of all the delays you just mentioned, and we've been married for five or six of those eleven. Although I've been in fairly constant touch with my offices in Boston, I really feel the need to get back there to see how things are going. I have a more than capable staff, but, since I'm the last of the male McGraths, it's my responsibility to run the organization. My two sisters aren't as interested in the business as I am, and Mother is getting old. I have to   return to Boston and I want to take you so you can meet everyone, my family members, all the cousins and so on. Besides, we haven't had a proper honeymoon."

Cynthia smiled up at him. "Why, William, that's a great idea and I was wondering when you were going to take me to Boston. The affair with Sir Julian and everything else prevented our getting away, so Boston could be our honeymoon. We'd love to go."

"We? Oh, yes, of course. By all means take Bridie. I suppose she has family in Boston who emigrated some years ago. Sure, she can come. Riordan and his staff can keep an eye on the Manor while you're gone. It won't be for a long time, but we'll be gone for a month or two, at least."

"Yes, we'll really be looking forward to it. And, William, you really have to get yourself a valet. Doing things for yourself just won't work. We can advertise here and bring one with us."

"Let's wait till we return to the Manor from Boston, then I promise I'll hire one, although, Jenkins does that for me in Boston. He's Welsh, but he may enjoy coming to Kildunlee."

"Well, we can certainly do that, and I'm sure this Jenkins will do fine. And, William, I can't stress enough that we're so excited to go to Boston, that it's hard to stay still. Believe me, we're jumping for joy."

"We, again? What is this 'we'?" he asked. "Is Bridie so excited about Boston that she can't contain herself? You couldn't have told her yet, could you? I've just mentioned going to Boston."

Cynthia smiled up at her tall, handsome husband, and reached up to put her arms around his neck. For just a moment, a smattering of rays pierced the gray clouds.

"You silly, silly sailor boy. My sailor boy. You haven't a clue, do you?'

"Clue? About what?" he asked her, his brow was furrowed in puzzlement.

"Several times, you have told me that you are the last of a long line of McGraths who own and operate your great grandfather Josiah's shipping line, haven't you?"

"Yes, I have. Oh, I see. You must be worried about whether I can support you in the style you've been used to. Don't worry, my love, my personal fortune is in the tens of millions, and the company is close to half a billion. You'll want for nothing."

"William, William, what am I going to do with you? The Manor brings in hundreds of thousands of pounds sterling a year and I have my own fortune, though not as much as yours. But, I've been thinking about selling the land to the tenant farmers so they won't have to pay rent anymore and the land will be their own. I don't need their rent money, or farm receipts anymore. I'd like to almost give it to them, but my solicitor says that's not within the law, and I'll have to charge them something. I was thinking a pound each for the purchase of their holdings. What do you think about that?"

"That's a great idea. Not many people around here think like you. The town loves you, Cynthia, and this will put you even higher in their esteem for you."

"Ah, but, William, they love you too, for all you've done for them during the war and since." She kissed him gently on the lips. "And we are very happy to have you here. Now. Today. In this spot."

McGrath looked around and saw no one. "We? There's only you and me here, Cynthia. We're alone."

"As I said, you've mentioned several times how you're the last of the line."

"I have," he acceded, nodding gently.

"Well, we have arisen to the occasion, and you're not."

"I am. There's no one to succeed me, but, perhaps one day."

"There is, William, there is. You noticed that we didn't use horses to come here today?"

"I did. We took the car."

"Right. Dr. McHugh told me no more riding, at least, not for now." She pulled herself closer to him, her lips against his ear.

"William," she whispered gently, "I'm carrying your child. And from the feel of it, I believe it's going to be a he. You're going to have a son, William; you're going to have a son. McGrath Shipping Lines will continue with him and I will give you many more sons, because I love you, Commander William McGrath, I love you dearly."

And Commander William McGrath, of Boston and Kildunlee, recently discharged from the US Navy, with honorable war service in both the European and Pacific theatres, buried his face in the blond tresses of his wife's hair, so she wouldn't see his tears of gratitude and joy.

30.

EPILOGUE

McGrath and Lady Cynthia, together with Cynthia's personal maid, Bridie, sailed from Southampton, in southern England, and landed in Boston almost five days later. Having so much baggage, to provide them for a long stay, they couldn't get it on an airplane. They stayed in Boston, doing the social whirl, for almost three months. Bridie, naturally, visited all her cousins, who "...had made the crossin'," and were now full-fledged American citizens.

But, toward the end of the third month, both Cynthia and McGrath felt the need to return to Kildunlee. In the meantime, McGrath's cousin, Dr. Gerald O'Connor, an attending Obstetrician and Gynecologist at the noted Massachusetts General Hospital, kept a keen eye on Cynthia's progress. His advice agreed with McGrath and Cynthia's idea that they should return to Ireland without delay, so there wouldn't be a problem with a birth at sea. Cynthia, McGrath and Bridie, this time with Jenkins as McGrath's valet, all went back to Kildunlee, having disembarked at Southampton, trained to Liverpool, crossed the Irish Sea and again trained to Galway, where they were picked up by several cars to accommodate each of them and all the luggage.

It was late in January of 1947 that Cynthia presented McGrath with twin boys, who they named Francis and Trevor, after their two grandfathers. All members of the family are doing well, but, unfortunately, six weeks after seeing his grandchildren, Earl Trevor FitzHugh passed away. Shortly after his Lordship's passing, life as usual and normal resumed at the Manor, and two nurses were hired to care for the twins, although Cynthia and McGrath were with them often and each day.

McGrath had the Irish telephone Service install four more telephones at the Manor, intentionally placing one in a downstairs back storage room now converted to his office, complete with Telex direct to McGrath Shipping headquarters in Boston. McGrath and Cynthia have lunch with Francis and Trevor as often as possible, and they spend time with them before dinner and at bedtime, when they are placed in the charges of their nurses, Nora and Rosie. They are all very happy.

Tim Kearney did not die, but made a generally good recovery and, because of his wounds inflicted by a pre-sumed psychopath, according to the Irish government, receives a pension from the government. McGrath aug-ments Tim's income so he is comfortable, as Tim can do only very light labor. Tim and Joe now have been amiably reconciled, realizing that they both were used as dupes. They are very good friends now.

Bobbee was never seen again. However, reports surfaced that there was a "...very attractive lady of Northern European heritage who had entered the highest social circles of Rio de Janeiro..." Delicate inquiries by Jean-Luc's associates at the Deuxieme Bureau suggested that this Northern European transplant resembles Bobbee to the highest degree. However, since at the time there was no extradition treaty between Brazil and Ireland, and also due to the fact that it would be extremely difficult for the Irish government to bring charges against Bobbee for lack of concrete evidence, no overtures were made to have Bobbee returned to Ireland to face charges. At last report, it was stated that the supposed Bobbee had invest-ed heavily in two coffee plantations, which had produced great returns, and she was doing extraordinarily well. Her engagement to a very wealthy Brazilian   businessman was shortly to be announced. It is highly doubtful that she will ever see Ireland again.

GLOSSARY

A Chara,	pronounced "ah kara," my dear.
Amadan,	Male idiot, pronounced "AM a dahn."
Ard riIrish,	High King in ancient times, pronounced ARD ri.
Bowsey,	Drunkard.
Ceili,	pronounced "kaylee". A party with music and dancing.
Clatter,	A large quantity.
Cuchillain,`	An Irish mythological hero, compared to Achilles; well known for his battle frenzy translated as riastrad. There are some variations on the spelling of his name. Pronounced, Koo HULL an.
Da,	Daddy or papa in Irish.
Drouth,	pronounced "drewth", thirst. Also, an alcoholic.
Duncher,	A tweed cloth cap.
Finn MacCool,	A mythical warrior-hunter of Irish mythology.

Fleadh,	pronounced "flah", a festival.
Hooley,	A party.
Is Tu Moghra,	I love you, pronounced as it is read.
Jar, or Drop,	of the PureA portion of Irish whiskey.
Niamh,	pronounced "Neeve", a woman's name.
Poitin.	pronounced "potcheen", moonshine.
Seanachie,	pronounced "shan a kee", a storyteller, sometimes one who can see future events.
Stocious,	Drunk, pronounced STO shius.

ABOUT THE AUTHOR

Laurence A. Booker, or Larry, as I prefer to be called, is a native of New York City and of completely Irish heritage. I spent four years in the U.S. Navy. After a cruise to the Far East aboard an aircraft carrier, I went to meteorology school where I learned about weather observations, and was then stationed in England for two years. It was during these two years that I got the idea for a small naval detail doing meteorological observations. I later tied this idea in to the D-Day invasion, but tie-in that didn't happen till I graduated New York University, moved with my family to Vermont, where my father had been born, took a master's degree at Castleton State College, and settled down to teaching Business on the high school level. My first book, *McGrath's Detail,* was the story of that small meteorological detail taking weather observations just prior to the D-Day invasion. It was published online. Many of our friends and neighbors here in our small Vermont town have asked me when I was going to write another book about the famous William McGrath. So, here it is, as he got wrapped up in a murder, and then some. My wife and I have two children who are both married and pursuing their own careers, so we are empty nest. Needless to say, this gives me ample time to think about writing, and to enjoy the Vermont countryside.

1/16

Brandon Free Public Library
4 Franklin Street
Brandon, VT 05733

51341630R00135

Made in the USA
Charleston, SC
16 January 2016